SF Books by Vau

LOST STARSHIP SERIES:
The Lost Starship
The Lost Command
The Lost Destroyer
The Lost Colony
The Lost Patrol
The Lost Planet
The Lost Earth
The Lost Artifactt
The Lost Star Gate
The Lost Supernova
The Lost Swarm
The Lost Intelligence
The Lost Tech
The Lost Secret
The Lost Barrier

THE SOLDIER SERIES:
The X-Ship
Escape Velocity
Final Odyssey

Visit VaughnHeppner.com for more
information

Galactic Marine

(A Traveler Novel)

By Vaughn Heppner

Illustration © Tom Edwards
TomEdwardsDesign.com

ISBN: 9798414565710
Imprint: Independently published

I must have still been drunk when I fell out of bed on Monday. My mind was hazy and I'd forgotten all about Juanita Bolivar's promise to meet me at the Red-Hot Chili Pavilion at six this evening.

I'd been executing the perfect campaign with her, working the angles to that most provocative moment last night when she'd finally laughed the way she does, flicking her hair to the side, and agreed to a date with yours truly.

But, as I said, when I fell out of bed on Monday morning, with my alarm ringing, I was not thinking about Juanita's perfect smile or the sway of her hips as she danced.

I was late, *muy* late for work as the lousy alarm had rung for Sunday.

It didn't help that I'd broken a ton of protocols lately, and if Master Gunnery Sergeant Hendricks wanted to make a big deal about it, he could. It would likely mean a dishonorable discharge from the U.S. Marines, which I wanted to avoid.

Do you hear that? *Avoid.* Two years ago, I would have died of shame if there had been a mere *suggestion* I might be dishonorably discharged from the Corps.

Two years ago, I hadn't been in that mix-up in Bhutan, of all places. Check it out. Bhutan, *Druk Yul*, or "The Land of the Thunder Dragon," as Bhutan was known: a tiny landlocked country in the Eastern Himalayas sandwiched between Tibet and India.

Our time there had been a bloody mess of ambushes and—

I shook my head before the bathroom mirror, rubbing my chin, feeling that the razor had done its job of making me presentable.

I was big and brawny, and yes, it had been crazy that the Marines had ended up in Bhutan, maybe even crazier that I had been there with them. My MOS was 0311, rifleman. The captain back then had once said I was a born warrior, but I figured he meant that as an insult, as we were supposed to be professionals.

Anyway, I ran out the door, hailed a taxi and muttered instructions to the driver in Spanish.

I know, I know, if you know anything about Marines on consulate duty, you must be scratching your head about my setup. I had twelve days left in Santiago, the capital of Chile. In twelve days, I would go home to the States, receive my honorable discharge and head out to Hawaii to start my life as a surfer-slash-beach bum. When I ran out of money, I'd find a job as a security guard or something.

You see, I planned on being free the way a knight-errant had been in the medieval chivalric literature like Gawain and Lancelot in the Arthurian cycle of the Round Table. The adjective *errant* meant wandering or roving. Probably, in the end, that meant I'd become a private detective. I wasn't going to be slaving away in a grind of a job, climbing a corporate ladder and toadying to the Karens and their lapdogs.

Bhutan had taught me so much. Consulate duty in Santiago had also shown me that—

No. I'm not going to complain. I'm going to tell you what happened starting on Monday, January 8.

My mindset that morning was fuzzy, although I remember telling myself to hold it together for another twelve days. A dishonorable discharge could complicate my future. Besides, I'd been a good Marine in Bhutan: the best, if you judged me by my fighting skills. The bastards there had learned the hard way that messing with the USMC was hazardous to their health.

Incidentally, Chile is that long narrow country that runs almost the entire length of the western side of South America.

It was summer now on the bottom half of the globe, a fine time to be here.

As the taxi pulled up, I thought about sneaking into the consulate building, but rejected that as unworkable. Instead, I sauntered in boldly, gathered my equipment in the armory and ran into Hendricks as I *clicked* the chin strap to my helmet.

"There you are," Hendricks said, scowling at me.

He was short, bordering on obese, and had wrinkles in his uniform, but he knew secrets that kept the right people off his back. Leverage, he called it.

His frown deepened as he took a better look at me. "What's wrong with you?"

I shook my head.

He pushed up against me, looking up. "Open your mouth. Breathe at me."

My shoulders twitched as I automatically started the motion that would shove him away. Then, the thought struck just in time: *You only have twelve days left. Don't screw it up, Bayard.*

That was me: Sergeant Jake Bayard, in case I'd forgotten to tell you.

Hendricks' scowl deepened. "Are you deaf? What did I just say?"

I breathed into the man's splotchy face.

He stepped back sharply. "I can't believe this. You've been drinking before work. Not even you can be that stupid."

"Last night," I mumbled, hating making any excuses to him. Soon, though, I'd never have to make another excuse in my life. I kept reminding myself of that.

"What?" he snapped.

"Last night," I said. "I drank way too much last night. Then I slept. Still sweating it out."

He stared at me, and I could see the wheels turning in his mind. "You know—" He stopped himself, knowing that I knew the rules. He shook his head. "You're lucky, Bayard. I don't know why, but you're going on a little jaunt today. It could be overnight. I don't know."

"What are you talking about?"

"Grab some extra gear just in case. Put in a few civvies, maybe some boots. You have an extra pair in your locker, don't you?"

"Yeah," I said. "What jaunt? You're not making sense."

"You know what DARPA is?" Hendricks asked, with an edge to his voice.

I stared at him.

"DARPA," he said slowly, as if I were an idiot. "Defense Advanced Research Projects Agency."

"What does any of that have to do with me?"

"That's the first intelligent thing you've said today. You have no idea what DARPA is, do you?"

I didn't care for his smirk, and my mind finally started to engage. In case I haven't said, I look like a big tight end, a football player, but I read all the time. Books gave me most of the ideas that drove others batty.

"DARPA is part of the DOD," I said. "They're responsible for developing emerging technologies for use by the military."

"Yeah, yeah," Hendricks said. "You're a bright boy. This morning, a DARPA scientist called and asked for you personally."

"Me? What for?"

"I already told you what for. Pack for an overnight. The egghead should be here in a few hours."

That was when I remembered about my date with Juanita Bolivar at six tonight. I absolutely could not miss that. She was the hottest girl I'd ever asked out. There was no way I was going to miss dancing with her. And more. I hoped.

"How long is this little jaunt supposed to take again?"

"How do I know? One day, two, maybe three."

"Uh…"

Hendricks stared at me, and he must have read my face. His broke out into a huge grin. "Just in case you don't understand what's happening, Sergeant, the DARPA scientist just saved your sorry ass. I could bust you for being drunk on duty, but I'm not going to, *provided* you hurry and get ready for your little TDY."

I needed to get out of this, but Hendricks had me, and I could see no way to wriggle out of the assignment without

4

ending up with that dishonorable discharge I know he was itching to stick me with. I couldn't believe it. I'd have to call Juanita and work something out. Hmm. I must have left my phone at home. I'd have to borrow one once Hendricks left.

I brightened as I realized how to do this. I'd talk the DARPA scientist into letting me go and have Townes take my place.

Besides, this sounded weird. How could a DARPA scientist borrow an on-duty Marine from the U.S. Consulate? It made no sense whatsoever.

"I don't understand this," I said, trying a last stab with Hendricks.

He cocked his head as if thinking about it. "You know, I don't understand it either. It's more than odd, but I'm guessing the scientist has major pull."

"What does he want me to do again?"

"I have no idea. Now, grab your gear so you're ready. I'm sure you'll find out soon enough what he wants with you. And Bayard—"

I waited.

"Lay off the sauce out there. Don't make us look bad. You understand me?"

Twelve more days, I told myself. After that, I'd be a free man.

-2-

After I packed, Townes and I had to move over a thousand boxes on the double, and I forgot about calling Juanita— thanks, booze brain.

Then, at one-sixteen in the afternoon, Hendricks raced into the conference room. "Set it down," he shouted at me.

I put down the big box I'd just lifted. Townes and I had to clear out thirty-two more before we were through. I was hungry, as we hadn't had any lunch yet.

For the record, Townes had just walked out with his latest box.

Hendricks, who was holding my duffel bag, threw it at me.

I grunted catching it.

"You won't need your helmet, baton or weapon," Hendricks said. "So, leave them here. I'll take care of them."

I unbuckled the baton and holster, setting them on a table with my helmet. Then, I trotted after Hendricks, who kept twining his thick fingers together. That wasn't like him. He usually showed a placid face to the world. He glanced back at me, and I realized he was sweating, with a hoggish look to his features.

"What's wrong with you?" I asked.

"Don't screw this up, Bayard. I'm passing on the warning to you."

I frowned, wondering who'd passed the warning on to him.

I would have asked, but Hendricks hurried through a side door into the main lobby. He used a sleeve to wipe his lips and slid to a halt before two rangy men wearing black suits and dark sunglasses.

I came more slowly, eying them. They were almost my height, with black shiny hair and an athletic quality to the way they stood. They struck me as gunfighters. They had expensive suits that fit perfectly and wore fancy shoes. I had no doubt each had an automatic in a shoulder rig.

"Keep out of trouble, Bayard," Hendricks said.

The two did not acknowledge Hendricks or me. They simply turned around and headed for the door.

"Go on," Hendricks told me. "They'll take you to the scientist."

Shrugging inwardly, surprised at Hendricks' servile antics, I followed the two. Which one was the boss? As in, which one did I have to convince to let me go?

I grinned, remembering again. Juanita Bolivar was waiting. I could practically see her swaying hips with my hands on them as we danced the night away.

There was a purring Cadillac SUV waiting outside. One of the two men had the back open. The other slid into the front passenger-side door.

I slung my duffel bag into the back.

The rangy man in black slammed the door shut, motioned for me to follow him and opened the back passenger-side door for me.

I slid in and he shut the door.

The driver was a third man in black with dark sunglasses. He wore a stylish hat and waited with his hands at ten and two o'clock on the steering wheel.

The other slid into the seat behind the driver, shutting his door.

"Uh," I said. "Before we go, I need to tell you—"

The Cadillac smoothly moved away from the curb, heading into traffic.

"Hey, wait," I said. "I have to tell you something."

All three ignored me.

"Listen," I said, putting my left hand on the side headrest of the front passenger-side seat. I figured the one riding shotgun

7

must be the boss. "You don't understand. I can't come with you."

The one riding shotgun twisted back to stare at me. I couldn't see behind the dark lenses, but the skin of his face seemed stretched tight, almost as if it was going to rip and reveal something sinister underneath.

"Are you hearing me?" I said. "I have a hot date tonight. It's taken me time to set it up. Townes is your man, not me."

"You are the one," Mr. Shotgun Seat said, using an accent I couldn't place.

"Would you listen for a minute?" I said, reaching over and grabbing his nearest shoulder.

It was like grabbing a hot band of steel. I'm not saying he was made of metal, but his muscles were taut and noticeably hotter than what I'd expected, as if his black suit were also a heating pad.

I released him, as he twisted more fully around as if he planned to do me harm.

I didn't like that—no, not one bit—and suddenly I didn't like him either. "Who do you think you are?" I said.

"Jake Bayard," he said, the strange accent more pronounced than before. "You are Jake Bayard, yes?"

"That's my name; don't wear it out."

He cocked his head as if he couldn't figure out what I'd just said.

"Never mind," I said. "Look, do you have a cell phone? I need to make a call."

"No calls," he said.

"Hey, bub, I have a hot date tonight. Do you *comprende?*"

"You are meeting Doctor Spencer today."

"All right, I get that. But if you guys would slow down for a second, I could get Townes to take my place."

"No."

"What do you mean no? Townes can help this Doctor Spencer just as easily as me."

"No."

It was weird. He talked as if English was his third language or as if he was slow in the head. But his physical competence

8

and presence proclaimed him sharp and dangerous. Then, it began to dawn on me what he was really saying.

"What's so special about me, huh?"

The driver and Mr. Shotgun Seat traded glances as if that were a loaded question.

"I don't want to get rough with you guys," I said, "but I really need to call Juanita."

"Jake Bayard," Mr. Shotgun Seat said.

"What now?"

He gestured to the man in the back seat with me. I looked, and what do you know; the other had pulled out a taser and aimed it at my midriff.

"Doctor Spencer needs your help," Mr. Shotgun Seat said.

I blinked in disbelief. This was crazy. Just what was going on with these three? "Are you kidnapping me?"

This time, Taser Man and Mr. Shotgun Seat traded glances. The leader reached into his inner suit and pulled out a document. He showed it to me.

"This is official," he said. "Doctor Spencer has need of your aid."

I noticed the Ambassador's signature on the document, which was a kick in the gut.

"Is this for real?" I said, deflated.

"Check it. It is quite authentic."

I studied the document, and realized he spoke the truth. Sitting back in bewilderment, frowning, shaking my head—

"Why did you feel so hot when I touched your shoulder?" I said.

Mr. Shotgun Seat stared at me, eventually saying, "Thermal gear."

"What?"

"Fever," he said. "I have a fever."

Was he making this up on the fly? "Why are you here if you're sick? You should be in bed."

"No."

"Okay, okay," I said. "You do what you want, and you're not going to let me go. Just let me borrow your cell then, so I can talk to Juanita and tell her what's up. That way, when I come back, I can still take her out."

9

He cocked his head. "We will ask Doctor Spencer about it."

"Yeah?" I said. "When?"

He cocked his head the other way. "Ten minutes from now."

I stared at him, glanced at Taser Man and realized there was something going on here I did not understand. The steely muscles, the heat Mr. Shotgun Seat had radiated, the stretched facial skin and pulling a taser on a U.S. Consulate Marine— why me? Why did this Doctor Spencer want me specifically? That did not make a lick of sense.

I folded my arms, noting that I was much brawnier than these three clowns. We moved through city traffic. When the car stopped...I'd watch and wait for a little while longer. But if this became any sketchier, I was going to be twisting a few heads or banging them together as if they were Larry, Curly and Moe.

3

Approximately twenty minutes later, the Caddy took turns that led to the Comodoro Arturo Merion Benitez International Airport, the main one for Santiago, a city of eight million. The airport was a beautiful place with plenty of palm trees, grass and sidewalks.

"You're planning on boarding a plane here?" I asked.

"Yes," said Mr. Shotgun Seat.

"Are we taking a short trip inland then?"

"Yes."

"Where to?"

He glanced back at me. "Doctor Spencer will tell you."

I'd been doing some figuring the past few minutes. Were these three SEALs or Delta? The more I thought about it and the strange accent, the more I realized they didn't have that feel. No, as I said before, they felt like gunslingers or possibly CIA operatives.

The driver didn't take us to an airport parking space—no surprise there—or head for the front of a debarkation area. He took a turn between two buildings and headed for an underground garage.

We sped past concrete going down, went through darkness and came back up on the other side.

The Cadillac came to a stop at a guarded gate. Our windows rolled down, and hard-eyed paratroopers wearing maroon berets and holding carbines stared at us.

I noticed that Taser Man no longer brandished his weapon. That was interesting. I didn't figure this was the place to make a scene, though.

A beret-wearing lieutenant waved us on. A bar rose to let us through, and the driver drove on through.

After a few more turns, the driver stopped at a four-engine turboprop military transport, a C-130 Hercules, which was parked on the tarmac. A C-130 was capable of using unprepared runways for takeoffs and landings, which would indicate some backcountry job. C-130s had been used in all kinds of actions throughout the years. This one had U.S. Air Force markings. At least that indicated a legitimate military mission rather than some shady gray or black operation.

The Ambassador's signature on the document also supported its legitimacy. Hmm. Apart from missing an eventful evening with Juanita, it seemed I had nothing to worry about.

So why did I have a bad vibe about all this? The semi-kidnapping seemed like the logical reason for my misgivings, but there were likely more.

The others had already climbed out. I did, too. A waiting Taser Man tossed me my duffel bag from the back.

"Hurry," the leader said. He and the driver stood at the bottom of the airstair, a set of steps folded out from the aircraft so we could board it.

I looked at the stair, glanced around, and then decided it was high time I talk to this Doctor Spencer. It was either that or run, which would likely end in my getting a dishonorable discharge.

I shrugged and began to climb the airstair. The three rangy operatives followed right behind, giving the impression they thought I might try to escape.

At the top, I peeked through the open hatch and saw that the cargo hold was mostly empty, with a parka-clad man sitting by his lonesome in a regular airliner cushioned seat bolted to the floor. That was weird. The man's parka was unzipped and he was busy studying a computer tablet. There was a second cushioned seat beside him and three more on the other side of the plane.

"You're sitting with Doctor Spencer," the leader said.

"Is that him?" I asked, jutting my chin at Parka Man.

"Do you see anyone else in here?"

The sarcasm made the leader seem normal, which was a relief. I felt my gut unclench, not realizing I'd been so tense. Maybe the leader really did have a fever, and that was why he'd felt hot before.

I picked up my duffel bag and headed for Spencer. It was time to start talking, wiggle out of this assignment, and make my date with Juanita a reality, if I could still pull it off.

The doctor was tallish and skinny, if his bony angular face was any indication, and he must have been in his mid-50s. He had thinning brown hair grown too long over a too-large cranium. Where his hair didn't cover, his pate showed weathered patches. He would have been better off shaving the hair. But that was his business.

"Doctor?" I asked, deciding to be polite so I could talk him into using Townes instead of me.

"Sit, please," he said in a reedy voice, looking up at me through his glasses. I'd expected them to have thick lenses, but they seemed ordinary enough.

I sat, placing the duffel bag between my booted feet. "Look, Doc, I have to ask a favor. I'm supposed to meet Juanita Bolivar tonight. Now, I appreciate you asking for me—"

"You'd best buckle up," he said, interrupting.

I'd been so wound up about convincing him that I hadn't noticed the retracted airstair, the closed hatch or that the engines, which had been idling as I boarded, were now revving.

The three operatives had already buckled into their seats on the other side of the hold. We faced each other across the way, and they were busy staring at me through their dark sunglasses. What was their problem anyway?

Then, the C-130 started moving.

"Hey!" I shouted.

Spencer looked up sharply from his tablet.

"I have a hot date tonight," I said heatedly. "I've worked hard to get Juanita Bolivar to say yes. The date's at six. I don't have time for this. Besides, Townes can do whatever it is as easily as me."

"Who?"

"Sergeant Dan Townes in the Embassy," I said. "We can trade places."

"Oh no, that is not possible."

"Are you hard of hearing or something?"

"Sergeant Bayard, I have gone to considerable trouble to secure your presence. Surely you realize that this…jaunt supersedes any romantic rendezvous."

I stared at Spencer. "How long is this trip supposed to take anyway?"

"A few days at most."

I groaned. "No, no, no. Juanita isn't going to wait a few days. I have to strike while the iron's hot."

"You are agitated for no reason. Women…they abound," Spencer said with an airy wave. "What we're attempting to do–" He shook his head, smiling self-importantly.

"Look, Doc," I said, seeing my date slipping away. "If you're going to be such a hard-ass about this, then loan me your phone, huh? I'll give Juanita a call and explain that I can't be there tonight. It's rude if I simply don't show up."

"I'm sorry, Sergeant. I simply cannot do as you ask."

"Well, you'd better have a quick change of attitude, *Doc*. I'm not staying in the Marines. See? So, you can't hold that over me for my good behavior."

"Sergeant Bayard, *please*. You make this sound ugly. And it is anything but. I asked for you specifically. Do you realize that? This is an honor, a great honor, believe me."

I looked around. I was sitting in a C-130 with a DARPA big shot from the Defense Department. We had the whole plane to ourselves, with custom seats no less. The Ambassador had signed for my temporary release. Spencer had asked for me and no one else but me.

No matter how I looked at that, it did not compute, and it finally made me curious. Maybe the realization that I wasn't going to see or be able to call Juanita alerted that part of me, the part that had been fixated on her lovely swaying hips, that something weird was going on and to pay serious attention.

14

"You win," I said, "for now. So, tell me, Doc. Why did you ask for me specifically?"

Spencer stared through his glasses, and it was the first time I noticed that his eyes weren't normal. They were a deep brown color, which was fine, but the eyes were definitely larger than they should have been, maybe fifty percent or so. And there were flecks of gold in them, and I swear one of the flecks sparkled, and then more of them did.

That was the weirdest thing. I started blinking, and a heavy feeling behind my eyes built in pressure. It made me sleepy and foggy, like I'd been this morning when I'd woken up drunk.

Spencer stared even harder, and the golden flecks shined. It felt as if he was trying to drill into my soul with his piercing stare. I had the feeling he was doing something…repugnant to me.

Even though the thought was preposterous, my discomfort and irritation grew. Did this scrawny, bigheaded dude think he was going to man me down with a dominating look and a freaky eye trick? Did he think his big-shot status would protect him from me? I was almost free like Lancelot had been. If someone ticked me off enough, I'd bop him one in the kisser.

Thinking such thoughts, I leaned toward Spencer as I locked stares, beginning to squint as if I aimed my IAR at him.

That was the M27 Infantry Automatic Rifle, a 5.56-mm select-fire assault rifle, standard issue when I went to Bhutan.

To my surprise, I saw the corners of Spencer's mouth quirk upward in approval.

The sparkling flecks—if they'd ever done that—ceased shining. His brown eyes still seemed bigger than normal, but it no longer felt as if he attempted to dominate me.

As Spencer took off his glasses, breaking eye contact, I rubbed the bridge of my nose. The sleepy, foggy feeling was dissipating, leaving a slight ache behind my eyes.

Spencer was studying his lenses as if looking for smudges. He mustn't have found any because he put the glasses back on and smiled at me.

"You're here for the simple reason that I need a… a grounded assistant, shall we say," as if nothing peculiar had

15

just happened, "one of sufficient size and… adequate mental toughness."

I quit rubbing the bridge of my nose, looking at him, wondering if the eye trick had really happened. Maybe it had been some kind of DARPA experiment, a thing he'd done with his glasses. Maybe he'd turned his glasses off or something, the reason he'd been fiddling with them.

"You need someone from the Embassy?" I asked, deciding to go with the flow.

"No," he said, "an assistant with your particular qualities."

"That doesn't make sense. I'm a jarhead, a regular rifleman on his way out. I don't have peculiar qualities. And how did you ever get the Ambassador to agree to this?"

"Bah," he said, with a wave of a skinny hand, as if that was the least of his worries.

"Okay… You can see I'm a big boy. I grant you that. But how did you ever determine my mental toughness beforehand?"

Spencer's smile grew. "That should be obvious. You're military. That means you've taken many tests while in the service, yes?"

I nodded. He was so right about that. I'd taken *batteries* of tests. Most of them had seemed utterly pointless, too. I would be glad to leave such useless activities behind.

"There is your answer," Spencer said.

I frowned. "You're saying you went through my records?"

"Not just yours, no. I examined *tens* of thousands of records and finally settled upon you."

I shook my head, bewildered. What was so special about me? I was big and excelled at close-quarter combat. Besides that, I often got into trouble like the kind I had with Hendricks earlier.

"Tell me this then, Doc. What do you mean by mental toughness?"

"Hmm, I'm afraid I've said as much as I plan to, at least at this juncture. You'll have to wait and see. I assure you that everything will soon become clear."

The C-130's engines had built up to a roar as we began racing along a runway. Our speed dramatically increased until we lifted and began to climb steeply.

There was an odd noise like gulping combined with a squeak. I glanced at Spencer.

He sat rigidly with his thin hands gripping the ends of the armrests and his head pressing back against his seat. Fine beads of sweat began to ooze upon his slightly bulging forehead and along his upper lip. Had he made that weird noise?

I don't know why I bothered with him, but I said, "You're going to be fine, Doc. These 130s are tough birds. Don't sweat it."

He didn't respond.

I gave him a few seconds more and then glanced at him again.

He must have noticed, as he managed to turn his face toward me, smiling in a grimacing way.

Soon, the angle of our climb lessened, and the roar of the engines changed to a quieter but constant growl.

Spencer exhaled with relief, prying his long fingers from the armrests. He felt around in his inner parka and pulled out a handkerchief, dabbing at his sweaty face.

"Takeoff can be quite stressful," he said.

"So is missing the best date of my life, you have no idea."

He nodded as if I was making polite conversation, stuffing the handkerchief back into his hidden pocket.

"Say," I asked, "where are we going anyway?"

Spencer's lips compressed into a thin line.

"After all this," I asked, incredulous, "you're not going to tell me?"

"Yes, of course, why not?" he said suddenly. "Antarctica. We're heading for Antarctica."

What did he just say? It surely couldn't have been Antarctica.

"You must relax," he added, "as it will be a long trip."

"Uh...are we headed to Chilean Antarctica? Is that why you needed someone from the embassy?"

"No, no," he said. "We're going much farther than that, almost to the South Pole."

I blinked with growing astonishment and disbelief. This was even nuttier than I'd anticipated. Why hadn't Hendricks told me ahead of time so I could have packed cold weather gear? It was summer in Chile, and I'd packed accordingly. This joker was talking about flying to the most inhospitable spot on the globe. I happened to know that very few planes flew over frozen Antarctica, and even fewer went near the South Pole. This was more than just a temporary *jaunt* into the Chilean countryside.

My hackles rose as my temper started to fray. I was already missing the date that would move things along, perhaps speedily along, with Juanita. Now *this?* No. It was too much. "Why am I here, Doc? You'd better tell me so this makes sense."

"Don't fret, Sergeant. You'll see soon enough."

"Hey, Spencer," I said, leaning toward him. "This is BS. No one said anything about going to Antarctica."

My voice must have risen with my temper. Spencer glanced in desperation at the three in black.

That made me suspicious. I looked at them, too.

All three were unbuckling, and one after another, they stood and started across the hold for us. None held a gun. I would have been surprised if they had. Bullets punching holes in the skin of the C-130 would have been *muy estupido*. Each held a taser, the little gewgaws aimed at yours truly.

"Have you kidnapped me, Spencer?" I asked. "Is that what is going on?"

"What nonsense," he said in a false but hearty tone. "You're to assist me on an important project. This is an honor, I assure you."

I frowned as I tried to reason this out. Clearly, I was just a Marine sergeant. The only thing I'd really done was get in a few wicked firefights in Bhutan. Spencer had talked about tests. Did I possess some hidden talent then? It would appear so. What could be in Antarctica, though, that needed me?

Still, I must have some leverage here. He wanted me and only me, out of thousands, he'd said. That gave me some room to maneuver.

18

"You're talking about a DARPA project in Antarctica?" I asked.

"Yes, yes, that is so."

"Is there a problem, Doctor," asked the leader of the three.

Spencer gave me a significant glance as he raised an eyebrow.

I'd be lying if I said I didn't think about getting up and plucking the tasers from the jokers in black. I'd had enough of their threats, and I could deal them plenty of damage even if jolts of electricity were flowing through me. I'd end up with the dishonorable discharge, though. Because after beating them senseless, I'd make Spencer turn the 130 around. The looming dishonorable discharge swayed me, although in retrospect, I wish I'd taken their tasers and shoved them up their collective colonic canals.

So, I remained seated. "Sure, Doc," I said. "I'll play along. For twelve more days, I'm still a good Marine. After that, well...you're gonna have to make it worth my while."

The three in black visibly relaxed.

"That is a good decision," Spencer said. "You will not regret it."

The three turned around as they put away their tasers and headed back to their seats.

I looked at Spencer. "So, what is this about, huh? Mind telling me that much?"

His thin nostrils flared. "I'm attempting to discover what this is about, Sergeant. Yes, that is *precisely* the question that needs answering."

4

Spencer gave me his nonsense answer, and then he clammed up tight as he studied a tablet. I debated grabbing and shaking him, making his teeth rattle if nothing else. Then, I figured he was a skinny prick with delusions of importance. Why give him the joy of pestering him, begging for info, while he acted smug and significant?

So, I shrugged. He wasn't worth the dishonorable discharge. None of these punks was worth it. The doctor played games but was clearly important enough to rate a C-130 for his lonesome. He was a big shot in DARPA. Okay. I'd done more than my share of hurry up and wait while in the Marines. It was standard operating procedure. I should have been used to it by now.

I sat back, closed my eyes and fell asleep.

I got up later and walked around, did some deep-knee bends and happened to look out a porthole.

What do you think I saw? It surprised the heck out of me. Two F-35s escorted us. They were advanced fighters, those two being Navy birds—I could tell by their markings.

I went up to the porthole, stood up on my toes and peered down. Far below, I saw what surely had to be the snow-white continent of Antarctica. I didn't see any blue ocean water anywhere either.

How far inland were we? Would a tanker refuel the F-35s then? Would a tanker refuel us, or had one already done so?

Hmm. As I said earlier, it was summer on the bottom half of the world. That meant it would be permanent daylight near the South Pole. What did that mean regarding the two F-35s escorting us over Antarctica? The fighters had changed the equation, showing me we were much more important than I realized.

Thoughtful, even more stumped as to why I was here, I returned to my seat, thumping into it.

Spencer had several tablets out: one perched on each knee and another on a parka-fold on his stomach. He'd zipped the parka he was wearing. I glanced at the tablets and saw mathematical equations with odd symbols scrawled everywhere on them.

We'd been in flight for hours. I'd missed both breakfast and lunch, and I was reaching my limit regarding all this secrecy. Besides, I was leaving the Marines in twelve days…what did I need an honorable discharge for anyway? I was going to live like a knight-errant, doing what I wanted when I wanted. Maybe it would be better to burn my bridges with the Marines, with any government involvement in my life.

"Doc," I said.

"Hmm?" he said absently.

"Why are two F-35s escorting us? It makes no sense. Who would possibly attack us while we're deep over Antarctica?"

Without looking up, he said, "The Soviets—er, excuse me. I mean the Russians might try."

"No way," I said. "I'm not buying that for a second."

Spencer looked at me quizzically. I wonder what he saw. Did he get it that I knew more than my mug might indicate? "You're right," he said. "I meant the Chinese. They're still Communists after all."

"Come on, Doc. There are treaties forbidding any fighting in Antarctica. The Chinese aren't going to risk attacking a transport plane like this 130."

"Ha!" he said. "Did the Second Lateran Council successfully stop Christians from using crossbows against each other?"

"What?" I said, annoyed.

21

"In 1139 A.D., at the Second Lateran Council under Pope Innocent II, crossbows were officially banned from use. That is, Christians were not supposed to use them against other Christians. They could still be used against infidels."

"What?" I said again.

"Tell me," he said in a prissy egghead way. "Did the anti-crossbow ban of 1139 work back then?"

"I have no frigging idea. I'm guessing probably not from the way you're asking, but who cares?"

"You are correct. The ban did *not* work. And the reason is that councils, treaties and bans cannot alter basic human behavior."

Why couldn't anyone give me a straight answer for once? Spencer must have an egghead's delight in showing off his knowledge, and thus his mouth automatically shifted into longwinded, detouring explanations.

I might have complained, but my stomach couldn't take any more. I looked around, realizing I hadn't eaten all day.

"Say, Doc, is there anything to eat on this flight? I'm starving."

Spencer scowled. "Are you avoiding the issue?"

"Aren't *you?*" I was too hungry and getting seriously irritated at not knowing the score. "Look, you shanghaied me, remember, and are taking me to the South Pole. There isn't even any Santa Claus to meet like at the North Pole. The least you could do is provide some grub for the trip. How about it? I need something to eat. Even a candy bar would help."

"No. You'll have to wait until we land."

I stared at him, no longer finding his prim ways amusing. "F-35s, men in black, a long trip to the South Pole—you'd better tell me what this is about right this instant."

"No, no, not yet. It is still too soon."

"Then feed me."

"No."

"Listen," I said in a deadly quiet voice. "Do you know I once punched a commanding officer in the face?"

For the first time after takeoff, Spencer looked alarmed. "Is this true? It cannot be true."

"It's true," I said. "I knocked out three of his teeth."

Spencer blinked several times as if trying to retrieve data. He shook his head. "I imagine you mean during your time in a combat zone in Bhutan. Your commanding officer never reported this. I have read nothing of this."

"He couldn't report it. He was dead."

"Y-You *killed* him?" Spencer asked, horrified.

"I did not. Bhutan nationalists killed him on the way back. I carried him, though, as I'd knocked him out cold. I carried him even after I found out he was dead. It's what we Marines do. Never leave a man behind. The brass flew his corpse back to the States."

"Why did you hit him?"

"Bah!" I said, staring forward and crossing my arms, knowing I should have kept quiet about it. What was wrong with me? I still felt sick in my gut for Second Lieutenant Shavers dying that day. It was my fault, mine, even though he'd been an idiot. We never should have gone up that ridge. But that wasn't the point. I knew better than to tell a prick like Spencer any of this. I might get more than a dishonorable discharge now. I might spend the rest of my life in Leavenworth.

"Now now," Spencer said, "this is important. I did not read this in any of your evaluations. Why did you hit your commanding officer?"

I knew I should shut up. But I was hungry, pissed and sick of this egghead and his three clowns. Maybe if they realized what kind of bad hombre I was, they'd turn around and I could still manage a date with Juanita. Yeah, it was stupid logic, but as I said, I was pissed.

I leaned toward Spencer, staring at him, remembering the awful incident. If Doc here reported what I said, I could always deny it, saying he was trying to get me into trouble.

"Shavers never should have taken us up that ridge," I said. "Then, he lost it and panicked when the nationals rushed us. You know what he did?"

Spencer shook his head.

"Called down artillery fire on us, the idiot," I said bitterly. "He got five of my men killed. He wouldn't give me the only radio either. He'd taken it after the radioman bought it. So, I

23

knocked him out, took the radio and stopped the barrage. We fought our way out of the ambush ourselves like I knew we could. I carried Shavers back, using my left arm and shoulder." I shook my head at the memory. "On the way back, the lieutenant took the bullets that would have dropped me. He ended up being my shield. Who says a good turn is never rewarded?"

"You're making this up."

I frowned as I stuffed the bitterness away. Yeah, Shavers got some good men killed, but I was responsible for him buying it.

Then, the doc's words penetrated my brain. "Why would I make this up?" I demanded, outraged. I'd told him something I shouldn't and this bastard didn't even believe me?

Spencer seemed to ingest that, and he grunted, saying, "I've already noted your insubordinate potentialities. I did not know you had put them into practice, however. You should have told your next-in-command what you did."

"Sure, I should have. What an idiot I was for forgetting. Oh well, it's old history now, so who cares? I'm leaving the Marines in twelve days."

Spencer was staring at me. "How did you explain the lieutenant's missing teeth?"

"We fought hand-to-hand before it was over. Them Bhutan nationalists were crazy bastards. Shavers must have lost his teeth then, right?"

"This is intolerable," Spencer said. "You *lied,* in other words?"

"You know, Doc. I did lie. I lie all the time. I might be lying now. I might keep lying. You sure you still want my help in Antarctica?"

"I don't know. If there were another suitable candidate—" He stopped talking, no longer meeting my gaze.

"A suitable candidate for *what?*" I said, not liking the sound of that.

Without looking at me, Spencer shook his head.

"Are you setting me up for something? That's the only thing that really makes sense. You wanted a jarhead no one would miss. That's the real reason I'm here, isn't it?"

Spencer looked past me, calling out, "It's okay. I'll settle this."

I glanced at the three jokers in black. They were up again and each gripped a taser. At the doctor's words, they put the gewgaws away and returned to their seats.

I was getting sick of their threats, and I wanted something to eat.

"Mr. Bayard..." Spencer said slowly, thoughtfully. "Here. I have been remiss. I see that now."

He reached under his seat and pulled out a black lunch box. The bastard had something to eat all along. He put the lunch box on his knees and opened it. He pulled out two sandwiches and a granola bar, handing me each one at a time, like a king bestowing gifts.

I could have said a lot of things. What I did was rip off the cellophane wrapper and devour a chicken sandwich in three bites, hardly chewing.

"You eat like a wolf," Spencer said.

I'd heard that before. "You got something to drink?" I said with my mouth full.

Spencer pried free a thermos bottle, handing it to me.

I unscrewed the top and tasted—lemonade. It was too sweet, but I guzzled half before devouring the second sandwich, ham and cheese this time. I drank the rest of the lemonade and sat back, tearing off the granola-bar wrapper.

When I was done with the bar, I said, "Got anything else in there? I'm still hungry."

He blinked at me, reached into the lunch box and pulled out a third sandwich, handing it to me. "This is the last one. So, I suggest you savor it."

I tried to. It was another chicken sandwich. Too soon, I was licking my fingers, the edge taken from my hunger. I could have eaten another six sandwiches, though.

"Now there's nothing left for me," Spencer complained as he stared into the empty lunch box.

"Well...thanks," I said. "I needed that," burping afterward.

Spencer put away the lunch box and studied me, and I had the feeling he came to a decision. "Watching you eat and hearing the story about the lieutenant—you're the one. You must be. It's obvious."

"The one what?" I asked, no longer quite so amped up.

Spencer rubbed his chin, and he nodded. "What I'm about to tell you is highly classified, top, top secret, in fact. Only a handful of people know the whole truth, and one of them is *not* the President of the United States. To be honest, only three civilians know about this, me being one of them."

I frowned. This was starting to sound scary. Now that I thought about it, the entire setup, what had been happening— was this something regarding national security? If so, I didn't want any part of it. I was leaving the Marines, wanting to take life on my terms and not anyone else's.

"I thought you belonged to DARPA," I said.

"No," Spencer said. "I'm a civilian contractor working under special license *for* DARPA. I'm the only one on the planet with the qualifications to do what I am."

"What a load of crap," I said, although without heat. The planet, this had to do with the frigging Earth? I looked at Spencer, noticing more than ever his oddly large cranium. I thought about that and how Mr. Shotgun Seat had felt hotter than he should be.

I wasn't sure I wanted to hear more. I just wanted off the plane, and I wanted to go home to Santiago, to the States, really. Instead, I had a feeling I was going to hear something that would forever change my life—for the worse.

5

Spencer cleared his throat several times before he started explaining. "My extended researched has shown me that you were or are the best candidate for the...the mission. We shall call it a mission, yes?"

"What are you talking about?" I asked.

He gave me a false smile. "By my calculations, you have a forty-eight-point-nine percent probability of withstanding mental domination by one of the...the aboriginals, shall we say."

"Huh?"

"No," he said, looking up at the ceiling, "we don't know they're aboriginal to Earth. Let us call them *psi-masters* for now. I think that's a more elegant term, don't you?"

"What are you babbling about? Aboriginal to Earth? We're *all* aboriginal to Earth."

"Possibly so, although I have my doubts," Spencer said. "Besides, that was not the important point. I'm surprised you missed it. I said *psi*-masters. Do you realize that psi is an abbreviation for the word psionic?"

I blinked at the DARPA-contracted scientist with his strangely overlarge brown eyes with golden flecks and his larger than average cranium. "Why don't you start making some sense, huh, Doc?"

"That is an excellent suggestion. Psionic relates to mental powers or paranormal abilities. Telepathy like reading minds would be considered a psionic ability or power. Mental domination would be another. The term psionic has gone out of fashion in the scientific community, as the concept is considered something of a joke. However, to our horror, we revived an actual psi-master. Many thought his survival would prove impossible. It wasn't, and he nearly overpowered the staff that revived him. What did happen was that seventy-six percent of the staff slew themselves before the others rendered the psi-master unconscious. We believe they killed themselves at his mental command."

"You've read too much science fiction," I said. "It's unbalanced your thinking. What are you talking about?"

Spencer shook his head. "Reality. I speak about harsh reality."

I should have been feeling good about now. Three sandwiches had taken the edge off my hunger. Instead, listening to Spencer, a cold sweaty feeling made it a chore to think. He couldn't believe I bought such an Area 51 story as that. It was ludicrous, absurd.

And yet...DARPA was known to be deeply involved with Area 51.

I glanced at the operatives, at the leader. His shoulder had felt like hot steel. He'd spoken in a bizarre accent. Two F-35s escorted the C-130 to the South Pole. If this was real, if an Area 51 story *could* be real...

"What does any of this have to do with me?' I asked in a quiet voice.

Spencer looked away, sighed and then regarded me more closely. "I have agreed to work with DARPA in this. You see...the men seated over there aren't here to guard you, but me."

I glanced at the three. They watched me as they had been doing from the start. They'd hardly said a word. Earlier, they had definitely moved to rescue him from me.

Yet, I realized something. Spencer was lying about them guarding him. That meant—understanding struck, and it struck relentlessly.

It reminded me of the time artillery fire had rained on us at the ridge in Bhutan, killing five of my men. The truth had felt like jelly, thinking through jelly, having such a hard time

28

realizing it was really happening: that Lieutenant Shavers was an idiot killing us.

My thoughts waded through jelly as I stared at Spencer, glanced at his watchdog goons and then back at him.

"When I first sat down," I said, "you tried to mentally dominate me."

"Yes," he said. "That is so."

I squinted through my jelly thoughts, squinted at him as if aiming an IAR between his eyes. I had the sick feeling his story was real. Something ignited deep in my chest. *You played with the wrong dude. I'm a born warrior, a Lancelot doing what he wants.* I gave Spencer a savage grin. "You tried to mentally dominate me *and failed.*"

"Not so," he said. "I simply did not use my full powers upon you."

The desire to hit him was strong. I could actually feel myself doing it. Instead, clicking into a higher more alert gear, I decided to probe, to learn, to study my enemy before I acted.

"Where did you get these psionic powers, huh, Doc? Did someone pump you full of gamma radiation or did you ride through space like the Fantastic Four?"

"I'm not at liberty to tell you."

"This… This is crazy stuff you're spewing." No, no, on the fly I decided on a different angle, a different way to go about this. "Supposing I believe you, Doc… What does any of that have to do with Antarctica?"

Spencer sighed and shook his too-large head. "I am…" He frowned, picked up a tablet, studying it, nodding, laying it back on his lap. "I suppose I can tell you now. We're well over halfway there and…"

He sat straighter, paused as if collecting his thoughts and cleared his throat for the hundredth time. "The truth is strange and fantastic in one respect and quite ordinary in another. I'm a product of crossbreeding, although I only learned this recently. I always knew I was different from others, but I didn't know why or how exactly. I've always known that my mother was an American. I only recently discovered that my father…I don't really know what he was, not exactly. Some would say he was a colonist from Mu."

29

Mu? I'd read about Mu before, supposedly an ancient sunken continent somewhere in the Pacific Ocean. Some claimed it had possessed an advanced civilization long before the dawn of human history. The goofballs making such claims, however, had as much credibility as those who believed in *Chariots of the Gods*. It was nutty talk, even more loony than Area 51 stories.

That got me suspicious. "Doc, are you making all this up off the top of your egg-shaped head?"

Spencer laughed sourly. "I could only wish that were the case. It would make my life so much simpler. Yours too."

"What does this have to do with me?"

"I'm surprised you don't see it."

"What does that mean?"

Spencer inhaled through his nostrils like a snooty professor, peering down his nose at me. "It's too soon for you to recognize the truth, is that it? In a way, I can understand. Learning the truth mentally unbalanced me for a time. I'm not surprised it is doing the same to you."

"I'm learning you're crazy," I said.

He smiled sadly, pityingly, shaking his head at me.

I wanted to punch him. I *ached* to punch him, to bash his smugness into smithereens.

"Perhaps if I told you what I've learned this past year, you'll understand. You'll see the connections to your own life." Spencer nodded, clearing his damned throat. I was getting sick of hearing that.

"You see," said Spencer, "my father died in 1968, gunned down as he tried to escape his confinement. My mother had been one of his keepers, a linguist working to translate his strange language. She grew to love him, and clandestinely made love to him one night. I think he used her, as his escape attempt occurred several nights later. In any case, I'm the product of their brief union."

What was this nut telling me? His dad was E.T.? No, his dad had been a psi-master. I stared at Spencer's slightly bulging forehead and greater cranium area. A sick feeling formed in my stomach. Where would this psi-master freak have

30

come from? The lost continent of Mu? Were we looking for saucer ships of Atlantis then? This was insane.

Worse, I heard myself ask, "This was supposed to have happened back in 1968?"

"My father lived in our era for three months and five days."

If Spencer had kicked me in the stomach, it wouldn't have surprised me more. I said in a small voice I could barely recognize, "What does that mean, *our era?*"

Spencer sighed once more. "In late 1967, a American Antarctica survey team found my father's stasis container and functioning support equipment. By luck or misfortune, they started the revival process. My father thawed and made it to a snow-cat, the only vehicle to survive an explosion, which destroyed everything else. The two men in the snow-cat were the only ones of the survey team to survive the expedition, although they committed suicide several years later."

"All this happened back in 1968?"

"No," Spencer said. "As I told you, in 1967 and 1968."

"Okay, okay, don't get your pantics in a bunch." My mouth was bone dry. I doubt it would have freaked me out any worse if Spencer had simply disappeared with the snap of his fingers. Could this be a true story? No way. But... "What happened next?" I whispered.

"The rigors of the snow-cat trip rendered my father unconscious. Other Americans recaptured him, imprisoning him. Soon, American scientists began experiments on my father, including my mother's attempt to piece together his language. Few believed the driver of the snow-cat about my father until they learned of the secret expedition. An interesting side-note is that many others experimenting and watching my father also committed suicide in later years. We now believe he mentally depressed them as an ongoing effort to resist their experiments, and the cumulative effect took time to work."

My eyelids felt gritty as I blinked them. "You must be making this up as you go," I said, "as your story has a huge hole. If your father was some kind of mind-master like you say, why didn't he just take over their thoughts and have them release him?"

31

"You surprise me," Spencer said. "Especially after watching you eat. That is an excellent question. The answer is interesting and rational. I think it's because he didn't know the language, not English or any modern Earth tongue. When he attempted telepathy on them, they just heard gobbledygook in their thoughts. Perhaps that was why he was so eager to have my mother teach him."

"That sounds like a stretch."

"I see," Spencer said. "And you understand the intricacies of telepathy, do you?"

"You got a point there, Doc. I have no earthly idea. All right, all right, you say that your mind-master father was a murderous bastard. What happened to your mother?"

"Fortunately, she is still living."

"Huh. So, what happened to you? Are you a witch like your father?"

"Psionics isn't witchcraft or anything resembling it," Spencer said in a huff. "It is extrasensory powers of the mind."

"Sure, whatever—and you have it?"

Spencer stared at me until he smiled sourly. "I lived a relatively normal life until seven months ago. No one knew about my differences. No one suspected. However, a recent exploratory team found another stasis chamber. This one was far below the ice."

"So what?"

Spencer stared up at the ceiling. "Scientists in DARPA read the old file on my father. They spoke to my mother, must not have liked her answers and made her take lie detector tests. Soon, they found and tested me. I was a professor at MIT at the time. Through their subterfuge, the scientists discovered that I possessed a latent ability I'd been unwittingly using most of my adult life."

For the umpteenth time, I noted Spencer's large cranium and protruding forehead. Then, I looked over at the three in black. They watched me. They were always watching me, and each of them wore his irritating sunglasses no matter what. Oh. The dark sunglasses—

"Do sunglasses stop you from doing your trick against them?" I asked.

32

Spencer noted where I looked, grew thoughtful and nodded. "The sunglasses retard the process, although they cannot fully stop it."

"There's something I don't understand," I said, regarding him again. "Why would DARPA allow you to pick me? No. The better question is: why do they let you run loose? It seems more likely they would have caged you just like your father, caged you and run a billion tests until you were dead. That would be how any sane scientist would do it. They'd never let you run loose."

A tic twitched his left cheek.

"Ha! That's it, isn't it? You escaped your minders and are on the run. You're a lone wolf running scared." As I said that, I realized how stupid it was to have let him know I figured it out. Now he knew I knew. It would have been better to have him think I was ignorant.

Desperation now filled Spencer's overlarge eyes. "I need your help, Bayard," he said thickly.

"My help," I said. "What can I possibly do to help you?"

He stared at me.

Shock struck, and I grunted as I folded as if someone had punched me in the gut. My old man had lived his life in orphanages, or so he'd told me. I'd never been to one, and the stories of his time in them had always been vague. My mother had died at my birth. My father had raised me until I was fourteen and then he'd been electrocuted to death in a freak accident in the middle of nowhere in Nevada—or so I'd been told. I'd bummed around on my own afterward, joining the Marines right out of high school.

"You're beginning to understand that you're different from others," Spencer said.

"My head is normal sized," I said.

He touched the bulging part of his forehead. "Yes, I'm different, but not in the same way as you. Do you have any idea how long it has taken me to find someone like you?"

"What are you saying I am?"

"A traveler," he said.

"Say it straight, Doc. What's a traveler? Are you saying my old man was one?"

33

"Ah, your father, you say?"

I clenched my fingers into fists, hating the way he said it.

"Don't you see?" Spencer said. "I want to find my father's people. I *need* to find them and I believe you're the key."

What in the world was a traveler? Could my old man have come from somewhere else than Earth? Did that mean I was part alien? I didn't feel alien. No. I was one hundred percent human. Then, what was Spencer saying?

"Sergeant Bayard."

I looked at Spencer, at his eyes. The flecks of gold in them shined as they had before. No, they blazed with glaring brightness, far brighter than earlier.

A wicked smile stole over him.

The pressure behind my eyes became intolerable. The fogginess of my thoughts made it hard to think.

"Listen to me, Sergeant. You're going to do exactly what I tell you. I've planned this for weeks and weeks. Now—"

I growled low in my throat, and I squinted at the bastard, mentally fighting the brightness in his eyes. I struggled against his dominating will that sought to subdue mine.

"Sergeant, you must listen to me. I lied about your mental toughness. You have a different quality I need. In reality, you're a *moron* like the rest of humanity."

I squinted as I struggled up to a standing position. My eyes smarted and my frontal lobes throbbed like crazy.

"Sergeant Jake Bayard," Spencer said in a loud voice as he stood up. *"Sit down."*

It was a command, and I felt the force of his will moving my knees. All the pent-up frustration of the past two years boiled in me, it boiled and surged against his control. It felt once again as if artillery shells exploded overhead, killing my friends as raining shrapnel tore them to pieces. I felt waves of dominating power flow against my mind. It seemed as if a hurricane force struck. I leaned into it, a physical action, and I saw Doc Spencer staring at me with his overlarge eyes shining.

Ever since Bhutan, I'd coiled tighter into myself. It was like a two-year windup for a pitch. Now, I cut loose and swung, putting everything into it. The knuckles of my right fist struck Spencer's jawline. The blow catapulted him off his feet so he

34

struck the floor with the back of his head. He arched up as if in agony, and then sank upon the deck as he twitched, twitched more and then lay very still.

The mental hurricane ceased as the achy feeling behind my eyes began to throb. My eyes watered, and I stared at Spencer and saw that he did not move.

Staggering, I knelt beside him and felt for a pulse under his jaw. He didn't have one I could feel.

I heard a rustle of sound behind me, and turned.

The three operatives stood there, their tasers aimed at me. Their thumbs pressed down. I expected darts and trailing lines. Instead, purple jags of force, like lightning, struck me. Those must have been a new kind of taser. As the energy surged through me—it was the last thing I remember.

-6-

My old man, my dad, had been a rugged individualist of the old school. He'd married a knockout of a doll, my mother, and as I'd said before, she died at my birth.

Nothing he ever said or did indicated that he held her death against me. But from around six years old on, I'd felt a great weariness and sadness from my dad.

I seldom saw him smile. He was a big guy with rock-hard muscles and never lost at anything...except maybe for life.

What did he do for income?

I have no idea. He never said. He never went to work like other fathers. Yet, we had money and we lived the middle-class life most of the time.

The few times we didn't, we went hunting in places like Alaska, the Amazon Basin or South Africa. He hunted with javelins most of the time, short three-foot things. Maybe the better name for them was darts. With his iron-barbed darts, he took down grizzlies, jaguars and yeah, even lions. The man could track and had skills like Tarzan of the Jungle. I'm not talking about swinging through the trees. He could follow spoor and creep up on anything.

My dad used to fix things, like old cars, buggies, a small airplane and our air-conditioner. He always chopped down an evergreen for Christmas. He loved Christmas, especially the story about how the three wise men outsmarted King Herod. My dad read that out loud from the King James Bible enough times I practically knew the story by heart. The wise men didn't trick Herod, though. God did that through a dream so the wicked king couldn't kill God's Son, the Prince of Peace.

My dad used to drink too much. He never picked on me, even when he was drunk. Those would be the only times he watched TV, just staring dull-eyed at the boob tube getting drunker and drunker until he passed out.

Three times that I saw, he got into a fight. He kicked ass each time, trashing three guys in an alley as we were going home from the movies in Baltimore. The three were big fellows and jeered at my dad, calling him a cracker and a white boy. They had knives and maybe two of them had guns. He had his fists. He left them crying with broken bones and severely massed noses. The second time was a mob in New York City. He kept tossing guys to the left and to the right. Finally, the mob rushed him and bore him to the concrete. Cops bulled in and pulled people off him. Two guys on the bottom were screaming: one with a broken arm behind his back and the other missing both his ears and bleeding profusely. My dad had torn off the ears Mike Tyson style with his teeth.

The last fight I know of was in Manitoba, Canada. Five lumberjacks rushed him with axe handles. They thought my dad had been smiling at their wives or something, or maybe they just didn't like him because he was an outsider. They were going to beat the tar out of him. He did something fancy to the first guy, who found himself on his back with two broken wrists. Then, my dad plied the man's axe handle like in the movie with the outlaw gangs of New York City and beat the snot out of the lumberjacks. By that, I mean—never mind. It was an ugly beating.

The Canadian government was going to take me from my dad because of that. Thus, we moved back to the States. My old man died in Nevada half a year later, electrocuted to death under mysterious circumstances.

Now, this Doctor Spencer, was telling me my dad was a traveler? What was a traveler, and how did that affect me? Why did Spencer think my dad had anything to do with his own bigheaded freak of a father? My dad never mentally dominated anyone, but he was the toughest person I'd ever known.

Mu...what had Spencer meant about colonists of Mu in Antarctica? Did DARPA have anything to do with any of this?

I was asleep, but I was thinking. Or I was the next thing to asleep in a mental fog that allowed me to ruminate about all this.

I hoped I'd killed Spencer. I hadn't felt a pulse under his chin. That didn't necessarily mean he was still dead. Wasn't he some kind of mind-witch? Could he fake his death?

Being a traveler was important to Spencer. If my dad had been able to *travel*—whatever that implied—did that mean I could do it too?

That must be it. I was a traveler, or I had the potential to be a traveler. The big question was, travel to where?

With the silent question ricocheting in my mind, I slowly lost coherence. It felt as if I was moving, being moved, but even that went away as I once more lost whatever semi consciousness I'd retained.

-7-

I began to cogitate again in a fuzzy way, as I grew aware of someone shaking one of my shoulders. I must have been stretched out. It felt as if I lay upon something soft, a cot, perhaps. The shaker proved insistent.

"What?" I slurred, my mouth feeling numb, my brain on strike.

He shook my shoulder again.

I opened my eyes, seeing the leader of the operatives on his knees beside me, his hot hand on my shoulder. The other two stood nearby, with Glocks in their hands. What had happened to their fancy tasers?

I realized a few things then. I was no longer aboard the C-130. I lay on a cot as I'd suspected. The ceiling showed metal and wood. I must have been inside a building. Had we made it to near the South Pole?

The leader climbed to his feet and glanced at the other two. All of them still wore their sunglasses.

I didn't see Spencer, but I wasn't looking around much, just staring up. I had fuzzy thoughts and couldn't move around much. Was that a property of being Tased or had they injected me with drugs?

The idea of drugs, forced injections—rage boiled in me, although it was a lazy rage, given my present state.

The three conferred in whispers, glancing back at me.

I noted the ceiling again and remembered some of what I'd read about base-building deep in Antarctica.

There was a standard doctrine for such things. This base surely hadn't been an exception. Light planes would have landed first on the snow and ice, with heavy transports parachuting supplies. Engineers would have come next and graded a proper airstrip with bulldozers so the heavy transports could land. At that point, they would have started to build the permanent base.

Heavy bulldozers would have scooped out huge trenches in the snow and ice. Afterward, engineers would build air pockets, roofing the trenches with steel arches. Prefabricated buildings would go up in the trenches. The bulldozers would then push snow onto the steel roofs. The ice and snow insulated the buildings from the hellish temperatures. During blizzards, men went outside with ropes tied to their waists so they wouldn't get lost, staying out for minutes instead of hours.

Everything—living quarters, labs, reactors, desalination plants, warehouses and garages—was constructed underground or in the trenches. The base personnel used ladders to get up onto the ice. If the base needed expanding, more prefabricated buildings would be flown in.

Antarctica and especially the South Pole region was a nightmare place even in summer.

I tried to sit up but gave up after a second, as I didn't have enough strength yet. I couldn't feel any pain to indicate injections. That must mean the purple energy in the fancy tasers had really done a number on me.

Why would two of them bother holding Glocks if I was woozy like this, and if they could knock me out at any time?

I turned my head, regarding them as they regarded me. "You boys worried about me?" I asked weakly.

None of them answered.

"Did we land near the South Pole?" I asked.

The leader opened his mouth. Before he spoke, though, he glanced at the other two. They nodded. He regarded me and finally took off his sunglasses.

I blanched at the sight.

He had red eyes like in a bad photograph, only these were real and not a result of lighting. Here was the reason for the sunglasses, not Spencer's BS explanation.

"Are you guys even human?" I asked aghast.

"Doctor Spencer is dead," the leader said, "slain by your wicked hand. You must now die in agony, screaming out your sin for all to hear. Otherwise, we would have dispatched you ourselves for your murderous deed."

My gut twisted, and adrenaline pumped through me. I began to shed some of my mental fuzziness and weakness. This time, however, I hid that as I faked the former loopy condition, letting spittle dribble from my mouth.

"Where...where did you guys come from?" I said, slowly moving an arm and wiping away the spit. "Not some laboratory, but somewhere off planet, right?"

"You speak about the Harmony. Yes, we belong to the Harmony. Doctor Spencer was going to..." The leader snarled silently. "You slew the son of a master. That was an evil deed of desperate wickedness."

I should have started blubbering in terror, as I was fighting panic in my heart. But like the Marine captain in Bhutan had told me two years ago, I was a born warrior. This was the type of situation that lubricated my brain and kick-started my interest. I felt woozy for more than just being Tased. Having my world-view trashed in seconds was hard on my inner sense of balance, of reality. But Spencer had already upset that earlier, and having a dad that went big-game hunting with barbed darts, taking down grizzlies and big cats—I wasn't exactly normal. Maybe having traveler genes had something to do with that, too.

"I get it," I said. "I'm a sinner. What I want to know is if you guys are human or not?"

The leader's red eyes blazed, possibly with indignation. "We are true men. You are substrata, a wild beast with bloody hands. If we knew how to return—"

He shut his mouth as the other two made odd squealing sounds like stuck pigs.

I stared at those two in shock. That hadn't sounded human, and it made his earlier iron-hard shoulder and hot flesh seem unnatural. It dawned on me that they'd just spoken in their native tongue. It was like nothing I'd ever heard, and I'd heard some strange stuff in Bhutan.

41

I studied the leader, his strange red eyes, and noticed that, like before, his facial skin seemed stretched too tightly. I had the uncomfortable feeling the skin might rip away and that I wouldn't like what I saw underneath: maybe scaly green reptilian hide.

Likely, it would be better for me if I kept talking, kept treating them as if they were remotely human. Keep up pretenses, in other words.

"Any of you boys know what happened to the F-35s?"

They stared at me, and I was beginning to wish the leader would put his sunglasses back on. There was something decidedly inhuman and devilish about the red eyes.

"F-35s," I said. "You know, the escorts flying beside us. What happened to them?"

They turned and stared at each other for longer than seemed reasonable. Imperceptibly, they became more alert, as if listening for sounds.

From on the cot, I cocked my head. The sound was faint; it would have to be coming through the snow heaped over the roof—if I was right about that. I heard the *whomp-whomp* of a big Chinook, a twin-engined, tandem rotor, heavy-lift helicopter. That was a CH-47 Chinook, by the way, one of the heaviest lifting helicopters in the world.

The three began squealing at each other in their hideous tongue. It was a wretched performance, and it became worse as I began to hear repeated sounds that I recognized as words.

Abruptly, they stopped squealing. The leader stepped back. The other two holstered their Glocks and lunged toward me, one on either side of the cot. They gripped my arms, and they had powerful holds for such thin guys. Worse, they literally radiated heat from their palms.

With grunts, they strained to lift me onto my feet.

Despite having felt stronger a few moments ago, I found myself sweating and gulping for air as I rose. The purple jolts—what had they fired at me before? I shouldn't have been this out of it. Groaning, trying to make my feet work, I stumbled as they helped me toward the door. I thought about that. I wore a shirt, pants and boots, but didn't have a coat.

"If we're going outside," I panted, "I need a parka."

42

They ignored me.

The leader was already at the door. He opened it, showing a wall of ice. We were in a trench, all right.

I felt the cold then as it drifted in from the open door.

It was summer at the South Pole, January 8—if this was the same day—the height of summer. But the South Pole was far colder than the North Pole during its summer months. There were three reasons for that. One, the South Pole was higher in elevation than the North Pole. Two, the ocean water—comparatively warmer than the surrounding land—was all around the Artic but was kept farther away by Antarctica's huge land mass. Third, The Earth was or is at aphelion in July. That meant the Earth was at its farthest point from the sun in an Antarctic winter and closest in the warmer Antarctic summer.

The first two reasons trumped the last one and meant that summer here was harsh.

To give you an idea, the average North Pole winter temperature was minus forty degrees Fahrenheit. The South Pole's winter average was *minus seventy-six* degrees Fahrenheit. The summer average was a regular thirty-two and *minus* eighteen respectively.

That meant it was extremely cold on the ice, and I only had on a shirt and pants.

"A parka," I said. "I don't know about you boys, but I'll die without a parka."

My helpers ignored the plea and propelled me toward the door. Their hot hands told me they likely didn't understand my dilemma.

I decided to heck with this—I wasn't going to let them freeze me to death. I let my knees unlock, dropping. I took them both down with me: them to their knees, me onto my stomach.

That didn't last. The leader yanked out a Glock and jabbed the pistol muzzle into the small of my back.

"Aw!" I shouted, arching in pain.

He knelt beside me as the other two scrambled upright out of the way.

"I'll cripple you by shooting out your knees," he whispered into my ear. He had the foulest breath I'd ever smelled. True

43

human my ass—this sucker was something else entirely. "The masters will still be able to torture you for many weeks as a cripple," he added. "Thus, I will not have sullied their honor."

"Uh…okay, I get that," I said. "I want to go topside, believe me I do. But I'll die without a parka. Doesn't the cold bother you?"

He seemed to think about that, finally saying, "The cold is uncomfortable but bearable."

"Sure. I get it. You're tough guys. Me? Not so much."

The other two squealed.

The leader looked at them and then me, nodding. "We wear thermal suits. I forgot that you do not."

He was lying about the thermal gear. I wondered why he bothered.

He climbed to his feet, looked around, went to a parka and threw it at me.

"Thanks, pal," I said, shrugging on the thick parka while remaining on the floor. "I won't forget this."

He snapped his fingers at the other two.

They surged forward and forced me to me stand.

The leader went to the door, leaning out and looking up. He scowled back at the others. "His delaying tactics are working. We will have to hurry. Are you ready?"

One of my minders squealed in reply.

The leader squealed back and dashed out the door, climbing a ladder.

My helpers hustled me to the door, and I managed to keep my feet under me.

Climbing the ladder proved difficult in my state and slow going. I also dragged my feet, figuring delaying was good if they thought it was bad. One minder climbed ahead and pulled at my parka hood, yanking me upward. The other climbed below me, pushing against my ass. I might have delayed more, but his hot-handed shoves against me were starting to make me mad.

We reached the top of the ladder, and the ice and the brilliance of the South Pole summer sun bore down upon me. The reflection off the snow and ice made it worse. I'd read

44

somewhere that a person could get UV burns from this stuff if outside in it for too long.

I squinted horribly, wishing for a pair of dark sunglasses. I saw a sun dog, a bright spot near the sun. I squinted even tighter, looking around to see what I could.

There was a runway and the C-130 parked near a smaller lighter cargo plane. Farther away, I could see burning wreckage. It might have been one of the F-35s. There was no sign of the second fighter. In the near distance, I saw icy mountains. Oh, and something else. There were snowy mounds, big things. Beyond the mounds was the top of a giant crane. Somehow, that seemed ominous.

I glanced back across the trench and then up. Three big Chinooks headed for us.

I found that strange. Antarctica didn't see too many helicopters. For one thing, a helicopter's range was much shorter than a transport airplane. It was also harder keeping a helicopter operational in winter weather. For both reasons, that meant the Chinooks must have come from a nearby base.

My keepers headed for the mounds of snow, hurrying as my boots and their fancy shoes crunched upon the icy substance.

I saw people then, honest-to-goodness humans in parkas with their hoods up and standing around. It was cold, maybe minus eighteen, maybe minus twenty-five outside. I really didn't know. I'd shoved my hands in my parka pockets, had my hood up and my eyes squinted nearly shut. The skin on my face hurt already with a prickly cold feeling.

We passed the ten-meter-high snow mounds, and I saw the crane better afterward. It was a big thing with a long cable into a large hole in the ice.

Those wearing parkas looked like mostly men with a few women, maybe thirty in all. Could they be the regular staff of the base? Most of the parkas had stars and stripes on them, U.S. Army personnel if I were to guess.

Looking at them closer, I had the sinking feeling Doctor Spencer had spent time with each of them, using his dominating power on them. Had Spencer used his power on the American Ambassador to Chile? Had he used it on the pilot of

45

the C-130? None of the Army people spoke to us as we passed them, although they all watched like hungry zombies. I don't mean they were already dead. I mean they had unwavering stares, but otherwise lacked all expression.

"What are we trying to do?" I shouted, seeing white mist spew from my mouth.

One positive thing about the cold was that it was helping me to revive faster. I already had better motor control but tried to fake that I didn't.

"Start it," the leader shouted.

Those nearest the crane reacted as if he'd prodded them with hot pokers as they went into motion. Seconds later, I heard the crane roar with engine noise and oily clouds puff upward. The cable moved, and an iron cage lifted into view from just inside the icy hole.

"Are we going down somewhere?" I asked.

The leader glanced back at the approaching Chinooks, the *whomp-whomp* sounds louder than ever.

The leader ran to one of the Army personnel. I heard him speak, and then all the parka-clad people began to move. They sprinted to stacked and waiting weapons, some of them crew-served heavy machine guns.

It was obvious they were supposed to attack the people coming in the Chinooks.

Soon enough, a few Army personnel pulled the iron cage onto the ice. They opened a door and turned to us.

My keepers propelled me toward it. I understood. They were going to take me down into the hole in the ice. Should I fight them? Was this the moment to make my last stand?

I decided against it. Even if I could overpower the three red-eyed quasi-humans—if they were even that—I would fail against the rest. Thus, I stepped into the cage with the two. Then, the leader joined us.

The zombie-like Army people closed the door, latching it, and they pushed until the cage swung over the hole.

I looked down and couldn't see a bottom.

The cage shook, and we started down, the crane lowering us by cable.

I should have stayed home this morning, phoned the embassy and told them I had a terrible hangover. I could have been getting ready for Juanita Bolivar then.

I looked down again. Was this really happening to me? Sadly, I told myself it was. What was down there? And how badly did I want to avoid finding out?

The cage kept heading down as we passed endless ice. I wondered about that and peered closely at the ice. It was smooth. What would have cut through the ice like that? A giant laser? No one had blasted the hole or chipped away at it manually, unless teams of people had polished or sanded the sides afterward. That would be ridiculous, though.

Anyway, that was the least of my concerns. My so-called true-men keepers radiated far more heat than a person should. An entire base of American soldiers did the hypnotic bidding of these aliens. That made these three my enemies. The hypnotized people were going to ambush other Americans.

I needed to prevent that. But how? I was at a loss to figure out the correct course of action.

Antarctica was big: over 13,000,000 square kilometers. That was about 40 percent larger than the continental United States. Most of the frozen continent was sheathed in ice up to 4000 meters high. The immense amount of ice had actually pushed some of the continent down to below sea level. If all the ice suddenly melted, the continent would turn into island chains. Interestingly, there were ice-free liquid lakes hidden under some of the ice. I think something like seventy percent of the world's fresh water was locked in the Antarctica ice.

What did that have to do with the base and my predicament? I did not believe the crane could lower us more than 4000 meters. That was as least as far as the cage would likely have to descend before we struck actual land.

I wondered due to one of the doctor's earlier comments. Spencer had said the aboriginal people of Antarctica might have been colonists from Mu. I couldn't believe that was possible. When had Antarctica been free of year-round ice? When had the Pacific Ocean continent of Mu existed? Long before men had been around—at least, given the usual time-rates as taught in the schools. What if what we thought about that—about Mu, anyway—was wrong? What if Mu had been around when Antarctica had been free of ice and that had been when men were on Earth? That would contradict the ice-core timelines scientists had developed.

Okay. Maybe I needed to bark up a different tree. Let me see…Spencer had said American explorers had found his psi-master father in stasis in 1967. Stasis was something like hibernation. Humanity didn't have that kind of stasis technology, however. Certainly, the three with me had never originated on Earth—

My eyes widened.

Spencer said his father had been in stasis. Could these three jokers have been in stasis as well, the ones found a short year ago? Why had Spencer gone to such effort to get me? To help him "travel," whatever that meant, was the short answer. It would seem, therefore, that these three did not know how to travel wherever Spencer was trying to get.

Hmm, traveling must *not* mean by some giant spaceship. Did we go down into the ice to search for more stasis-held…people? Or was there something else down here, perhaps something to help us travel?

The cage kept remorselessly heading down, the light dimming around us as it did.

Spencer had talked about Mu and ancient Antarctica, and the leader had said something about the "Harmony." Our planet did not belong to it, at least not that I knew about anyway. What was the Harmony?

As I watched the ice pass—or as we passed it—I thought about possible ways to travel to other planets. After all, I've read my fair share of science fiction, doing a lot of the reading while in Bhutan.

One way to get to another planet, either here or in another dimension, was through a gate. I'm talking about a sci-fi idea. There had been a whole TV series about people going to different planets through star-gates on Earth. Could that be what this was about? But…why would a gate need me? Had my father had come to Earth via a gate on a different planet?

I had no idea. But supposing that I was on the right track? Was this the time to try overpowering my keepers? Three of them and one of me—normally, I'd like the odds. I wasn't sure how groggy I might be, though, and who waited for us at the end of the line.

I debated with myself, frowning, tensing—until the bottom of the cage struck ice, jolting us against each other. My two minders tightened their grips on my arms.

The leader spoke into a wrist radio.

Seconds later, the crane ceased lowering cable onto the top of the cage.

The leader opened the door and pulled out a flashlight, turning it on. His beam of light showed a long tunnel through the ice heading down at a slant.

"Go," he told me.

The minders kept hold of me, shoving, propelling me ahead. Seconds later, they let go.

After straightening from my stumble, I looked back at them.

None wore sunglasses. Their eyes seemed redder than before, glowing in the darkness, making them seem more demonic than ever. I shuddered. Could they see in the dark better than a normal human? Were these three demons in some Biblical fashion?

I held up an arm as the leader shined the flashlight in my eyes.

"Go," he said. "We will follow you."

The two former minders had their super-tasers out again, aimed at me. I didn't want to take a second shocking. I was still recovering from the first.

With a shrug, I faced forward and began to trudge through the ice tunnel. At least moving should warm me up. Standing in the cage had started me shivering.

50

After ten minutes, I did feel warmer, and I kept heading down, slipping now and again.

I soon lost track of time. I was hungry, not fully recovered from the purple jolts and still shivering. I felt winded and realized some time later that we must have walked five, maybe six kilometers already.

"Wait," the leader said, as he looked at a small handheld instrument.

I stopped, leaned against a tunnel wall and slid down onto my butt. After a few seconds, 1 felt around and realized I touched stone, not ice. We'd made it onto Antarctica bedrock. That was interesting—and ominous.

The three conferred softly in their squealing tongue. One of them took out a tablet, and they studied it together, their squeals becoming more agitated.

I lay down on my back and closed my eyes. I was beat. For a moment, I could see Juanita's swaying hips in my mind's eye. I sighed. What rotten luck.

As I lay there thinking dark thoughts, it occurred to me that I should be feeling claustrophobic. Hundreds of thousands of tons of ice were above me. What kept the ice from sinking onto us and crushing us like bugs?

I sat up and looked at the three.

One of the minders was putting away his tablet.

The leader shined his light on me. "Get up," he said. "We must continue. We have another hour of trekking at least."

"Who made the tunnel?" I asked.

"No questions," he said. "You must walk."

"Look, bub, I'm tired and hungry. I'm cold—"

He turned to the others and squealed.

They charged me, pulling out their tasers. Red jolts of something lashed from them.

It was like having red-hot pokers pressed against my skin. I shouted hoarsely and jumped to my feet, stumbling away from them.

The leader squealed again. More red jolts lashed me.

I stumbled away, yelling at the pain, and then I figured I'd had my fill of this. I put my head forward and began to run. I

51

was big and heavy, but I could book it when I needed to, and this felt like one of those times.

I must have taken them by surprise.

"Stop," the leader shouted.

I didn't stop. I kept racing down the tunnel. His flashlight gave me illumination until I reached a Y-fork. I took the opening on the left.

"No!" the leader shouted, his voice echoing in the tunnel. "That is the wrong path."

I grinned, running harder, knowing it was a risk. I could dash myself unconscious if I ran into a wall. I still felt the red-hot poker stabs of the jolts of…electricity maybe.

I heard the leader yell one more time, his voice even fainter than before.

It was pitch-black now, and a feeling of claustrophobia finally did hit. I immediately slowed down and then put my hands in front of me, feeling ahead into the darkness. I walked for a time, bumped against a wall and felt around. There was an opening to the right. I took it. I had no idea if I passed other openings. On impulse, I went up to a wall and smelled it, smelling granite.

I was no longer maneuvering through ice. I was feeling my way through a pitch-black corridor or tunnel in stone. Had had the red-eyed freaks or psi-masters made the tunnels? Or had I reached an ancient tunnel system made by someone or something else?

One thing was for sure, the three so-called true humans hadn't known which way to go. They'd consulted a map. That would seem to indicate there was a complex tunnel system down here.

I stopped and cocked my head.

What if I wandered down here for the rest of my short life? I might starve to death or die of dehydration.

I shivered. I was cold, hungry and thirsty.

What was the right choice? Did I turn around or keep going? Staying in one spot wouldn't solve a thing.

I felt in my pants pocket for a coin. I'd flip it in lieu of deciding myself. But I didn't even have a coin. I had nothing but the parka, the clothes on my back and my boots.

Forget this. I made my decision and continued to forge ahead, seeing what I could find.

-9-

I wandered through the stygian tunnels for what must have been hours. Several times, I heard the grind of heavy stone against stone. Was a rockslide in progress, forever trapping me down here?

I kept going, hearing the rock-on-stone sounds again. Some of the grinding noises came from ahead, the others from behind. By that time, I was staggering and reeling. Then, I realized what I'd been hearing: heavy rock doors sliding open and closed.

Did that mean someone was guiding me? I shuddered as I thought about that. Did some*thing* guide me instead? Did this thing open passages that were otherwise hidden? Who would have constructed such passages and stone doors? *When* would they have done this and what kind of power moved the doors today?

I began inhaling like a maniac, treasuring each breath, thinking it could be my last. None of the air tasted stale, however. So, that was a positive.

My state of exhaustion eventually drove away the fear, as I no longer had the strength to worry. Instead, I reeled as I dragged one boot after the other. I no longer heard stone doors grind open and close. I no longer feared recapture, as I was beginning to understand that I'd never see the surface again.

I debated lying down and giving up. As I mulled that over, staggering forward, I knew my dad would never give up. He would never surrender. Could I do less?

My throat was raw. I was beat. And thoughts of courage no longer stirred me. Man—

Just then, I saw a faint red glimmer in the distance. It was a hellish glow, to be sure, but it was better than reeling through darkness until I died.

I barely had enough strength to wonder what the three red-eyed devils were doing. Were they still trying to track me? Had they found any of the closed stone doors? If not, had they backtracked to the surface? A different thought intruded. Red-eyed devils and a hellish home deep in the subterranean world—maybe I'd found a gate to Hell.

Fear made me quail until I stubbornly shook my head. This wasn't a gate to the Lake of Fire. The three would have known it then, and they'd used a computer slate for a map. They had freakish features, but I did not believe they were Biblical demons but merely strange men with delusions of superiority.

My stomach began to unclench as the red glow provided me with illumination so I could see my surroundings. There were rock walls beside me, reality, and my gut relaxed even more until I happened to notice that there were lines etched into the walls.

I stopped and stared, my mouth hanging open as my bafflement grew. The red illumination showed more than etched lines, but painted and chiseled pictures upon the walls. They depicted men riding what I took to be floating rafts. Beams angled down from one sky-raft. The beam reached mammoth riders, men carrying lances.

I rubbed my eyes in astonishment. Who had chiseled the images? Why bother making up such BS as this? It was either think that or believe artists in the time of mammoths had drawn this. That would make these tunnels what—six thousand, ten thousand years old?

I forced myself to keep walking as I studied the images on the wall. I saw pyramids and sphinxes, slaves dragging massive blocks of stone with overseers plying whips. There were more mammoth riders and some riders on giant pterodactyls.

I shook my head. That had never taken place on Earth. Even given a pterodactyl big enough to ride, the laws of gravity, muscle-power and aerodynamics precluded such a thing.

As I neared the source of the red glow, the wall images changed, becoming more science fiction. I saw what I'd call drill-tractors using lasers to bore through ice. Men floated with packs on their backs. Other men with big heads herded people to a fire. Others fought with rifles. I saw what must have been a spaceship and many stars. The closer I came to the glow, the more high technology I witnessed in the wall art.

I realized abruptly that I'd long ago unzipped my parka and taken off my hood. I carried my parka, and yet I sweated.

Just how deep had I traveled?

I recalled reading somewhere that deep gold mines in South Africa were hot.

I inhaled. Was the air closer down here, staler than before?

Maybe I was too lightheaded to know. Despite that, it occurred to me that Spencer had changed his story on me several times. What he'd told me at first about his father hadn't matched the later tale. Had the whole thing been a pack of lies?

No. Spencer had had a larger-than-normal head. His eyes had really held little golden flecks that had glowed several times. I'd felt him trying to mentally dominate me.

With a grunt, I shook my head, trying to shake out my worries and growing fear. Spencer had chosen me for a reason. If his words could be trusted, he'd gone over tens of thousands of records to find me, the son of a traveler.

I exited the tunnel, entering a *huge* area. I gaped in disbelief. I stood in a vast domed area or what seemed like a domed rock area. In the center of the chamber was a huge obelisk like the one in Washington D.C.

The obelisk was a tall, four-sided narrow tapering monument with a *pyramidion* at the top. A pyramidion was the uppermost capstone of an Egyptian pyramid or obelisk. There was odd script and symbols along the obelisk's sides, while the pyramidion up there glowed with the hellish red light.

I approached the obelisk, gaining an idea of its size: bigger than the one standing in Washington D.C. As I neared, I realized that while the obelisk itself was made of stone, the pyramidion on top appeared to be made of a large crystal.

What powered the pyramidion or capstone? How long had it been running? Who had built this place and the obelisk?

There were no answers.

My approached slowed, but I continued to advance just the same. I felt a *thrum* then. It originated from the pyramidion. The *thrum* was powerful and seemed as if it should have been louder. I could feel it pulse through my body each time.

I stopped, worrying suddenly about radiation poisoning. I laughed a second later, and I did not like the sound of insanity I heard. If that thing pumped out radiation, I was already a goner.

I must have dropped the parka, as I held up my hands, palms aimed toward the pyramidion high up on the obelisk. I began approaching faster again.

Warmth engulfed me, and strength. I had become incredibly fatigued by this time. That now slid off me like water. Then, I heard a sound, something different from the soft but powerful *thrum*. The new sound penetrated my brain and senses.

I cocked my head, trying to understand.

I didn't understand what the structure or the mind behind the pyramidion was trying to ask, but I realized it questioned me.

"Hello," I said.

The effect of my voice was electric.

The *thrum* powered up to a *throb*, a fast cycling of energy. I heard gears shift and a *whine*, as if the glowing pyramidion was building up power.

I almost stepped back, and I think now that if I had, the pyramidion would have slain me.

The sense of intelligence from the thing grew. I did not understand, but I realized it was judging me. It wanted to know—

I grunted as a narrow ray from the pyramidion reached down and struck my eyes. I bent my head forward but that didn't stop it. I could *feel* an intelligence running through my latest memories. It sensed my running through the tunnels, my *zaps* from the red-eyed devils with their tasers.

The intelligence seemed pleased at that, but I sensed it thought the memories might be a trick.

My latest memories continued to roll backward until I relived striking Spencer on the jaw. Elation filled me—no, no, the intelligence behind the pyramidion was elated at the image of Jake Bayard striking and killing Spencer. It believed that a monumental feat, worthy of praise.

I have waited an eon for a Traveler of at least the Third Rank to show himself. Your father was Second Rank. I do not know why he couldn't find the travel unit. There must be something wrong. Perhaps it is the work of the Krekelen. From voices in the ether and deep calculations, I believe the curse to have originated at Tynar. You must hurry there and challenge the evil ones, rallying the downtrodden and leading them into purifying battle.

I staggered back as I cried out, realizing the thing thought I was a galactic badass like my father. I didn't mind that part, really, but this *purifying battle* sounded iffy, especially the part about leading the downtrodden. Did it think I was Spartacus? That hadn't ended well for the escaped gladiator, as the Romans crucified Spartacus and his men, thousands of rebellious slaves and gladiators nailed to crosses along the side of the main road, or as they called it then, the Appian Way.

The *thrum* of the pyramidion reached out once more, soothing me, drawing me back to the obelisk and then closer yet.

Abruptly, the crystal pyramidion glowed brilliantly, lighting up the mighty cavern. I saw pictures up there as if I was in some ancient Sistine Chapel spying paintings and etchings greater than those done by Michelangelo. The scenes were breathtaking and marvelous. Mammoths and men, beautiful women, sky-rafts with—

I frowned. What was *that* I saw? It—

A thicker beam reached down from the pyramidion, engulfing me. I raised my hands, not knowing why I shouted with joy. Then, I noticed my left hand. It had begun to fade, to dissipate. Was the beam devouring and destroying me?

My left hand, I was fixated on it. As it faded, it began to waver, waver more and stretch impossibly as it reached up for the pyramidion.

I looked at my body, and it, too, was fading, wavering and then stretching toward the glowing, pulsating pyramidion.

Perhaps I shouted again, in horror this time. It was difficult to think. Then, all of me seemed to move upward toward the pyramidion, heading to it as a wavering, fading, stretching thing.

I entered the pyramidion and shifted direction in an instant. It shot me upward, outward, and I burst through land and ice as I stretched beyond the South Pole of Antarctica. I felt myself heading upward into orbit, not as a body but as some kind of mysterious force projected...beyond, far beyond Earth into the stars, racing for—

I had a moment of recognition, although I had no idea where the thought originated. Certainly, it could not have been me. In a star-gate fashion of some enigmatic manner, the pyramidion was sending me—

I wasn't sure where.

I had the vague notion of the southern constellation of Carina and the second brightest star in Earth's nighttime sky: Canopus. I vaguely remembered reading somewhere that Canopus was a little over 300 light-years from Earth—

An interruption occurred. That hurt. I had no idea what caused the interruption or what would happen now. The feeling in me—

A new thought struck as a force, or an energy perhaps, redirected my path. My target was no longer Canopus, but much nearer: Epsilon Eridani.

That was a star in the southern constellation of Eridanus. Epsilon Eridani was a mere ten point five light-years from Earth, the third closest individual star visible to the unaided eye.

Going there was a mistake. I felt it, but I did not know how I felt it or why I should know. It was my last coherent thought in this form as I began a fantastic journey through time and space, hurtled from the wonderful planet of my birth.

-10-

My eyelids fluttered as I stretched and groaned. It felt as if I'd been asleep for a long time. I turned over—in an instant, all that had happened to me came flooding into my memories. I froze, realizing I was stretched out on a soft surface. I opened my eyes.

A red substance dissipated or dissolved from under me. I grunted as I fell several inches, hitting a hard surface.

I looked up in time to see the red dissipating substance sucked upward into wide funnels. I heard a faint sound, but that ceased almost immediately.

The funnels were low overhead. If I sat up, my head would bump against them. I appeared to be in a small chamber…no. I was upon a raised dais in an alcove. The dais had embedded coils with a clear, plastic-like sheathing covering them.

I wore the Marine uniform that I had in the embassy in Santiago, Chile. They were the same as I'd worn deep in the subterranean complex in Antarctica near the South Pole.

My last memory was of me fading and stretching, leaving Earth and—

I found that I couldn't breathe as I crawled out of the alcove, rolling onto tiles in a larger room. There was light, artificial light in a large octagonal chamber.

I sucked down a breath as I climbed to my feet. I swayed, blinking, slowly turning and looking around. I wasn't sure what I expected. There were panels to one side with colored blinking lights. The lights had flashed in sequences but now cycled down as if something was coming to a stop.

I touched my torso, and then pinched my right forearm. That hurt all right. I was awake, and this struck me as a cold and bitter reality. Could I allow myself to believe I'd used a star-gate, say, or a travel unit, and reached another planet? That struck me as utterly impossible.

Still, I remembered thinking about Epsilon Eridani, a Sun-like star 10.5 light-years from Earth. A ray had struck me from the crystal pyramidion, guided by an unknown intelligence. That hadn't been a gate, a portal, but a travel unit as it had suggested.

"Matter transmission," I said. "Long-range teleportation. That's what *traveling* is."

I frowned. Could matter teleport 10.5 light-years from one spot to another? That seemed preposterous. The accuracy needed was beyond stunning. Hmm, perhaps travel units acted like lightning rods, accepting the body in transfer if it was in the vicinity. Still, the power needed and the idea...had the pyramidion turned my body into energy and shot that toward Epsilon Eridani, and had that energy reformed into matter here?

I laughed shakily. I was being silly. Such a thing could not possibly have happened. Yes, Doctor Spencer had been different, seemingly possessing psionic abilities. The three black-suited men with red eyes and hot skin—

I swallowed audibly. My father had been a traveler, at least according to crazy Doctor Spencer. That did not mean a star traveler through mysterious forces, did it?

What was the Harmony they spoke of, then?

I determined to prove to myself that this was not a strange planet circling the Star Epsilon Eridani.

Ah. There was a door to my right. I headed there, examined it and finally pushed, because there was no handle. A block of stone slid forward, revealing smooth stone to the sides. That merely made a door-sized recess, but did not give me egress from the chamber. Before quitting with the block, I pushed again, and it moved farther, sliding out of what proved to be a short hallway.

61

Green light shined from out there.

I moved out of the hallway, seeing the block as a stopper more than a door. I walked upon a stone floor…my step slowed until I stopped, staring in panic at the sky.

The sky was green, a dark green, quite unlike the blue of Earth's sky. Stars shined up there and two bright moons, each half again as large as our moon. On the distant horizon, the edge of a sun peeked, possibly Epsilon Eridani.

I concentrated in order to continue breathing. This was impossible. Did I seriously believe that I'd crossed—?

I moaned in dread as the sick truth slammed home. Earth did not possess such a sky. It did not have two small moons. Our sun was much larger, too.

My heart was beating fast, the thuds like hammer blows in my chest. I felt grossly alone and lost. I was stranded on a foreign planet, under a strange sun. I wanted to weep. I wanted to rave and gnash my teeth. I almost clawed my skin to make it bleed in deep furrows.

Instead, I closed my mouth. If this was real, I had to believe that I could go home again. But before I did that—

I moaned again because I had ceased looking up at the sky and studied my surroundings. For the first time, I realized that I stood atop a monumental structure of stone, something like an even bigger Aztec step-pyramid, perhaps five times the size of the biggest Aztec or Mayan temple as found in Mexico and Central America on Earth.

I looked back and saw that I'd exited a relatively small block temple on the top of the step-pyramid.

I moved to the edge of the top of the pyramid. The ground was far below. It would take at least an hour to reach it as I attempted to negotiate giant-sized stone steps, levels or tiers.

Then, I noticed what lay beyond the pyramid.

"What in the…?" I whispered.

There was a huge, raised road made of paved blocks of cyclopean size. Along it on one side were low drooping trees with purple hanging fruit. The raised road led to a vast city of giant obelisks, plinths, colossal domes and spires, pyramids, raised terraces and gargantuan piles of heaped stone and blocks. The City of Monuments spread far into the distance, seemingly as large as Los Angeles.

A dry wind stirred, and I noticed that beside the road and beyond the City of Monuments was a great desert of red stirring sand that blew endlessly in shifting patterns.

I did not see any life: any birds or bats, any animals and certainly no people.

I breathed deeply, purposefully. The air had a different quality that I did not recognize at first. It was dry, dusty and holding that...

I sniffed experimentally, and shuddered with growing dread. The quality to the air—it was dead—not putrid decay, but a long or distant death that must have happened ages ago, perhaps when Columbus was sailing his three ships to America for the first time.

I'd escaped from subterranean death in Antarctica and hot-handed death from the three red-eyed "true men." But I may have reached Epsilon Eridani to find a new kind of death from loneliness and fatigue.

The weight of the realization—

"Hey," I said loudly. "What kind of pussy are you, Bayard? You're a traveler. You reached a new world. Let's see what's here before you die of fright."

The sound of my voice, the encouragement, and the idea I was my father's son in ways I'd never known—it was time to explore this place and see what I could find.

To that end, I glanced at the ceremonial block building I'd exited. I had an immediate aversion to going back inside. Thus, I would climb down the step-pyramid, use the raised road and trek to the City of Monuments.

-11-

In retrospect, I might have ginned up some courage and searched the small block building before I departed the pyramid. I was taking plenty of risks doing it this way.

It took longer than I'd expected to climb down. The sun climbed higher into the sky as I did, turning the heavens into a lighter green color. The stars disappeared from view, and the moons both became fainter as one sometimes sees the moon on Earth during the day.

The temperature climbed as well, turning from pleasant to hot until it had to be one hundred or one hundred and one degrees. I'd reached the raised road by then, and I was sweating, my garments soaked. I needed a hat, some eyeshades and water, lots of water if I was going to survive.

I'd noticed shimmering quite a distance from the road, reflections of what might be water or possibly useless sheets of volcanic glass. It was on the other side of the road as the trees and quite a way off. Still, there was no way I was going to last without a drink. I didn't see the possibility of water anywhere else.

I studied the red sand that shifted beside the cyclopean blocks that made up the road. It was at least thirty feet down from here to there. If I dropped, I wasn't sure how I could climb back up to the road.

Thirst caused me to slide onto my stomach, slip over the lip and stretch out as I hung from the edge of the road. The blocks were heating up, making this uncomfortable. I pushed and

64

dropped the remaining distance, hitting the sand with a grunt and rolling.

I would have lain there, letting the pain subside, but the lousy sand was already too hot. That meant I jumped to my feet, realized there was no shade anywhere, and struck out for where I remembered seeing shimmering in the distance.

Down here, I realized there were sand dunes and depressions everywhere.

The sun rose higher yet and the heat—I panted in desperation, sweating worse than before and moving fast, feeling the heat radiating up from the red sand.

If I was wrong about the shimmer being water, I was going to die of dehydration soon, meaning, my planet-hopping days would end in hours.

After another twenty minutes' trek and my thirst becoming desperate, I broke into a staggering run. I'd been an idiot. The heat was baking me, the red sand absorbing the heat and radiating it back to me and the hot air. If there was water out there, I would live, if I reached it in time that was. If there was no water—

I laughed with glee as I crested a large red dune. Below was a stand of the trees with purple fruit, like the ones I'd seen on the other side of the road.

Their apparent lowness, however, had been a deception caused by the cyclopean road of outsized raised blocks. The trees were huge, towering over me once I reached them. I staggered gratefully under the leaves, gaining a reprieve from the baking sun and hot sand. I went to a vast warty trunk, the temperature dropping considerably to something more tolerable.

Several pieces of the huge purple fruit lay on the red shadowed sand.

I was so thirsty that I decided to see if the fruit had moisture. The nearest piece was the size of a big watermelon, and it had tough leathery skin. I clawed and tore at the skin, finally creating a tiny rent. Thrusting my fingers into it, I tore it wider. I could feel moisture in there.

I thrust my lips against the opening and smelled, then tasted gingerly. The juice was incredibly sweet. It didn't burn my mouth. If it was poison…then it was a subtle poison. I would die of thirst in any case. Thus, I sucked and sucked, and finally began to squeeze the great leathery thing. That helped, and soon I was able to slake my raging thirst.

Refreshed and strengthened, I collected the other pieces of purple fruit. I put them near the tree trunk—

I heard a crack of thunder such as I've never heard in my life. It shook the trees and shook me as I staggered from side to side.

I expected a deluge of rain to pour. Instead, flashes of light brightened the already bright and cloudless day.

Advancing toward the bright flashes, with a hand shielding my eyes, I approached the edge of the tree's shade. The flashes came from the direction of the giant step-pyramid, the one where I'd arrived.

I saw great red bolts reaching from the heavens and lashing the top of the step-pyramid. The bolts writhed with cosmic fury, gigantic crashes of thunder shaking the world.

I expected the red bolts to split the step-pyramid asunder. That did not happen. Instead, as the red bolts dissipated, a huge red cloud of particles circled the top of the monument, spinning around it faster and faster. Then, the spinning particles poured down into the top of the pyramid, vanishing from view.

Frowning, I began to wonder if my arrival here had caused a similar display. If that was so—I backed away, heading into deeper shadow under the trees.

If this had happened when I'd arrived, might a new display mean a new arrival? And what would be the logical conclusion?

My eyes narrowed. Could the three…"true men" have used me? Could they have known that stone doors would open for me in the subterranean complex in Antarctica? Had the opening and closing been a tribute to my genes as a traveler? Perhaps they had been tracking me as I fled from them. That would explain how easily I'd gotten away from them.

I admit, I was making some huge assumptions here. But the assumptions fit what I was seeing better than anything else I could figure.

What would be the best thing to do? Wait and watch to see if I saw the three climb down the step-pyramid?

I shook my head.

If I were right about this, they would have the advantage, as they would conceivably know more about all this than I did.

Supposing I was right—"I need weapons." Nodding—"The city," I said. "If there are weapons here, they'll be in the city."

I heaved a sigh, gathered my fruit and hurried to the other side of the trees. It was time to make plans and execute—on the double.

-12-

I was on an alien planet, and that night, I decided it must indeed be a world circling the Star Epsilon Eridani. I recognized many constellations, and that would seem to indicate I had not traveled too far from Earth. I'm talking in galactic terms.

The trek across the desert was brutal. I found stones in the shifting red sand and hammered several together until I had a hand-sized rock with a sharp edge, like a stone axe-head. This I used to slice open the leathery fruit.

The meat of the fruit was edible and tasted like a cross between a peach and honey melon.

I did not see anyone climbing down the giant step-pyramid, but I lacked binoculars and seldom had a good angle.

I camped on the sand below the City of Monuments, listening to the empty wind and feeling lonelier than ever on a world all by myself.

After a nap that might have lasted a quarter of the night, I searched for a way up into the city. I did not come upon any insect, animal or person. The world felt barren, long dead but for the fruit trees and some grasses I'd seen. Near dawn, I found winding stairs leading up. I devoured my second huge piece of fruit, with one left. Then, I ascended the stairs, reaching the floor of the city as the star or sun once again began to climb into the sky.

The sun had never truly disappeared. And I realized that I must be on the top or bottom of the planet, just as I'd been at the South Pole of Earth.

I started exploring the various obelisks, plinths, terraces, stone piles and ziggurats. I found murals in some of them, mausoleums or tombs with human stone faces and hieroglyphics in others. Just like in ancient Egyptian pyramids, there were stylized pictures on many walls, but these showed dinosaurs and wooly mammoths with riders, sky-rafts and giant pterodactyl riders, spaceships, rocket blasts and one mural that had to be a mushroom cloud and myriads of dead people.

If this was a world or planet of the Harmony, it was a harmony of death.

I stood before some of the pictures as if I were an art lover, trying to decipher the deeper meaning of the pieces. The people looked ordinary enough; their faces that is, but they wore odd styles of garments. One mural had beautiful women with zigzagging black hair and exotic dresses. I'd seen that type before, and finally remembered reading about Cretan ladies back in ancient times. These pictures here were like those I'd seen in a book about ancient Minoan Crete.

Could people back in those days on Earth—I'm talking far back—have traveled from one world to the next? Maybe the stories about Atlantis were true. Maybe Mu had existed on Earth. Instead of spaceships to these places, humans had used matter transmitters, a form of long-distance teleportation. Maybe those of Atlantis and Mu had colonized the stars, and then some kind of natural or unnatural disaster had sealed Earth from the Harmony.

Really, I had no idea. I was puzzling my way through the City of Monuments, looking for weapons, clothes, transportation, anything that might help me against the three so-called "true humans" possibly dogging my step.

After three-quarters of the day spent doing this, I concluded that this was a City of the Dead. The monuments commemorated a long-lost people who no longer existed.

I would dearly have liked to know more about Spencer's father, the one found in stasis somewhere in Antarctica. Had the psi-master been an old resident of Mu, or had he visited Earth from another planet?

The three "true humans" had spoken about the Harmony. That indicated more than one planet. Besides, wouldn't a traveler visit many planets?

Why had my father landed on Earth? Why did it seem that he'd never known how to leave?

An hour later, as I exited a giant ziggurat, I realized I had no idea if that was true. Maybe my father had exiled himself. Maybe he'd been content to live his remaining days on Earth. I didn't really believe that. He'd been too sad for a self-exile. I had a feeling others had cast him onto Earth. The question was, who were these others, and why had they exiled my father?

What was the deal with this planet, though? Why had the pyramidion sent me here? Or had something diverted me to an unintended destination? It was maddening knowing so little.

I slept fitfully, sheltered beside a tower, waking up as whistling wind kept interrupting my sleep.

In the morning, I devoured my last piece of huge fruit, drinking my fill. Then, I started my tour again, spending half the day examining new places. I studied murals and hieroglyphic wonders.

Coming out of an obelisk, I saw motion far down the street in the direction of the original step-pyramid. I froze, staring hard, and definitely saw a man in a black suit and hat.

Slowly, I slid back into the doorway. My heart jackhammered in my chest. One of the so-called true humans was out there. He, at least, had followed me from Earth.

I was glad now that I'd carried my sharp stone with me.

Squinting thoughtfully, I decided they had definitely used me. They had not known how to cross worlds, or could not have found the pyramidion I'd used.

I shook my head. None of that mattered. Doubtlessly, they knew I was here and were hunting for me.

Grinning savagely, I decided to turn the tables on them. I wanted answers. I wanted to go home. They would have their super-tasers and Glocks. I had a true heart, and I was a U.S. Marine. I cracked my knuckles and almost ran out of the door to chase him down.

"No, Bayard," I said. "This is the fight of your life. It's time to think this through."

That felt right. I sat against a wall and tried to make a plan. Several minutes later, I gathered my resolve and crawled to the door on my belly, peering down the street.

I did not see any of them.

Breathless, determined, knowing that failure was a lonely death on the Planet of the Dead orbiting Epsilon Eridani, I began what was to this point the greatest campaign of my life.

-13-

The Epsilon Eridani sun began to head for the horizon when I zeroed in on my adversaries. I was in a recess in a pile of rocks, hiding in shadows when I saw all four of them. Yes, there were four of them, not three, as Doctor Spencer trailed the three "true humans."

You skinny bastard, I said to myself. *You never died. You faked it.*

Spencer's head jerked up.

I squinted, and on impulse, I looked away, only watching them with my peripheral vision.

The four of them huddled together. I could imagine them jabbering like mad. Spencer must have sensed my thoughts and was telling them about me.

"Right," I whispered.

Maybe they also had some kind of tracking device and could follow my footsteps. I shook my head a few moments later. Why would they have gone by the raised road then? They would have jumped down to the sand as I did, and I was fairly certain they hadn't done that.

For some reason, they were hunting me. I nodded. The reason seemed evident. They were stranded on this Planet of the Dead just like me. Yet, Spencer might believe that I, as a traveler, could find a way off sooner than they could. Of course, that was sheer speculation on my part. No... It was logical speculation given the information I had.

I inhaled and focused on the problem at hand. How could I sneak up on one of them…and do what? What was my ultimate goal?

Information. I needed to know…more.

I realized something else, too. Hunting them made me feel less lonely, which surprised me on several counts. I was surprised at my self-awareness and that—

"Bah," I whispered, with a savage shake of my head. I was a loner and—

Ah, I was like a WWII Japanese soldier. If any particular enemy had made the U.S. Marines what they were today, it was the WWII Japanese. They had fought with extreme valor and insane courage, literally insane because they'd been deadly suicide soldiers, kamikazes. A Japanese soldier of that era had loved his emperor and would fight beyond all usual expectation. Some of them had found themselves stranded on lonely islands in the Pacific Ocean after the war. For years, many of these Imperial Japanese soldiers had fought on by themselves, raiding farmers and creating mayhem. When people had gone into the backcountry with loudspeakers, telling the hiding soldier in Japanese that the war was long over, the soldiers figured it was a trick. Some had only surrendered thirty years later.

Well, I truly was alone on the Planet of the Dead. I would take a leaf from the Japanese playbook and fight on as a lone U.S. Marine. I would defeat my enemies no matter how long it took or how hard it was. It didn't matter that a sharp stone was my best weapon—

"Wrong," I whispered. "My best weapon is me."

I flexed my hands and headed toward the enemy, deciding the pall of night—or what passed for night here—was the best time to capture and interrogate one of them.

***

Several hours later, as I continued to keep my thoughts blank, I crawled across the stone floor of the city. When thoughts of mayhem involving Spencer crept into my mind, I

73

quickly diverted, thinking about dancing with Juanita Bolivar. I imagined her swaying hips, her laughing face—

I had to stop doing that because I was getting a boner.

Then, I heard a scape of noise, and froze. The noise…came from the left.

Only one moon shined tonight. The other wasn't in the darker than normal green sky. The star or sun had half-sunk into the horizon. A huge ziggurat blocked it from view.

I heard muttering from the other direction as the scape.

This was just great! They'd zeroed in on me. Maybe my mental games hadn't done anything to hide me from Spencer.

I jumped up and charged to the left, running down a lane created by an obelisk on one side and a vast pile of stones on the other.

A voice rang out. "He's heading for you, Melchior. Look out!"

I recognized Doctor Spencer's voice. I had my sharp stone, realized this Melchior would be ready for me, and tossed the stone underhanded ahead of me so it rattled past a corner.

A purple discharge of energy struck near the skittering stone.

I swung around the corner of the obelisk and saw the man in black aiming with his taser. He was canted away from me, staring at the stone.

I surged toward him. He raised the taser—I launched myself airborne in a flying tackle. A bolt of purple power flashed over me. I struck him with my right shoulder, catapulting him off the stone floor. We went down hard, him ahead of me. I heard bone-snapping sounds, a vicious grunt and a mewl of pain. He bounced. My knees struck the stone floor, and I wrapped my hands around his hot neck. As we slid to a halt, I choked him fiercely, twisting and grinding, pushing my thumbs against the hollow of his throat. He flailed. I got a knee on his chest. I swear I heard thudding feet heading toward me, but no purple bolt flashed against me yet.

Knowing I had only seconds, I released him from my right hand, cocked a fist and slammed it hard against his face. I did that a second time, adding more force this time. The back of his head slammed against stone, and he went limp.

74

I searched frantically in the dark, drawing his Glock from its holster, getting both hands on it and rolling to the right.

Now, a purple taser bolt flashed past me and hit him. He thrashed and groaned.

I aimed by reflex and fired. A spear of flame jetted from the muzzle.

My target screamed in agony, staggering and going down.

I laughed in a demented way, getting my feet under me. Shuffling to the one called Melchior, I grabbed the back of his shirt and dragged him with me. I still wanted those answers.

"Bayard!" Spencer shouted from hiding.

I kept dragging as I scuttled backward, the Glock aimed where I faced.

"You need me, Bayard," Spencer shouted.

I didn't believe that. I looked to the right, then to the left and just happened to glance at Melchior as his eyes opened. I might not have noticed it, but his eyes glowed with the sinister red color. He flailed, and grabbed my left ankle.

I reacted. I wished I hadn't, but I did, as I was more than tightly wound on a razor's edge. I shot him in the face. He slammed back and then started thrashing, releasing my ankle as he did.

"Bayard, stop," Spencer shouted. "You don't realize what you're doing."

I backpedaled and had a feeling Melchior's last compatriot had circled around and was going to attack from behind.

I spun that way, and sure enough, the last one of them ran around a corner.

I pumped three shots into him. He went down fast and hard, and something clattered from his left hand. In the moonlight, I saw that it was a computer tablet.

I ran at him, scooped it up and sprinted to a random location, trying to throw Spencer off.

"Bayard!" Spencer shouted forlornly. "Come back. You don't understand. You need us."

Were any of the "true humans" left? I wasn't sure. I needed time to think, to assess carefully. So, I kept running, wondering what kind of prize I'd taken. If Spencer was right and I did

75

need them or him, I could always find him later. Right now, I wanted to see if I could do this myself.

-14-

My paranoia ran deep as I slunk farther into the City of the Dead. I felt as if Spencer and more of his hot-skinned Red Eyes were around every corner. I no longer thought of them as true humans, realizing they had made a pathetic joke, one I no longer accepted.

Had the three Red Eyes been the extent of Spencer's backup? Or had the doctor brought more of them across? I'd taken out three of them. One had died for sure, the one I'd shot in the face. I might only have wounded—badly wounded—the other two.

I crept into the doorway of a smaller ziggurat, squatted low and took out the computer slate. It looked like an old-style Kindle with those tiny buttons on the bottom.

I pressed various buttons. Squiggles, lines, odd equations and—that had to be cuneiform script appeared, what the ancient Sumerians and Babylonians had used, pressing the cuneiform symbols into wet clay tablets.

What did that mean? That the Red Eyes used cuneiform writing? That the ancient people of Antarctica or Mu had used it? Could Spencer read the cuneiform script or had he needed Melchior to do it for him?

I kept pressing buttons and combinations of them to see if I could find something I understood. My frustration grew until I felt like smashing the thing.

"Don't do it," I told myself.

I nodded, working to keep my temper in check. I had to reason this out. Going off half-cocked definitely was not the answer. The United States Marine Corps had been my kind of outfit because I'd often solved a problem by attacking it. If the problem yelled in agony when I hit it, that was all the better.

I put the tablet face down on the stone floor. I leaned out the door, searching and listening. I heard the moaning wind. I did not see anything move—until I did. I looked up and saw a shooting star. It crossed a quarter of the night sky before winking out.

Seeing that, a great sense of loneliness filled me. It twisted my stomach. I was stranded on an alien planet. I might die here, would likely die soon, too, as I was out of food and water.

I grunted softly. It was time to return to the trees and pick up some more of the purple-skinned fruit. Would I remain here for years, slowly going mad in my loneliness?

I drew deeper into the doorway, pulled out the Glock and checked it. I had five bullets left. Well…that was better than no bullets.

I picked up the slate and continued to press combinations of buttons. Abruptly, I began to see pictures of obelisks, step-pyramids and plinths. These rested under a blue sky. Then, that changed, and I spied some under a green sky like this planet during the day. One of them was the giant step-pyramid where I'd arrived. The other—

My heart sped as I studied this giant obelisk. Other monumental structures surrounded it. This one was in the city. Well, it was in *a* city. Did that mean the City of the Dead?

Something about the obelisk stirred me. I had no reason to suspect that to be a logical response. Rather, I felt it in my heart, my bones. Could my traveler genes—if I possessed them—have sensed something about the obelisk?

I grunted, shaking my head. I had no real idea. I was—

"To heck with this," I whispered.

I had nothing to lose by trying.

I considered my options and decided I needed food, which meant the great trees and purple-skinned fruit.

It was still dark. Thus, this was probably the best time to collect what I needed. To that end, I gathered my Glock and slate, slipped out of the door of the ziggurat and headed back for the stairs I'd used to reach the city from the red desert sands.

***

Toward the end of the night, I heard a whisper in my mind.
Jake Bayard, can you hear me?
"Spencer?" I said aloud.
You can hear me. Good. Now, listen, Bayard—
I thought about Juanita Bolivar, drowning out Spencer's telepathy with mind's-eye pictures of her swaying hips and seductive smile. I heard him plead. Then I became more explicit about what I thought concerning Juanita.

In time, the pressure of his telepathy departed. I felt it go because a sense of deep despair suddenly lifted from me.

I scowled at his mental intrusion and then I laughed because I'd gotten rid of it. Spencer was running scared. He must not like this world any more than I did.

That was both good and bad. If I couldn't figure out how to leave, how to get back to Earth, could Spencer help me?

I entered the desert as the main star began to rise into the sky.

I traveled for days until I reached a tree out in the sands, drank my fill from old rotting fruit and gathered several extra pieces of the big watermelon-sized things, the riper ones. Then, I hiked back to the city and started searching for the obelisk I'd seen in the computer slate.

The only interesting thing during that time was a dream on my third night on the planet. In the dream, Doctor Spencer and I once again sat in our seats in the C-130. The buzz of the engines was loud in the dream, making it hard for me to hear anything Spencer said.

"Listen, Bayard," he shouted, leaning toward me.
I stared at Doctor Spencer.
"We must work together," he shouted.
I cocked my head, hearing the pleading in his voice.

"This is the wrong world," he said. "Everyone is gone, dead."

"The Planet of the Dead," I said.

"Yes, yes, that's right. Everyone here is dead, long dead."

"How did they die?"

"I have no idea."

I had the feeling he was lying, but I didn't care to know enough. Instead, I asked, "Was this world part of the Harmony?"

In the dream, Spencer licked his lips, hesitating before saying, "You must return the tablet to me. I need it."

"The tablet?" I asked.

"Bayard—"

"You bastard!" I shouted. "You're in my dream. This is a dream, isn't it?"

"I'm searching for my father's people. I want to—"

"How long was your father in stasis in Antarctica?" I shouted, interrupting him.

Spencer looked at me blankly.

"Why is everything so old?" I shouted. "Did colonists leave Earth before our world's history began? Was your father in stasis for thousands of years? I wonder if he ever wandered the stars like my father did."

"Calm down," Spencer said. "We have to—"

I jumped out of my seat and shouted to myself, "Wake up! This is a dream. Wake up!"

My eyes flashed open and my head jerked. I looked around in bewilderment. I was in the doorway of a giant tower. The sun was beginning to climb into the sky. I was in the City of the Dead, having woken myself from the dream.

Bayard, I heard in my mind.

With a shout, I collected the slate, Glock and the last piece of purple-skinned fruit. I fled out of the tower and ran deeper into the city. I was beginning to suspect that Spencer could only use his telepathy on me if he was nearby. I was going to put distance between us.

A gunshot sounded.

I whirled around.

Far down the lane, I saw a man wave with both his arms at me. Two men in black suits stood with him, one of them lowering his pistol. If those were the Red Eyes I'd shot…they must possess fantastic recuperative powers.

I stared at them: Spencer and two Red Eyes. It was weird seeing people. Part of me longed to join them. I was sick of being alone on this alien planet. Then, I realized Spencer had been using me from the beginning, setting me up time after time.

"All right, you bastards," I said. "Let's see if you can keep up with me."

I turned, and I started to run, deciding to make this an endurance contest.

-15-

To remain hidden from them better, I traveled at night and slept during the day. What made it easier was that the night wasn't pitch-black with the two moons shining so brightly. The city was endless in extent, though. The monuments surely ran to hundreds of thousands and possibly a million or more. It was incredible and mind-boggling.

What had compelled the people to expend such effort? Was this some kind of hub planet where others in the Harmony journeyed to bury their important dead? Had those of Antarctica been part of that? Who had paid for the endless construction, and why on such monuments?

The next night, I found an unusual structure quite different from the rest. It caused me to stop in dread as I studied it. Then, like a sleepwalker, I advanced toward it, climbing stone steps to reach a large, raised area of stone flooring and giant menhirs.

A menhir was a large upright stone. There were many on Earth, particularly in Wales, England and parts of France. These were huge, each towering fifty feet at least. The combination looked like a giant Stonehenge, with great flat rock laid upon the menhirs in a circular pattern as in the pictures one sees of Stonehenge on Earth.

There were some differences from Stonehenge, size being the most obvious at first. The alien Stonehenge...I kept blinking, believing the pattern of this place had significance or direct relationship to the menhirs on Salisbury Plain in Wiltshire, England.

Then I noticed a difference in the menhirs themselves. Instead of chiseled rock, each menhir here was a smooth black monolith with a sheer or precision surface.

I knocked my knuckles against one. It had the sound and feel of rock, but the smoothness and precision gave it the feel or sense of a machine.

Then, the monoliths or menhirs began to hum softly, as if it had taken time for them to switch on from the rap against the one.

I was tempted to run away. My mouth was dry, and I found that my limbs trembled. I backed away from the monolith I'd rapped. I did not realize it at the moment, but I backed toward the center of the entire edifice.

As I did this, the humming intensified. It was eerie, causing my nape hairs to stir. Being alone and trapped on this dread alien world made the sensation much worse than otherwise.

I feared Spencer or his Red Eyes would hear this, or maybe sense it. I gulped, lowered my head to race away—when forms began to materialize before each monolith.

I heard a squeak. It might have come from me. In fact, I'm sure that was what happened.

"Ghosts," I whispered. "I'm seeing ghosts."

The forms were universally a ghostly white color, and they continued to enlarge and take on greater shape.

As I stood petrified in the center of the alien Stonehenge, the forms became people, each before his or her monolith. They were all different from the other, some amazingly different.

I saw tall, black-skinned men and women dressed in metallic uniforms, each of them with several holstered sidearms. One man was a squat Sumerian type and wore a toga with a wreath of flowers on his bald dome. I spied Nordic warriors with spear-like instruments, with blinking lights on them to indicate technological items. One of them sat upon a wooly mammoth as from Earth's last Ice Age.

I peered more closely at the mammoth and rider. The mammoth was much smaller and so was the man sitting behind his knobby head.

I frowned severely. Was that a miniature man and beast?

It was so odd that it galvanized me into staggering toward him. I closed the distance, and he seemed to peer off at place far from us.

"Hey," I managed to say.

He did not look at me or give any indication that he'd heard me.

I blinked, surprised, and my wits began to tumble back into place. Squinting, looking at him and his mammoth more carefully—

In a moment, I moved briskly to him and dared to reach out. My hand sank into the ghostly mammoth.

That frightened me again. Was it wrong to touch ghosts?

Then, I noticed wavering like a bad TV reception.

I did that again, and the same thing happened. Could...could these be holographic images projected in front of their particular monoliths? Had my reaching in upset the imager?

I laughed with relief, nodding at the obviousness of it. I viewed ancient holographic projections of...heroes, prophets, great statesmen? I would have loved to know.

I moved back to the center of the giant Stonehenge and slowly rotated, examining each holoimage in turn.

Abruptly, they disappeared. Moments later, new holographic images took their place. These showed various suns and a highlighted planet or two in the star system.

A feeling of awe came over me. Were these star systems and planets part of the Harmony? Did this show the kind of people on each planet?

I snapped my fingers and rotated faster, searching for the sun and Earth. Each image showed the planet from an orbital distance, the planet rotating and displaying its continents and oceans.

I did not see Earth. I looked again more slowly this time, but there was no representation of Earth. That had to be important and mean something critical. I did not know what, though.

I swallowed in a dry throat. Shouldn't I try to get this information back to Earth? Might this not be important to our planet, to all humanity?

"Of course, it's important," I whispered.

Suddenly, great flashes occurred in all the holographic projections I could see. I feared the alien Stonehenge had short-circuited. I turned to view the other images, and similar flashes took place there as well.

One by one, the images of the star and special planet wavered and then disappeared. In its place was cold space, a representation of it.

I frowned. Did this indicate a great disaster in the past?

"What just happened?" I said. "Are you computers or AIs that can understand me?"

Slowly, the representations of cold space disappeared. In moments, the monoliths were as I'd originally seen them.

I rubbed my jaw, debating options. Finally, I left the alien Stonehenge. It couldn't help me get home to Earth. But it would be wise to remember this as best I could and tell someone useful if I ever arrived back at our lovely, alive planet.

-16-

I drank the juice and ate the meat of the last piece of purple-skinned fruit, hurling the final bits of leathery skin from me. I was exhausted after two days of hard maneuvering through the endless stone city. It had been two days since I'd fled from Psi-master Spencer and his goons.

I'd spent the time alone, ruminating or simply walking and sightseeing, although I found nothing as interesting as the alien Stonehenge again. I searched for the obelisk pictured on the Red Eye's slate, but hadn't seen it anywhere. The gargantuan extent of the city awed me. And I believe I'd started to absorb of the essence of this place, that the aura had spoken to me in some supernatural manner. The extent of passed time here...I'd begun to believe the last person had died when Hammurabi had been making his famous code in the Land between the Two Rivers on Earth, something like 1750 B.C.

The loneliness I felt was matched by the sense of great antiquity. There was another thing. I hadn't found a single skeleton or piece of cloth or tool, weapon or—

I raised my head higher. In the distance—

I broke into a trot as hope filled me, hurrying toward a massive familiar obelisk. Other towers and terraces surrounded it. As I trotted, I pulled out the slate and studied the pictured obelisk.

I laughed in a half-strangled way. That was it, dammit! That was my prize.

86

"O God," I prayed. "Let that be a matter transmitter device. Let it send me back to Earth, or to anywhere with people. Amen."

I laughed once more. Then, I closed my mouth and concentrated on getting there. I had to slow down after a while as I sweated too much, was out of fruit and felt dog-tired.

***

The targeted obelisk and surrounding monuments staggered my imagination. They were much larger than the other stone structures in the city. Whoever had built these giant ones had obviously aligned them in precise angles to each other and to the center towering monument.

It took me longer to reach them than I'd originally foreseen, as their size meant I'd seen them from farther off. I was more exhausted than ever, dragging my feet and on the verge of weeping in desperation and defeat.

If this didn't work—I barely managed to shake my head. I refused defeatist thinking at this point. I would slog on to the end—

"The beginning," I said, correcting my negative thought.

I did not sense Spencer or his Red Eyes. I did not sense anything but for deathless age.

I never wanted to be on another Planet of the Dead again. There was a grim feeling of finality to this world. It was oppressive to the spirit and wearying to an intense degree.

The last lap proved a struggle as I climbed the immense terraces and tiers, moving like a mouse in some gigantic house of the gods. The people of the dawn time had been great beyond us. Those of Mu and Atlantis had dwarfed the thinking of modern man. The city proved that. The powers of the mind they'd developed—

I laughed dryly, shaking off the feeling of tininess. I was a U.S. Marine, dammit. At least for another—I paused in my climb and ticked off fingers. I had ten more days in the Corps. Then, I would get my honorable discharge. I thought it was ten more days anyway.

Finally, I climbed up the last terrace and staggered toward the dwarfing obelisk. This one made the one in subterranean Antarctica seem like a toy.

"Hello!" I shouted at it. "Are you a matter travel unit? Are you awake? Do you understand my speech?"

I fully expected silence, and despair to envelope me. Instead, the pyramidion high up there began to glow with a sinister red color.

I stood openmouthed, watching as the stone turned redder and then transformed before my unblinking stare into a giant capstone of crystal.

Could this really be happening? Maybe I was just imagining it.

"Earth!" I shouted. "I want to go back to Earth."

A red beam flashed from the pyramidion and struck my face, my eyes.

I cried out, averting my gaze.

Alien gobbledygook sounded in my mind, making it into a question.

"What?" I shouted. "What are you asking me?"

The alien gobbledygook sounded once more, an insistent chatter, becoming angrier the longer I answered in English.

I'm not sure what would have happened if the tablet in my hand hadn't begun squawking in a similar tongue as I heard in my mind.

I looked down at it. "What are you saying?" I shouted.

There was a purr in my mind: a feeling of rightness from the pyramidion.

"Did you tell it to send me back to Earth?" I shouted.

The tablet did not answer me.

Suddenly, I had a bad feeling about this. I shook the tablet. "Get it to talk in English. I'm pressing one. I'm pressing one for English."

The beam from the giant capstone changed intensity. I could feel it changing me. I raised my left hand, and I saw the flesh begin to waver and stretch upward.

It was happening. This was a travel unit. It could not understand me, though.

"All right, I can't stay here anyway," I said. "Let's do this. Let's go."

As before in subterranean Antarctica, my entire form wavered and stretched, and headed up to the pyramidion as a flow of energy. And in an instant, I felt myself shot up into the heavens, into space. I was heading to a planet, which I hoped would be Earth.

-17-

The less said about the world I reached the better. It was a nightmare planet, although upon my arrival it seemed like an Edenic paradise.

I awoke like before in a small alcove under similar circumstances, resting upon red energy. The energy dissipated into low funnels above me and I fell several inches onto something hard.

This time, the octagonal chamber possessed a stone door with a latch. I turned the latch, and the stone door swung open soundlessly on hinges.

The scene before me was different this time. Charred remains of...vines and leaves, I supposed, smoldered everywhere on the top of what I assumed to be a step-pyramid.

Exiting the temple chamber, I moved gingerly among the ashes of thick vines, walking upon a stone floor. Soon reaching the edge, I discovered this was indeed a step-pyramid, as big as any on Earth, but not as large as the one I'd exited on the Planet of the Dead.

The other difference was a veritable blanket of old twisty vines and leafy growth covering the entirety of the step-pyramid. The scorched remains on top likely meant that great bolts of red energy from the heavens, from the Planet of the Dead, had seared the growth formerly covering the top.

I looked back at the boxlike temple I'd exited. Burned and smoky vines lingered on it as well. And like before, I did not want to reenter the chamber. Except…the feeling was stronger this time, a searing compulsion.

Swallowing, intimidated—I shook my head, trying to restore my equilibrium. The ashy remains of vines and leaves up here—

I looked around and exhaled in relief, immediately feeling much better. The star in the sky looked remarkably similar to our sun. And the sky was blue instead of green, although a lighter blue than I'd ever seen on Earth.

It was at that point I felt a greater pull against my muscles, suggesting that I weighed more here, that the planet was bigger or more massive than Earth, thus exerting more gravity. I would not say considerably more gravity, just enough that I noticed the extra drag.

Clouds floated in the sky, and a flight of small birds brought a smile to my lips. The sight of rolling green hills in the distance, a wandering river through a lush valley of grass and narrow trees—I sighed with contentment.

The world was alive. I saw birds…although I did not see any animals yet. The beautiful scenery suggested I should have seen—

What a minute. What was that? I laughed with delight. In the far distance, people, I definitely saw people. There were a hundred or more wandering through the grass, picking…flowers, I supposed, a community effort.

I shaded my eyes from the sun and peered into the far distance. It was hard to tell, but it looked as if they all wore heavy fur coats. That struck me as odd. It was pleasant weather, maybe in the high 70s or low 80s. Why wear coats on a day like this?

One other thing troubled me about their behavior. Surely, intense lightning had flashed and booming thunder sounded. The charred and smoking remains up here proved that. The people out there did not seem curious about the step-pyramid in the least, but…studiously ignored it as if the pyramid did not exist.

Frowning, I switched my attention back to the pyramid.

I examined the steps leading down to the ground. Under the heavy growth of flowery vines, they seemed normal-sized.

91

Despite the vines, I should be able to climb down without too much trouble.

Suiting thought to action, I started down.

The way was steep, and the vines proved more troublesome than I'd realized. I took my time, not wanting to strain or sprain anything. To my delight, I discovered that I felt refreshed upon starting instead of weary. Transferring seemed to have filled me with energy again. That was something at least.

As I neared the bottom of the pyramid, I noticed huge weeds growing up through cracks in the surrounding paving.

Using my feet, I pushed huge vines aside and examined the step underneath. The block was cracked and looked worn with great age.

This was an ancient structure, an abandoned structure as some on Earth used to be in Central American jungles.

Earth, would I ever get home? Would I ever get to dance with Juanita Bolivar? I turned and looked at the top of the pyramid. Would I ever see Doctor Spencer and his Red Eyes again? On that score, I hoped not.

As I neared the bottom of the pyramid, I noticed motion quite different from the wandering people in their heavy fur coats. I stopped in surprise and laughed with delight and relief.

An air-car swept across the lush grass of the valley. It was a rectangular-shaped car with a windshield where you'd expect and two people sitting behind it. The car floated several feet above the grass, keeping uniformly at that height. It came fast toward the pyramid, which meant fast toward me.

So, this planet had advanced technology. I would presume until I learned differently that the pyramid had announced my coming with flashes of lightning and horrific thunder. I didn't see how it couldn't have done that.

What would be the correct course of action on my part? I glanced at the computer slate in one hand and the Glock tucked into the waistband of my pants. I transferred the Glock from the front to the back. I would keep it out of sight for the moment.

I glanced at my shirt and pants. They were worn and dirty, and my climb down the vines had made them even worse. My boots looked dirty as well. I imagine I didn't look much like a

Marine anymore, maybe more like a bum. Still, I jumped down the remaining way, standing, dusting myself off while I could.

Did they know about travelers on this world? Hmm. What if they knew as much about travelers as we did on Earth, which was to say, nothing at all?

I shook my head.

"Keep your composure, Bayard. Use your wits." I grinned to myself, wondering what Hendricks would think about that. I had to fight to keep the smile in place. I missed the short obese consulate bastard.

The air-car began slowing down as it approached. I noticed that both riders wore jackets and clear goggles. They each wore bright green shirts under their jackets...I blanched. They had green faces and green hands.

As the air-car neared, I realized the two suckers had green scaly skin like lizard or serpent people. They also had red glowing orbs that reminded me all too much of the Red Eyes.

My breath came quicker, and a feeling of unease touched me.

The two had faces you'd expect on lizard or serpent men, with bulging or protruding eyes and wide obscene mouths. The faces were also wider than they would be on a human.

"Great," I muttered, "this is just great."

The air-car whined as it slowed and then settled onto the cracked and weedy paving a considerable distance from the pyramid. As the machine turned off, the two riders behind the windshield stared at me in what seemed like shock.

"Hello," I said in greeting, waving.

The two...I decided to think of them as Ophidians, which seemed more elegant than serpent men. They stared at each other. I saw their mouths open and move. They had fangs like serpents, and they both reacted at once, opening a door, stepping out and standing.

They were thin and tallish, although not as tall as I was, and they moved with deceptive and hideous serpent liquidity. One held a two-pronged instrument with a line attached to a pack on his back. The other had a flat device that might have been a handheld weapon. He held it loosely, not quite aiming it at me, but ready to, it felt like. He had a slender three-fingered hand, a scaly thing with talons. I loathed the clawed hand and instinctively loathed him—them.

The two moved sinuously, warily toward me. The two-prong-holding Ophidian hissed to the other as if speaking.

That was when I noticed what lay on the hood of the air-car. The sight was shocking, and it surprised me I hadn't seen it sooner. The strangeness of my surroundings must have caused me to overlook it until now. Or there must have been too much to take in at once for me to concentrate upon it.

Tied to the hood of the air-car were two dead humanoid creatures. They were big, furry like apes and tied down as if they were deer. Ordinary looking rope held them. Each throat had been expertly cut and possibly the blood drained. The eyes were glazed and sightless.

"Whoa, whoa," I said, stepping back from them, feeling my gorge rise in my throat.

The one holding the two-pronged instrument glanced back to see what I'd noticed. He stared at the dead people on the hood and hissed to the second Ophidian. That one nodded sinuously and quick, almost as if he were gulping a mouse.

Then, they resumed their vile approach, coming with quick lizard steps and the slight swaying of their heads upon necks longer and suppler than a human neck.

I must have been in momentary shock. The furry people—I remembered those I'd seen in the grass. Now that I thought about it, those people had wandered around as if they were cattle in a field. They must not have been picking flowers, but some kind of food plants, and eating them.

I had the unpleasant sensation of realizing all of this in an instant. This world was nothing like Earth. If the people had been human once, they'd reverted to animals or to an animal-like existence.

The approaching Ophidians—did Red Eyes look like that when they weren't wearing human-skin disguises?

The one holding the two-pronged instrument hissed at me as if I could understand him.

That was too much, and I lost my composure. It fled, as I had the grim feeling these two figured I was an animal that was getting too big for its britches. I was wearing clothes and

94

walking in places I should not. Why wasn't I out in the field with the others?

Maybe these two were game wardens or cowhands. I really didn't know.

"No," I said.

The two stopped.

I reached behind me, yanked out the Glock, aimed it at the first Ophidian and shot him in the head, his sloping forehead. It was a great shot. He dropped like a sack.

I aimed at the second Ophidian.

He fired his little gizmo as he hissed like a kettle, and a flash of something darted past me. Seeing his buddy go down must have shaken and disrupted his aim.

I shot him in the face, more of a nose shot. He didn't have a nose; well, he had two slits, and the bullet struck there. He flipped back onto the paving and began flopping and twisting around like a snake.

I had three bullets left. Thus, I wasn't going to waste one putting him out of his misery, not after he butchered those two people. I—

I stood there dumbly. What was I going to do now? I was on a world where humans were animals and serpent people or Ophidians ran the show. This was not good, no, not good at all.

-18-

I decided on a few obvious moves, starting with dragging the two dead creatures to the vines, stuffing them out of sight. One thing I noticed was the temperature of their skin. They were not hot to the touch as the Red Eyes had been each time.

Hmm...that seemed to indicate differences between them. The wideness of the Ophidian heads was another thing. If anything, the Red Eyes had narrower heads, and they certainly hadn't moved with serpentine sinuousness.

What had caused the glowing redness of each of their eyes then? That had to mean something, that they had something in common.

Before stuffing the two out of sight, I checked their garments, coming up with some coins, keys and lint, which all made them seem normal. I took off the two-pronged instrument and pack, through some quick experimentation discovering the combination was a shock rod. That inclined me to believe these two had been cattle ranchers, the furry humans out there the cattle.

The flat handheld device was a gun of sorts, shooting little darts. It had no recoil—I test-fired it—and thus must have shot the darts by springs.

I headed to the air-car, blanching as I eyed the two throat-slit people. One was female, which made the sight more grisly. Steeling myself, I examined them, their heads in particular. They did not look like regular *Homo sapiens,* but big hairy Neanderthals with a heavy ridge of bone for eyebrows.

I hadn't thought Neanderthals were idiots, but comparable to *Homo sapiens*. I'd read somewhere that we had Neanderthal DNA in us, indicating inbreeding between our species during prehistoric times. If these cattle people were an example of Neanderthals, that wasn't a good thing for us.

Still, I didn't know the furry humans out there were of subhuman intelligence. Maybe the Ophidians had started with regular Neanderthals and only let the stupid ones breed, slowly lowering the IQ of the race on this planet.

I climbed into the air-car, studying the controls. They were easy enough, and I soon began flying.

I parked at the river, untied the two dead people and dragged them off, pitching them into the water and watching them float away.

After a second, I made the sign of the cross. "Go in peace," I said solemnly, "rest in peace."

Did the hairy Neanderthals have a religion and believe in the Creator God? Had they originated on Earth? If so, had Jesus died for their sins, too?

I looked up at the clouds and began shaking my head. Weary and dispirited, I walked back to the air-car. I was out of luck being here. I was—

"Hey, Bayard," I said to myself. "You have to get it together, man. You have to think." If I sank into depression, I was done for. I had to psych myself up to do what needed doing.

I reentered the air-car and studied the vehicle's monitors. They were behind round glass shields. According to them, the vehicle had a full tank. At least, I took it that way.

Maybe the right thing to do was to find another step-pyramid or obelisk and see if it could transfer me to another planet. I did not want to stay on this one.

I looked back at this pyramid. The vines and leaves—it looked like a hill, nothing more, well, except for the burned top.

I closed the driver's side door and started the air-car up again. It was time to look at the herd of people.

I reached them easily enough. The furry Neanderthal-looking people grazed through the plants, picking off seeds and nibbling them. They hardly noticed me, a few glancing up—

A big boy suddenly bawled with terror.

All of them jerked up then.

He stared at me in the air-car, pointing a dirty hand with long, yellow fingernails. He bawled again, stamping his feet, and grabbing a fistful of dirt and hurling it at me.

Then, they all were picking up dirt clods, hurling them at the air-car, or at me in it. I guess they didn't like seeing me in the driver's seat, or they didn't like that I wore clothes like a serpent man.

The herd began running at the air-car, bawling with rage, hurling whatever they could. Yes, one of them grabbed some crap like a chimpanzee in a zoo and threw that at me too.

"Stop it!" I shouted.

A few of the nearer ones stopped as I spoke. They stared at me in terror, backing away.

"You're people," I shouted. "Why are you acting like animals? Why do you let the Ophidian bastards kill you whenever they feel like it?"

A few more stopped what they were doing and backed away.

Others charged up behind them, screaming animal insults and hurling dirt clods mostly.

Realizing I couldn't reason with them, I took off, opening up to see how fast the air-car could go. I left the herd behind, which did not stop running after me no matter how much distance I created between us.

Then, terrific flashes of cosmic red lightning zigzagged down from the heavens. Awful thunderous booms shook the world.

I immediately grounded the air-car, throwing up dirt as it slid to a stop. I swiveled around, watching the lightning through narrowed eyelids.

As it had on the Planet of the Dead, the bolts swerved toward the step-pyramid, hitting the top, but doing nothing harmful to it. In seconds, a swirling red cloud circled the top, to be sucked down out of sight in seconds.

"Doctor Spencer," I said to myself. "You came after me, huh?"

What was the right thing to do now? It would take them some time to collect themselves, maybe for the mechanisms inside the pyramid to reform the red energy into bodies.

I glanced back at the herd. It had vanished, likely taken off to other parts after that display. Maybe they would show up again. Maybe having this happen twice in near succession was too much for them.

Was the pyramid in the backcountry, so only a few cattle ranchers would come to investigate? Or would teams of Ophidian scientists soon descend on the area?

I rubbed my chin, thinking.

"Strategize, Bayard," I told myself.

I nodded, deciding to do just that. I wanted to leave this planet. I liked it even less than the Planet of the Dead. Now, I could take the air-car and search for a vine-covered hill, and investigate it. Or...

Doctor Spencer and his Red Eyes knew much more about all this than I did. How did I know that? I didn't, really. It was my gut decision. Thus, I would have to successfully do here what I'd failed to do on the Planet of the Dead. I needed to capture one of those suckers and interrogate him. I had a better chance of that here because I had an air-car and a weapon with more than a few shots. Well, hopefully more than a few shots.

I stood on the hood of the car, studying the surrounding terrain like a good Marine. I decided that hill over there would give me a good vantage point over the area.

I soon started up the air-car, reaching the hill in relatively short time. I parked on top, tore some big ferns down and used them to hide the air-car. Then, I found a good spot to watch and started to wait to see what would happen next.

-19-

Twenty minutes passed before anything happened. Then, one moment, the area was barren. The next, I saw the herd of grazing people.

I squinted at them in the distance. Ah. They must have been lying down in the tall grass, hiding. The twenty minutes was the span of time they could remember, or something like that.

They picked seeds and ate them, slowly grazing, a few possibly looked at the pyramid from time to time.

Maybe a half hour after that, three balloon-wheeled vehicles appeared far to the left. The step-pyramid was to the far right.

I studied the vehicles. They were like bigger than normal armored personnel carriers. Each had a long-barreled gun, maybe around 30-mm in size, I guessed.

Did they use gunpowder, or were the cannons driven by giant springs? I had three bullets in my Glock, plus my dart gun, neither of which would do much against the APCs.

I turned my attention back to the pyramid. Ah-ah, I saw people on top...three of them. That likely meant Spencer and the two Red Eyes. I kept my gaze on them, noting them standing still on the edge. Were they watching the balloon-wheeled vehicles or the herd of grazing people?

"Think, buddy-boy," I said to myself.

I was stranded on an alien planet, one that I loathed. The dominant life-form was Ophidian, lizards who herded and killed Neanderthals, probably for meat. Three heavy APCs headed for Spencer. I had an air-car—

I realized I only had one reasonable option. I was going to take it, or die trying, as the saying went.

The air-car started up beautifully. I'd expected Mr. Murphy to screw with me about now. He had not. I lifted, the torn ferns dropping away.

Instinctively, I flew low down the other side of the hill as the approaching alien APCs. Once on the valley floor, I opened up the air-car, speeding lickety-split for the step-pyramid. I didn't bother looking back. What would it matter? I was either going to do this, or I might well end up as Thanksgiving dinner on some Ophidians' table.

Could the air-car negotiate the vine-covered pyramid? I planned on finding out as soon as I reached it.

***

Bayard? asked a voice in my head.

"Yes, it's me, Spencer. I'm in the air-car heading for you. I'm coming to rescue you from the Ophidians."

What did you say?

"Look, I don't know if your Red Eyes are really serpent men in disguise, but the serpent men or Ophidians on this planet eat Neanderthal cattle. You can see a herd of them out there."

I've seen them. Are you sure about your conclusions?

"One hundred percent sure," I said. "There are two dead Ophidians stuffed in the vines at the bottom of the pyramid. I killed them. I did it because they had two dead Neanderthals on the hood of the air-car I'm flying. They were tied down like slain deer."

How disgustingly barbaric.

"Ain't it just," I said. "Are your goons Ophidians in disguise?" I knew about the different size of heads between the two, but Spencer didn't know that, and I was curious about the hot-skinned Red Eyes, what he'd say about them.

That is not the issue.

101

"The heck it isn't," I said, closing on the pyramid. "If they're disguised serpent men, or reptilian creeps, they might decide to throw in their lot with the dominant species here. They might kill you and surrender to the Ophidians."

Is that why you're trying to reach us first?

"I want to get back to Earth, or at least to a different world, Spencer. This one is bad mojo for the likes of us."

You think I know where the travel unit is on this planet.

"You or one of your goons does," I said.

You are perceptive and clever, Bayard. I congratulate you on your reasoning abilities.

"Now you have me worried, Doc. Have any of you used these travel units before your time on Earth?"

No. We are all native to Earth, although my…companions were in stasis units in the subterranean complex in Antarctica. They are from my father's era.

"And he was a colonist from Mu?"

Such is my belief.

"Do you trust your companions?"

Not altogether… Especially not on a planet full of…you say serpent people rule this world?

"Sure do. You can either believe me or find out the hard way. Frankly, I suggest you gun down your companions—to show your good faith to me—and we hightail it off this world."

I lack enough information to do that just yet. In any case, we need Charmalos, the most perceptive of my companions. But listen to me, Bayard. This is quite important. My companions heal unnaturally fast. Unless their brains are destroyed or severely smashed, they will revive. In some manner, they have improved on the regeneration abilities of lizards. Are you certain the two you slew and stuffed in the vines will stay down?

"Very," I said. "I destroyed their brains. Do you believe me, you treacherous bastard?"

Yes. I'm afraid I do. I'm afraid Charmalos has been less than forthright with me. They are seeking something other than what I seek. But we need him just the same.

"Are they disguised serpent men or Ophidians?"

He paused a moment before he said, *Indeed.*

I wish I knew if Spencer was telling me the truth or not. Should I trust him? Could I get him to trust me?

"Your companions have human-skin disguises then?"

It took Spencer even longer to answer. *Yes, yes, I've said as much.*

"What were serpent men doing on Earth back in your father's time?"

I have not yet deciphered the truth of that. Charmalos seeks something. We will join you, Bayard. Can you fly that car up to us?

"I'm going to try."

Good. Say nothing about Ophidians to the others. Let me convince you to join us in front of them. We will try to depart this world before Charmalos realizes the truth and double-crosses me.

There it was. The deal. Would Spencer keep his word, or was he saying all this to lull me? I had no idea. But I didn't see as I had much of a choice. Thus, I psyched myself up to fly the air-car up the freaking pyramid.

I could feel them watching me fly up the tangled vines on the step-pyramid. The air-car whined and stuttered in flight, shaking. I expected it to quit any second. Then, we'd be up the proverbial brown-watered creek.

But the air-car made it as I performed a race-car trick, flying straight up for twenty feet, sliding forward and coming down hard, jarring me as my teeth snapped together.

The engine sputtered a moment, and then purred again.

"Ta-da," I said, raising my hands as if showing off.

The two Red Eyes did not look amused. One aimed a taser at me, foolish as I sat protected behind the windshield. The other had both hands on his Glock, aiming at me as his red eyes glowed with extra venom.

"Hey guys," I said. "Spencer offered me a deal. I'm taking it. Didn't he tell you about it?"

The Glock-holding Red Eye glanced back at Spencer.

I told you to let me talk you into joining us. Now, you've made Charmalos suspicious. That is never wise, as he's already as suspicious as a nun in a whorehouse.

I considered shooting Charmalos in the brain as he glanced at Spencer. But I refrained, as I'd expose myself for a second to the taser-holding one.

I did take a close look at each of their heads. The Red Eyes had narrower, angular heads compared to the two Ophidians I'd slain. How could they be the same species of serpent creep? Did that mean Spencer had been lying to me? Were they playing a charade for my benefit? I should just shoot the three of them and be done with it.

For those of you feeling I was morally repugnant for thinking such thoughts, you ought to consider my situation. I was alone on a freak of an alien planet, surrounded by human-eating Ophidians. I was desperate. Frankly, I was beyond desperate. I felt like a drowning man who would think nothing about climbing over others to save himself. Was that a pretty picture of me? No. But it was the truth, which holds its own charm. At least, that was how I thought about it.

I wanted to go home. That I even had coherent thoughts showed I had plenty of punch left, but with a survivor's sort of morality in operation.

"I note that armed vehicles are approaching," Spencer said to me. "Have you had any truck with them?"

"What?" I said.

"Are the armored-personnel people friendly?" Spencer asked, giving me a significant glance.

It took me half a second. "No," I said, finally getting his drift. "They've already tried to kill me. We have to get out of here."

"What about the grazing people yonder," Charmalos said.

"What about them?" I said.

"They strike me as docile, as cattle-like."

"Yeah, so?" I said, barely keeping myself from asking if he felt like eating human steak.

"You are highly agitated," Charmalos said. "What is the reason for that?"

"Because I don't trust you guys," I said. "You tried to kill me on the last planet, remember?"

"You slew Melchior," Charmalos said. "He was my brood brother, and I am sworn to—"

"Your brood brother, huh," I said, interrupting. "Well—look, dude, we're up the creek, and the cavalry is coming to kill us. You want to bury the hatchet and work together, or do you want to fight it out before the enemy arrives?"

"Is he lying about them?" Charmalos asked Spencer.

"No," Spencer said.

To me, it looked as if Charmalos wanted to ask Spencer if *he* was lying about saying that. Maybe their working relationship had deteriorated over the past few days. It would have been under a ton of stress on the Planet of the Dead. The Red Eyes were supposed to have popped out of stasis, I'm guessing down in the subterranean complex in Antarctica. They were possibly as old as Spencer's father. How had they and Spencer ever come to an agreement in the first place? When had the Red Eyes or Charmalos learned English?

"I need the tablet," Charmalos told Spencer. "Without it..." He shook his head.

I picked the Kindle-looking tablet off the passenger-side seat and tossed it over the windshield at him.

Charmalos stared at the airborne tablet in shock, released the Glock and grabbed at the tablet with both hands. He clutched it as the gun clattered against stone, and he held the tablet against his chest as if it was a holy object. That he would disarm himself to catch it showed me how important the tablet was to him.

"Well?" asked Spencer.

"First, I have to know what world we have arrived at," Charmalos said.

"You don't have much time, eh," I said. "We either work together, or I'm leaving before they arrive."

Charmalos squinted at me, and his skin disguise looked as if it was going to rip free. "Perhaps we should earn their goodwill by capturing Bayard for them."

"Not this time," Spencer said.

Charmalos turned to stare at Spencer.

My patience was nearly gone. I itched to aim and fire, knowing I had to go for a brain shot to finish the creep.

Charmalos finally relented with Spencer and began to manipulate the tablet, shaking his head as he did.

I glanced back to see how far the APCs were. They'd passed my hill, and the guns were moving on turrets I hadn't noticed earlier and aligning higher to aim at us.

"Spencer," I said.

The doctor ignored me as he watched Charmalos.

The other Red Eye froze and lowered the taser beside his right leg. What had he been doing that he suddenly froze? I recognized it, as I realized he had a new position relative to him, the windshield and me. He must have moved stealthily while I'd looked back at the Ophidians. Now, he was pretending that he hadn't been getting ready to shoot me, glancing at Charmalos as if checking up on him.

"Saddoth," Charmalos said abruptly. Had he been watching his brood brother and me out of the corner of his eye? Did he pronounce it like that to distract me?

I didn't trust them, not a bit. This was BS, and if I made the wrong move, they'd hand me over to the Ophidians.

"I believe we have reached the planet Saddoth," Charmalos said.

"And?" asked Spencer.

Charmalos looked past me at the three balloon-tired APCs. He switched his concentration and seemed to look at the grazing herd. Lastly, he regarded Spencer. "It is obvious that you are withholding information. You have clearly spoken telepathically with the traveler beforehand. He must have discovered a secret you do not wish to share with me."

The other Red Eye said a single squealing word to Charmalos, and I had the sense he shifted his gaze toward me as he said it.

Charmalos did not reply, but waited as he studied Spencer.

"Saddoth," Spencer said, as if tasting the word. "That sounds like a name one of your people would give a planet."

"Not necessarily," Charmalos said.

Spencer licked his lips and seemed to be avoiding looking at me.

"I should point out that Saddoth is nearly twenty-six light-years from Earth," Charmalos said.

Spencer paled, his eyelids blinking rapidly.

The other Red Eye slowly moved his feet, perhaps thinking I wouldn't notice. He maneuvered so a jump or a leap would take him past the windshield and give him a direct line of fire at me. It seemed as if his taser hand tensed, his fingers readying.

Sweat pooled under my armpits as my gut twisted and tightened. I must have been an idiot to come up here. But how else could I return home to Earth? I wanted to leave this awful planet with its people-eating serpent men.

Think, Bayard, I told myself. *Think and act before you're dead.*

From what I was seeing, Spencer needed Charmalos because only the chief Red Eye seemed able to retrieve data from the tablet. That meant—or I thought it did—that I needed Charmalos and his tablet to find the launch point from this hell world so I could get home. I'd have a hard time watching one of them, two was nearly impossible while three—the taser-armed bastard shifted again, and I watched him gather himself and tilt his wrist so the weapon—

No! They'd all tried to kill me on the Planet of the Dead. Under their skin disguises, they were serpent men or Ophidians, at least according to Spencer. Given a chance, they'd probably pull out forks and join the aliens of this world to feast on my flesh.

Panic boiled in me. If I didn't take charge—and do it immediately—I was a dead man.

Something snapped in me and I went into overdrive warrior-born Marine. I could feel the second Red Eye coiling his leg muscles for a jump.

I grabbed my Glock, raised it over the windshield and fired two quick shots even as the Red Eye brought up the taser and lowered himself to leap.

The gunshots must have surprised Charmalos and Spencer, as they did nothing but gawk.

The taser-armed Red Eye jumped then, but awkwardly, landing on the hood of my air-car. His head—it was a gory ruin. He jerked and spasmed, sliding off the hood to flop onto the stone floor of the step-pyramid.

Committed, and having barely forestalled my recapture, I was already climbing over the windshield. I jumped off the hood over the dead Red Eye. My Glock had one bullet left. I was hoping Spencer and Charmalos didn't realize that.

"Game over," I snarled, leaping beside Charmalos and sticking the barrel of the Glock against the side of his head. "I can kill you, if you want, or you can live and leave Saddoth with us."

You shouldn't have done that, Spencer said in my head.

"You want to talk to me, you use your voice," I shouted at Spencer. "He was getting ready to taser me."

You are mistaken. He would not have done anything. That was a bitter mistake and will prove costly.

"If you try more telepathy on me," I shouted, aiming at Spencer, "I'm shooting you next."

Spencer nodded abruptly as if slapped, taking a step back from me.

I shoved the barrel of the Glock back against Charmalos' head. "What's it going to be?" I said, at the breaking point of losing it. I had to get a grip, and I had to do it now.

Charmalos was staring at the dead Red Eye. I couldn't blame him for hating me. But that wasn't the point.

I heard a loud whoosh and then two more in quick succession. Looking back, I saw rocket-propelled rounds zooming toward us. Springs may have launched the 30-mm shells. Rocket power gave them extra boost.

Charmalos jerked away from me, made a spin move and slashed at me with his left hand. I barely caught the motion in time, instinctively twisting aside as his razor-sharp fingernails parted the torso area of my dirty shirt.

I shouted and clouted him with the Glock, hitting him on the side of the head. He staggered. Remembering I only had one bullet, I scooped up his fallen Glock, aiming both weapons at him.

The three 30-mm rounds flashed over us, barely missing as they hissed with rocket power.

"I'll drive," Spencer said. "Charmalos, no. Do as he says. It's our only hope for surviving the enemy."

Charmalos panted and glared at me as he rubbed his head where I'd struck. He still had the tablet. With deliberate slowness, he headed for the air-car.

I scrambled ahead of him, piling into the back seat. I'd killed his brood brother. I had a mortal enemy in Charmalos. But if I hadn't done what I had, I'd have ended up as a turkey dinner for the Ophidians as they all had a grand feast to celebrate their alliance with Charmalos and Doctor Spencer.

I felt soiled for the brutal attack, but I was glad to be alive just the same as my gut kept clenching. As I said, my nerves were frayed and fraying still. Charmalos wasn't human, but one of them, an Ophidian from a race that *ate* people.

I heard more whooshes, more rocket-propelled rounds. Then, Spencer used the controls, raised the air-car and sped for the other side of the step-pyramid.

-21-

"What are you, Charmalos?" I said, from the back seat, his Glock in my hand and aimed at the back of his head. "You're not human. You're a serpent man, aren't you, an Ophidian?"

Charmalos turned to the side and stared at Spencer. "You sold us out. When it came down to it, your promises were worthless."

"Not true," Spencer said. "He's guessing about you."

"No," Charmalos said. "He's too stupid to have guessed all that. You betrayed us, betrayed the alliance we made with your fathers."

"I didn't betray anyone," Spencer said, sounding freaked out. "You were thinking about betraying *me*. This is Saddoth, a planet of your people."

"A planet of what my people may have become over time," Charmalos said. "Do you have any idea of the passage of time?"

"What are you talking about?" I said from the back seat. I kept thinking about what Spencer had shot into my head. Had I been wrong about the second Red Eye? No, no, I couldn't believe that.

Charmalos ignored my question. "I cannot trust you, Doctor. After all we have done for you, after all we told you——"

"Everything you've done was for your own self-interest," Spencer spat angrily.

111

"I have made an error trusting you," Charmalos said, "believing you had the fiber of your father. The psi-masters of old were men of their word and composed of ruthless steel. Their progeny are soft and spineless, weaklings who fold at the first sign of pressure."

Spencer glanced sharply at Charmalos. "And yet Mr. Bayard here has defeated you repeatedly."

"Luck. Coincidence. Animal cunning. Serendipity."

"Don't play your word games with *me*. I've done my part. And don't forget that I'm a product of two worlds, the present America and the blood of my father. I'm learning, and I've been acting with ruthless determination. Look how I collected Bayard from the embassy. But you're right about one thing. Saddoth frightens me. What Bayard told me—Charmalos, here your people eat humans. I want to reach the land of my fathers. This isn't it."

"I cannot help you any longer," Charmalos said. "I cannot give you the coordinates to the next travel unit. My brood brothers are dead, slain by the animal killer in the back seat. We are far beyond helping the rest of my brood in the stasis tubes in Antarctica. We shall never reach Earth in their lifetime."

"Why not?" I said from the back, pushing the barrel of the Glock against the back of Charmalos' head. I'd had enough of his inhuman arrogance.

"Haven't you told him?" Charmalos asked Spencer.

"Told me *what?*" I said. "What are you talking about?"

"You don't know for sure," Spencer told Charmalos. "You're guessing about the time dilation effect."

"Tell me what?" I shouted. "Why can't we go back to Earth?"

While ignoring the Glock, Charmalos looked back at me with his devilish red eyes. "The travel units do not work as they did in the past. Once, they used to make nearly instantaneous transfers, somehow compensating for the usual speed-of-light principle of time dilation. The compensating function deteriorated, or so I believe. When you traveled to the Planet of the Dead, it took ten point five years to make the

112

journey. Saddoth is sixteen light years from there. That thus took another sixteen years."

"What?" I said. "You're lying."

"Nothing lasts forever," Charmalos said. "The Harmony of the past...I think it has shattered, was shattered long ago."

"How do you know any of this?" I said.

"He doesn't know," Spencer said. "He's guessing. It's all guesswork."

"You are monkey-brained creatures," Charmalos said. "We were the geniuses who invented space exploration. We designed all this. We showed the apish humans on Earth long, long ago. It was a mistake, all a mistake."

"What's he talking about, Spencer?" I said.

"I'm not sure," Spencer said. "He has his ideas about...the past. They're quite different from what DARPA deciphered from the subterranean complex."

"You mean down in Antarctica?" I said.

"Yes, yes," Spencer said. He peered at Charmalos. "Listen to me. We must continue world hopping. We can't end it here. We must keep looking for the Hub."

Charmalos was staring at Spencer. "Why did Bayard shoot my brood brother in the head? Why did he finish him off? Did you tell him about our recuperative abilities?"

"Of course not," Spencer said.

Charmalos opened his mouth and made hissing sounds that could have been Ophidian laughter.

We sped along a grassy valley, having passed many herds of hairy Neanderthal grazers along the way. We'd outdistanced the three APCs. So far, we hadn't seen any new ones. We hadn't seen any more step-pyramids either.

"Are you a scientist?" I asked Charmalos.

"We both are," Spencer said. "There is a Hub World, Tynar at the star Canopus. There, we will find the capital of the Harmony. Once there, we can bid them to come to Earth and admit us into the galactic union. Think about that, Bayard. We can change everything."

"I am thinking about it," I said. "And I don't like what I'm thinking. What if this Tynar is run by his kind? Earth would become a giant gourmet meal for the Ophidians?"

"You have betrayed us," Charmalos told Spencer. "You've broken the ancient accord."

"Don't you understand?" Spencer cried out. "You might have sold us out to your people here."

"Not you," Charmalos said. "You're a psi-master. You are more than human. You have always been superior to the common ruck of humanity."

I could see where this was going. I could see I'd have to kill Charmalos any second now. *He* was losing it. I needed to know something, though, before I blew his brains out.

"What's a traveler?" I said.

They both ignored me, although I saw Spencer's shoulders hunch. What did that mean? Were these two playing an elaborate charade with me in order to get me to do something for them?

"Where did my father come from?" I shouted at Spencer. "Why did the pyramidion in subterranean Antarctica warn me against the Krekelen?"

Charmalos swung about to stare at me.

"Oh…" I said, feeling mule-kicked as understanding blazed in my mind. "That's what you are, aren't you? *You're* a Krekelen. Spencer has been selling out the human race working with you guys. Or have psi-masters been doing that all along? Did you Krekelen breed the psi-masters back in ancient Mu? Did you breed them to become your cattle ranchers over the rest of us?"

Charmalos shifted in his seat.

"Don't try it," I said, aiming at his head again.

Charmalos' door swung open. He must have been fiddling with it, not getting ready to jump me as I'd suspected. Squealing, he threw himself out, falling, hitting high grass and tumbling over the ground.

I took several potshots as we passed, but I don't think I hit him. The bastard got away.

Spencer was staring at the open passenger-side door as if he hadn't expected something so bold.

I don't know what I would have done next if nothing had changed, but in the distance, I saw several tall vine-wrapped…obelisks, those had to be obelisks. Had Charmalos been secretly guiding Spencer there, or was this uncanny luck?

I leaned over and clouted Spencer on the side of the head with the Glock. He shouted in pain. I did it again. He slumped at the controls and the air-car began bucking.

In those few seconds, I climbed over the division between us, managed to get his door open and pushed him out. The son of a psi-master had sold out humanity to the Krekelen. I couldn't trust him anymore.

Climbing behind the controls, I headed for the obelisks. I would have liked to know more, but I was out of nerve, trembling at the idea of entering an Ophidian's stewpot. I sat hunched behind the controls like a maniac, ready to commit any crime to leave this God-forsaken planet of the serpent men.

-22-

Did I get lucky? I suppose that was a matter of opinion about what constitutes luck. Perhaps dying on Saddoth would have put me out of my misery, but I don't think that would have been a good thing. Having hiss-laughing Ophidians march me to the cooking pot would have been mental agony and torment. Having Charmalos watch would have made it a hundred times worse. Having Spencer in my head, chuckling about what a fool I'd been would have caused me to rave like a lunatic.

Fortunately, I grounded the air-car before the vine-covered obelisks, jumped out with my meager belongings and raced to them, the central biggest one.

I looked back and couldn't see any sign of Doctor Spencer or Charmalos. What I did see was enough of a cause for concern.

Four air-cars zoomed across waving grass, heading toward me at speed. Far in the distance behind them lumbered at least a dozen of the balloon-wheeled APCs. If nothing else, we'd stirred up the local constables.

I didn't have much time to leave Saddoth before the Ophidians captured me.

"Hey!" I shouted up at the central obelisk. "I'm a traveler. You have to get me out of this mess. I want to go Earth. But if you can't do that…Tynar, send me to Tynar."

Nothing happened expect that a small bird tweeted at me from the top of the obelisk.

116

I looked back, seeing the air-cars spreading out as they advanced toward me.

"Obelisk," I said, turning back to it. "Can you understand me?"

Speak this name to it, a voice said in my mind.

I clutched my head. "Is that you, Spencer? Are you using telepathy?"

Speak the words I tell you.

"Why?" I shouted. "I just threw you out of the air-car. Why would you help me?"

I'm not helping you. I'm helping me, you idiot. You're the trailblazer. Don't you realize that yet?

"The Ophidians will never let you follow me, Doc."

We'll see. Remember, I'm a psi-master.

"What's your game? Are you screwing me doing this? Are you screwing humanity?"

Do you want to live or die?

"Screw you!" I raged.

You're out of time, Bayard. Choose.

I twisted back and saw the approaching air-cars. Then I shouted at the obelisk the words Spencer had put in my mind.

The capstone of the obelisk flickered with a reddish light. The little bird must have sensed something just before that happened, as it flew away.

"That's it. That's it," I said, cry laughing. And I repeated the words Spencer had given me.

The pyramidion or capstone blazed with red light, and the vines around it up there ignited with fire. A ray beamed down, and the obelisk surged with a thudding sound.

Could it still do this? Was it too broken down? What had I told it to do?

The light blazed upon it with greater intensity, and the beam changed color.

My hand—the process had begun. "Where did you send me, Spencer? Tell me before it's too late."

I heard him chuckling in my mind. *You aren't going back to Earth, Bayard. No, it's onward and forward. You're heading for the Hub World.*

"Tynar?" I shouted.

117

Tynar that orbits Canopus, Spencer said in my mind.

My body wavered and drifted up toward the pyramidion as the sequence of events ran through their customary manner, shooting me—it felt as if I curved in orbital space. I did not understand. A process started that seemed to be sending me back to—I blanked out then, remembering no more.

***

By slow degrees, I revived, with red energy surrounding me. In a moment, the energy flowed upward into funnels. It was old hat by now, familiar territory for me.

I grunted as I hit the floor of the dais, and rolled out of the alcove. This time, things looked decidedly familiar in this octagonal chamber.

I moved to the block door with the latch, and turned it. The stone door swung open on hinges, and I viewed the charred remains of vines littered on the outer and upper stone floor of the step-pyramid.

My mouth opened in shock, and I had the dreadful sensation that I'd landed back on the ziggurat of Saddoth. Swallowing, I gingerly stepped out and looked around.

With a groan, I realized Spencer had double-crossed me. I was still on Saddoth, the planet of the Ophidians and hairy cattle Neanderthals. As I walked across the top of the ziggurat, I saw the original herd of Neanderthals serenely eating seeds. They were farther than last time, but still distinguishable.

"Think, Bayard," I said aloud. I was embarrassed how I'd freaked out earlier. I'd panicked instead of staying cool under fire. I was determined to never let that happen again. I would indeed become the warrior born.

Hmm. During the final air-car ride, Spencer and Charmalos must have been feeding me a line of BS. I'd killed his brood brother—I shook my head. Charmalos and his brood brothers were always going to screw me. I'd lost nothing acting before the taser-armed Red Eye had rendered me unconscious. Here was the thing. Why would Spencer send me through the obelisk again to begin here once more?

Maybe he'd launched me in order to keep me out of the hands of the approaching Ophidians. Okay, why do that, why bother? What did he gain from it?

Despite examining the angles, I couldn't figure it out. So…was Charmalos really an Ophidian? Spencer had said yes, and Charmalos had pretended to be one. Why had Charmalos bailed out of the air-car then?

Thinking about it, I nodded. He'd done it when I'd called him a Krekelen. That was important. What was a Krekelen? Charmalos was, clearly. But why bail out of the air-car because he was one?

I nodded again. He must have thought I'd known more than I had.

Okay. I'd leave that aside for the moment. Spencer and Charmalos needed me. Being a traveler must be the key. They'd pretended not to hear me about that, although Spencer had given himself away with the involuntary hunching of his shoulders.

I exhaled with frustration. There was so much I didn't know about all this. I looked around—

Far off in the distance, I spied dots. Those could be air-cars or APCs.

What should I do?

I swallowed hard and started down the vine-covered step-pyramid. I had to hide, or failing that, I had to blend in. How could I blend in among moronic hairy Neanderthals?

As I negotiated down the steep vine-covered steps, a plan began to form in my overheated imagination.

-23-

My plan was to join the herd if I could, to blend in for a time and thus escape the Ophidians. That would mean going native, naked. I'd be throwing away the advantages of clothes and boots, but give myself time to come up with a better idea.

However, as I put the plan into operation, doubts assailed me.

I'd reached the river where I'd released the two dead Neanderthals before and found a place to hide my embassy uniform, socks, boots, underwear—I stripped naked, deciding it was time to go native: moronic hairy Neanderthal native that is.

Would that disguise me from the Ophidians? I had grave doubts, but I also knew that species arrogance might assist me. Would the Ophidians be able to tell the difference between a Neanderthal and me? Certainly, Neanderthals would be hairy and have a different kind of head. But I was big, and I was naked and would be shuffling among them…if I could pull it off.

As I began my trek along the banks of the river toward the herd, air-cars reached the step-pyramid.

I went onto my belly and peered between reeds, observing. One of the air-cars was bulkier than the rest, more of an air-truck. Two of the Ophidians wore silvery suits from head to toe and began to ply the steps with fire, burning flowery vines.

A few men with machetes could have cleared the way faster, but hey, these were serpent men, and they probably

120

enjoyed spewing fire. Maybe they were natural pyromaniacs, akin to dragons.

Eventually, the two silver-suited pyromaniacs climbed the cleared steps, stretched the hose between them and the air-truck and continued to burn vines until the entire path was clear to the top.

By that time, a caravan of balloon-wheeled APCs and other bigger vehicles arrived. It was a regular cavalcade. They parked, and Ophidians in long red robes debouched, climbing the steep steps.

Time passed, and I grew anxious. I wasn't hungry yet, might not be for a while because I'd gone through the red-energy process. That always filled me with renewed strength. But I would need something to eat soon enough. I debated heading to the herd. The Neanderthals might see a difference in me, though, and that might cause a commotion. The commotion might alert the Ophidians. Thus, I would wait and continue to watch.

The Ophidians carried machines from the biggest vehicles and manhandled them up the steps to the top of the ziggurat.

At that point, a new set of air-cars arrived. They came from the direction Spencer and I had left earlier. The air-cars landed and several Ophidians forced someone to climb the steep stairs.

I couldn't be sure, but they might have escorted Doctor Spencer up there. It would seem his psi-mastering abilities weren't helping him much. Would the Ophidians eat him later, or would they be smart enough to keep him around for a time?

It did surprise me the serpent men didn't escort one more up the step-pyramid. What had happened to Charmalos? Could the tumbling fall have killed him? I could hope, but I doubted it. Was he hiding then?

I had no idea.

What was a Krekelen? It must have been bad back in the day when whoever had built the subterranean complex in Antarctica. The intelligence behind the obelisk had warned me against the Krekelen. What extra sort of power did a Krekelen have? Had Charmalos exhibited such a power?

With a shrug, I continued to watch and wait.

121

The serpent men and possibly Doctor Spencer spent several hours up there on the step-pyramid. Only as the star or sun headed for the horizon did the mass of scientists or priests, or whatever, head down the stone stairs for the parked vehicles.

Did Spencer know what he'd done, that the vine-covered obelisk had sent me right back where I'd started from? If he did know, why hadn't he tried to use telepathy to speak with me? Was this too far for him to reach?

I had mixed feelings regarding Doctor Spencer. I hated being alone on the Ophidian world, and I distrusted him. I did not fully believe what he'd told me while we'd ridden in the air-car, either.

As the sun bloated on the horizon, the massed caravan headed away, going in the direction Spencer—if he was out there—had arrived.

Soon, the last balloon-wheeled vehicle and air-car was gone. I climbed out of the reeds and proceeded toward the milling herd. They were even farther off than before.

I left the riverbank and trekked across the grassy plain, my feet unaccustomed to going barefoot for such an extended period outside. There were occasional pebbles and stones, and they always made me wince or hop off them. If I stayed here long, I hoped my feet would toughen up.

The sun disappeared, and stars began to twinkle overhead. These twinkled more than I recalled stars doing on Earth or the Planet of the Dead, for that matter. That indicated something.

A tiny, blue-colored moon appeared, providing a bit more light, but not much.

I finally halted, and I grew aware that it wasn't especially chilly. It must have been two hours since the sun or main system star had set.

I looked up at the twinkling stars again.

I decided this planet had a much thicker atmosphere than Earth did. The thicker atmosphere caused the apparent twinkling and the thicker atmosphere kept the heat longer than a thinner atmosphere would do. This region must also be near sea level.

Mountainous regions on Earth cooled faster because of the thinner atmosphere.

The river had curved back so it was near again. I trekked there and climbed down the bank, gathering soft reeds, yanking them from the ground and making a bed. I pulled enough to exert myself, wondering if I'd need bedcovering later during the night when I cooled down.

I nestled in the reeds, staring up at the stars. This was quite unlike the Planet of the Dead. I'd forsaken my clothes and wandered around naked. It was an uncomfortable feeling, but not half as uncomfortable as dreading the possibly of becoming a meal for the dominant Ophidians of Saddoth.

Tomorrow…I'd have to join the herd, see if it was possible anyway. I'd have to watch them eat to get the knack of it. Hopefully, the seeds proved edible for me like the purple-skinned fruit in the red desert on the Planet of the Dead had been.

I might have stayed awake most of the night, worrying, but the exhaustion of wandering naked soon claimed me. I fell asleep, dreading the morrow.

-24-

I stirred in the morning, feeling the rays of Saddoth's sun. That meant I'd slept past dawn. I blinked from the light, and then a humanoid shape blocked the light.

That brought me awake even quicker. But before I could rise, two more humanoids joined the first. They each aimed—

I rubbed my eyes, seeing clearer, and felt the pricks of spear-points pressed against my chest.

Before me were three hairy Neanderthals in crude loincloths, with animal-skin pouches hanging from leathery belts around their waists. They each held a stout spear in thick, wide hands. The spears had smooth flintheads, ground or sanded stone held by leather thongs and a splice in the end or the front of the wood that made up the pole of the spear. The three did not have beards or mustaches, but hairy faces along the chin and forehead. They had heavy bone ridges over their eye sockets and black eyes.

To my shock, the eyes showed intelligence.

The center Neanderthal—the biggest of the bunch, certainly bigger than me—opened his mouth. "What are you?" he grunted.

I blinked with astonishment, dumbfounded that I understood his grunts and guttural speech. I also realized that he did not speak English. That was interesting, as I'd always been a one-language American, only knowing a smattering of Spanish words, even though I'd tried to learn in order to meet more Chilean hotties.

"Are you one of the beef cattle?" he asked, pressing the spear-point, causing blood to well on my chest.

"No," I said in English.

He cocked his head.

The other two jumped back, removing their spear-points from my chest.

"Hold your ground," he told them.

"He speaks like the Masters," one said.

"They are not Masters," he said. "They are the enemy."

I concentrated—I figured I could do this. Then, I grunted in a guttural way, saying, "They are not Masters, but Ophidians."

The leader squinted with his beady eyes, but he eased some of the pressure from the spear-tip. "How do you know our tongue?"

"I have no idea how I know," I said.

That made him ponder, and he finally asked, "Did you arrive from the ziggurat?"

I should point out that he did not use the exact word "ziggurat." But for the ease of rendering my tale into a story instead of a treatise on alien diction, he used the word for ziggurat or step-pyramid.

"I did," I said, making sure to use his guttural tongue.

"You are from…elsewhere?"

My astonishment grew. "How do you know about that?"

He growled angrily, and then removed the spear-tip from my chest. He thumped himself a mighty blow on the chest. "I am one of the Original People."

"I, uh, I'm not sure what you mean by that."

"I mean that my ancestors came from…" He squinted suspiciously at me. "Do you know the word I wish to use?"

"I'm from Earth, if that's what you mean."

He cocked his head and scowled more. "You are from dirt?"

"No. Earth is the name of my planet."

"Dirt is an odd name for your world."

"Isn't everyone here from Earth?" I said, deciding to change the subject.

He scowled once more. "Are you claiming you are one of the Original People?"

"I have to know what you mean by that before I can answer you."

He eyed me, and he scratched his cheek. "Why are you hairless?"

"It was how I was born."

"Stand up," he said.

I did.

"You are small."

That was rare for anyone to say of me, although I did stand a little shorter by an inch or inch and a quarter than him. He had bigger shoulders, which was even rarer for me to find. That he had a deeper chest surprised me most of all. He was a veritable bull of a...a Neanderthal. I was taller than the other two, though.

"Are you weak, as well?" he asked.

I remembered the slightly greater gravity, and decided I did not want him testing my strength.

"What's your name?" I asked.

He snarled, leveling the spear at me. "Do you wish to use witchcraft against me? Is that why you wish to know my name?"

"No. Exchanging names is an act of friendship."

He curled his upper lip.

I slapped my chest. "Here, I'll show you. I'm Jake Bayard."

"That is your real name?"

I nodded.

"Jake Bayard of Dirt?" he asked.

"Of Earth," I said.

"I do not fear your spells either. Thus, you can call me Bok."

The other two stared at Bok with surprise.

"And them?" I asked, indicating the other two. "What are their names?"

"They are Ferals. They are not of the Original People."

I was beginning to get an idea of what Bok might mean by Original People. It seemed that people, Neanderthals, I'm guessing, arrived on Saddoth from elsewhere, maybe Earth. The Ophidians must have enslaved many of them, turning them into cattle over time. Bok was part of the original group, never

126

having undergone the bred stupidity of the cattle people. These other two were Ferals, perhaps some that had escaped from the Ophidian-kept herds. Granted, that was plenty of guesswork. But there was a sense of rightness to it. Perhaps whatever property of the ziggurat that had given me the native human tongue here, had also subconsciously imparted some of the world's history.

That was an even larger stretch. Why hadn't that happened the first time? Maybe I hadn't triggered the right process. Maybe that was another reason Spencer had sent me through again. Perhaps he'd triggered the right protocols the second time that infused my mind with the correct knowledge.

"Do the Ophidians hunt the Original People?" I asked.

"With vigor," Bok said. "They hate us and often use their magic to aid them in tracking us. When they can, they seize our champions for their gladiatorial games, pitting us against bred fighting slaves."

"Ferals?" I asked.

"Some of the fighting slaves do escape their captivity." Bok pointed to the Neanderthal to my right. "He was a fighting slave of Vulthoom, having slain eleven others in the arena. Now, he thinks himself good enough to mate with one of the Original People. What do you think, Bayard? Are you good enough?"

"Of course," I said.

"Aeeiii!" Bok cried. "Do you hear, Qal? He is your better."

Qal snarled, and he jumped back from me, leveling the spear-point at my chest.

"Will Qal attack me when I'm unarmed?" I asked.

The champion of eleven bouts snarled, thrusting his spear at me for an answer, and would have run me through if Bok hadn't been quicker. He smacked the shaft of his spear directly behind the other spearhead, knocking it so the sharp stone only gashed my side instead of impaling me.

That awoke me from my stupidity. I was bandying with a Neanderthal killer wanting to mate with some prized maiden of the Original People. Of course, he was going to run me through while he could. Why would I think he'd play by the Marques of Queensbury Rules of fair play? Qal was an arena champion, and that probably meant he'd do anything he could to win.

"First blood," Qal cried, as he jumped away from Bok, but hunched at me.

I backpedaled and tripped over the mass of reeds I'd used as a bed last night.

Qal snarled with glee, his eyes alight, and he stamped fast at me, lunging.

I had no idea if Bok was going to intervene a second time. Instead, I rolled frantically, Qal's stone-tipped spear thrusting against the reeds and dirt where I'd been.

I scrambled to my feet faster than I ever remember, bleeding from my side, with my heart racing and my mouth dry, realizing this was a fight to the death.

"Fast," Bok said. "You're fast, Bayard of Dirt."

That usually surprised people about me. I could move much faster than my large bulk implied. But Qal had to weigh as much as I did, as he had more meat on his Neanderthal bones and his bones might be denser due to the greater gravity and his non-*Homo sapiens* heritage.

"Not fast enough for Qal." The eleven-time arena champion stamped at me again, and he leapt to the left even though he hadn't thrust. He laughed a gritty laugh, and his black eyes blazed with murder-lust as he watched me shift aside.

I tried to understand what he'd done: maybe making strange moves to see how I'd react. Yes. He was an eleven-time arena champion. This was his style of battle. I couldn't just grab my Glock and fire as I'd done to the Red Eyes I'd slain yesterday. Was this karma come to bite me in the ass?

As I thought furiously, Qal rushed and thrust. Fortunately, my reflexes were still operating. I skipped back farther than ever, barely staying out of spear-tip range.

"I am better than you," Qal said. "I will kill you."

"Give me a spear and we'll see who's better," I shouted.

"See how he makes excuses," Qal told Bok. "He is not a killer. He does not deserve Tina."

128

I couldn't believe this. I was fighting over a Neanderthal dame named Tina. That was a kick in the pants, although not mine, as I was fighting to the death buck-naked.

"Bok, is this fair?" I shouted.

"A warrior makes his own rules," Bok said cryptically.

Qal snarled with glee and began to stalk me as he hunched with his spear leveled for a quick thrust. He would be ready for me to try to grab the spear behind the stone head. He would have faced that before.

So, what could I do? Well, stop whining to myself for one thing.

I backed up faster, feeling mud squish between my toes. Crouching, I scooped up mud with both hands.

Qal snarled and charged.

I flung my handfuls of mud at his face and dodged as best I could, the razor-sharp edge of the stone tip slicing skin and making blood spurt.

Then, he was past me, crying out from mud in his eyes. I did not hesitate, but shouted a savage cry, jumping at him, wrapping an arm around his neck and flinging myself crossways behind him. I went down and flipped him backward so his hairy feet went flying. I twisted while he was still airborne, trying to break his neck. That did not happen. His bones felt like iron bars.

Releasing him, I bounded up, looked around and saw his spear lying on reeds.

He groaned in pain, hurt but not out as he gathered himself and began to rise.

I rushed to scoop up the spear, reversing the hold and spinning around to face him. He stumbled at me. I shouted and thrust at his chest. The stone-tip entered, stuck and then snapped, likely against one of his iron-hard ribs. Yanking the broken weapon from him—

He bellowed and charged, his big hands held wide. I clouted him on the top of his head. The spear bounced off his skull. He crashed against me, and we both went flying. He tried to grapple. I proved quicker, slipping from his grasp because I sweated horribly. He had a fierce grip, however, tearing skin from me as I slithered away.

129

I picked up the spear shaft again. He climbed to his feet, grinning vilely with blood on his teeth. Blood oozed from the wound in his chest, but not enough.

"Man of Dirt," he snarled, coming at me.

I whaled against his right ear, clouting him hard. He winced, stumbling sideways, crying out. I followed, hitting him on the other ear.

He bellowed, lowered his head and once more charged me.

I barely skipped out of the way, bashing against his back as hard as I could with the shaft of the spear. He didn't seem to feel it. He whirled around, bellowing hoarsely, charging once more. I skipped out of the way and hammered at one of his knees.

He went down, twisted around and began climbing to his feet.

I was winded, sweating copiously, and realized I needed something sharp to kill him. He wouldn't stop until I did. Continuing to hammer against him would likely wear me out before it finished him.

"I win!" I shouted, deciding on a new tactic.

"No," he said, shaking his hard-skulled head. "Qal will kill you. Qal will twist off your head and piss down your neck."

Did he think that was original? I gripped the spear shaft—

"Bok has decided," the big guy said suddenly. "Bayard of Dirt has won the match."

"No!" Qal said, turning to Bok.

"You have a chest wound," Bok said. "You will only slow us down." He ran at Qal and thrust brutally in the throat, throwing him to the ground and removing the bloodied spear.

Qal gurgled as blood jetted from his throat. He tried to rise but crashed back against the bloodied reeds. He stared at Bok, gurgled more—more gore gushed and he sputtered as he died.

I was too exhausted to do anything else but drop my spear and clutch my knees with my palms. I sucked down air, sweating as if someone poured water over me. I'd never fought such a savage hand-to-hand duel. Qal had been tougher than anyone I'd ever faced.

"You are weak and lack stamina," Bok told me. "But you are a clever warrior."

130

Even though I found it painful, I straightened to regard Bok.

"Qal thought too highly of himself," Bok said. "And he insulted my sister Tina before we left. That is what happens to those who insult her, to those who earn my hate."

I glanced at the other spearman. He nodded as he gripped and leaned against his upright weapon.

"Can you travel?" Bok asked me.

"Yes," I said.

"You have heart, if nothing else," Bok said. "Come, we will leave the Slave Lands. We came because we saw great flashes of lightning and heard distant thunder even though there were no rain clouds in the sky. The ancient legends say— never mind. I will take you to the Chieftain and see what he has to say about a hairless outlander who walked out of the Ziggurat of Ubo Tan."

Without further words, Bok and the other headed for the river. I hurried after them. I was with people, not just cattle, but would their Chieftain accept me among them or would he have me slain out of hand, as Bok had just slain Qal? Or did it mean something grand that I'd walked down from Ubo Tan?

Yet, if that was so, why had Bok let Qal battle me to the death?

I was confused and tired, but glad that I was no longer alone on Saddoth.

-25-

As gruesome as it sounds, I should have stripped Qal of his loincloth and belt before leaving his corpse, but I couldn't force myself to do it. Instead, I trudged naked after the two hardy Neanderthals, with only a broken spear for a weapon.

They picked up a water-skin each after splashing across the river. I slung Qal's water-skin over my shoulder.

They used cover, slinking whenever an air-car appeared and going to ground and hiding when balloon-tired vehicles drew near.

Bok and the other did not have sandals, but walked on toughened feet. They moved relentlessly no matter what kind of terrain we crossed. I did okay most of the time, but over rocky ground, I was forced to pick my way.

"What is wrong with you?" Bok asked. "Why do you mince like a shaman?"

"My feet hurt," I said.

"Let me see." He grabbed an ankle and yanked my foot up, prodding the sole with his fingers. "You have soft feet like a baby."

"Thanks a lot," I said, yanking my ankle out of his grasp.

He glared at me as I hopped from him. Then, he laughed. "Bayard of Dirt with soft feet, you are a strange man. How did you ever defeat Qal?"

"I'm tougher than I look."

"No, no, you are weaker. You tire fast and you hobble through the land. If your feet start to bleed, you will leave

132

tracks. I will have to kill you then, so the…what did you call them?"

"Ophidians," I said. "It means snake-like creatures."

He nodded vigorously. "Ophidians are like snakes. They are vile and treacherous, and sly. They hate the Original People."

"Because they know you're better than they are," I said.

He stared at me. "How did you come to learn the secret truth?"

"It's self-evident," I said.

"Not to the…Ophidians."

"No, not to them," I said. "But as Ophidians, they believe the lie."

Bok turned to the other. "Bayard is soft, but he is…smart, very smart. We must make sure to bring him home alive. The Shaman and the Historian will want to hear his words."

That night, I slept like one dead. In the morning, I ached all over. After a long drink, I climbed to my feet and hobbled after Bok and the Feral. It took an hour before I could keep pace with them.

The land had become rockier with sparser vegetation. Once, an air-car traversed the area. It had a radar dish on the back that swiveled everywhere. Were the Ophidians tracking sounds? The dish didn't strike me as an infrared or thermal sensor.

We remained in a ravine until the air-car had long passed.

Near noon, Bok slew a deer-like animal, spearing it at a watering hole. He produced a flint knife, expertly skinning part of it and hacking out choice pieces.

"Have you ever eaten raw flesh?" he asked me.

I shook my head.

"That must be why you are so weak." Bok thrust bloody meat at me. Then he sat cross-legged and began to gnaw his piece with gusto.

I also sat cross-legged, small stones sticking against my butt. I held the raw flesh and glanced at him.

He ate his meal, but he watched me sidelong.

When in Rome, I suppose. I inhaled, steeled myself and tried to keep my gag reflex at bay, and I tore off a hunk of bloody meat. I chewed fast, trying not to think about it. I should have chewed better, but I didn't. Then I tried to swallow and realized the hunk was too big. Closing my eyes, I spit out the meat and used my teeth to tear a smaller hunk that I swallowed like a giant pill.

Look, I needed sustenance. I needed to eat. If I didn't, I'd get weak and faint. That would never do. So, I ate what Bok gave me and worked to keep from complaining. There were several times I thought I was going to gag, but I did not. I was a U.S. Marine. I did what I needed to stay alive and fit for battle.

Too long of a time later, Bok declared he'd had enough. We all swilled water, picked up our spears and started again.

I nearly heaved then. Instead, I forced the bloody food to stay in my gut. The water helped, as I'd been able to rinse the blood out of my mouth.

"Stop," Bok said.

We did.

He pointed behind me.

I looked, seeing bloody smears on the hard ground, mine, I'm afraid. I'd sustained a few gashes to the soles of my feet. I gripped my broken spear, wondering if I'd have to fight to the death again.

Bok shook his head and looked at me frankly. "You helped me, as I hated Qal and he had it coming. Your fight gave me the right to finish him. Thus, I am going to help you. The reason is that I want to hear your tales of Dirt. You will speak of it later, yes?"

"Oh, yes," I said.

He untied a pouch and pulled out a wadded piece of tanned hide. With his flint knife, he proceeded to slice wide strips. Finally, he handed me the results. "Tie them around your feet. They will act as skin."

I sat down and gratefully tied the wide strips around my feet.

The other watched and began to laugh.

"No!" Bok shouted at him.

"But he is wearing foot-skins like a woman," the other said.

"He is not of our world," Bok said. "He is an outlander that walked down the Ziggurat of Ubo Tan."

"He is a weak outlander," the other said.

"He will toughen up as he eats more raw meat," Bok said. "Then, he will thrash you for having laughed at him. He will crush your skull as he crushed Qal's."

"You slew Qal," the other said.

"All right," I said, with both feet tied with leather. "You and I, let's fight with our hands." I was tired of his mockery, and quite unused to it concerning my physical abilities. It was time to change my rank around here.

The other looked at Bok.

"You laughed at him," Bok said. "That was a mistake."

"If we fight," the other said, "we must use spears."

"Do you fear to face me with just your hands?" I asked.

He scowled thunderously. "I do not fear a soft-footed outlander like you."

I exhaled. I was tired and not in any mood for a fight. But I was not in any mood to get constantly insulted either. I had an idea I'd never last in a Neanderthal tribe if they thought I was a weakling. Thus, it was time to use some Marine training on him.

He tossed aside his water-skin, spear and knife. Then, he held his arms wide and flexed his thick fingers. "I will choke him," he told Bok, "but I will not kill him."

Bok nodded impatiently.

I shook my arms and twisted my neck around, trying to get limber. I had an idea hitting a Neanderthal in the bony face would be a bad idea, as I'd break my fingers. A few combat hand-to-hand moves ought to take the starch out of him.

He bellowed suddenly and charged, rushing me for a grapple. I judged the moment, grabbed an outthrust wrist and flipped him over a hip, a basic but useful move. He went flying, hairy feet up in the air, hit hard, tumbled and sprawled onto his back.

After a second, he snarled, whirled onto his hands and knees and glared me. He jumped up and rushed again, and I did the same thing as before.

"What are you doing?" Bok asked me.

135

"Fighting," I said.

"Why do you not run in and kick him in the head when he falls down?"

"This is more fun," I said.

The Feral climbed warily to his feet. "Can I use a rock against him?" he asked Bok.

Bok looked at me.

"If he uses a rock, I can use a rock."

"You heard him," Bok said.

The Feral tore a big rock from the ground, needing both hands to carry it, and he charged me, holding the rock high overhead.

I set myself. He heaved. I dodged, feeling the heavy projectile barely miss my head. It would have killed me if it had hit. The extent of his hurl impressed and shocked me. The sucker was much stronger than I realized, more with an ape's strength than a human's.

He must have expected another flip and came more slowly. Instead, I ran at him and gave him a flying mule kick against the chest. He catapulted backward. I landed on my feet.

Then, I scooped up three baseball-sized rocks. As he climbed to his feet, I hurled them one after another against his head. I couldn't believe the punishment he could take. Only after the third rock square against the forehead did he slump dazed to the ground.

He remained on his hands and knees, blinking, perhaps trying to put together a coherent thought.

"I can keep this up all day," I said.

"Do you yield?" Bok asked the Feral.

"I yield," he said, drooling and wiping his mouth. "Bayard is tougher than he looks."

Bok nodded sharply. "The Chieftain will be interested in hearing that."

"Why?" I asked, feeling good about the victory.

"Because the Chieftain, my uncle, hates outlanders," Bok said. "He will be glad to watch our warriors beat you to death."

"What?" I said. "Wait a minute. I thought we were friends."

"We are," Bok said.

"And you're going to just let your uncle kill me?"

Bok shrugged. "What else can I do? Besides, after the fight, we will all feast on your heart to gain your cunning."

"Whoa, whoa, whoa," I said. "That's uncool. That's—"

"Are you going to run away?" Bok asked. "Because if you are going to run away, I will have to tie and carry you back."

"No, I'm not running away," I said. "We of Earth are too brave to run."

"I am glad to hear that."

"I'm just sad that you're not going to learn how to defeat the Ophidians."

Bok scowled. "What are you saying? You know how to defeat them?"

"You bet, I know."

"Could you teach us?"

"If you agree not to kill and eat me."

"I am not Chieftain. It is not my decision."

"Would you like to be Chieftain?" I asked.

Bok blinked several times. "My uncle is a mighty warrior. None has defeated him in twelve long years. I am not as powerful as he, although I am a strong warrior."

"I can teach you how to defeat him," I said.

"No. That is impossible."

"It isn't," I said. "We of Earth are champion warriors. We know skilled methods of combat. You have already seen that."

Bok turned to the Feral. *He* will tell my uncle what we plan when we return. Then the warriors will feast on both our hearts."

I turned to the Feral. "What's your name?"

"His name is Feral until we agree to make him a tribal member," Bok said.

"Then how about this?" I said. "When Bok wins, he will give you a name."

"I would want a name," the Feral said.

"What name?" Bok said.

"Yakov."

"That is a strange name," Bok said. "But I will give you that name if you keep silent about our plan."

"I will keep silent."

137

Bok turned to me, soon beginning to nod. "We will travel another day. Then, you shall begin to teach me, man of Dirt."

"It's a deal," I said.

"Then, once I'm Chieftain, you will teach us how to defeat the Ophidians."

"Yes," I said, much less certain about how to do that.

-26-

The next morning, I taught Bok a few basics about leverage. I used pre-Yakov for the examples, as I didn't want to create any enmity between Bok and me by tossing him around. We practiced in the mountains under some bushy trees, keeping in the shade.

Bok stopped after his third attempt where he failed to flip Yakov as I had. "This is not working," Bok said. "Why is that? What secret are you keeping to yourself? Do you fear that I will be able to master you as easily once I know all your tricks?"

I shook my head.

"There is something you're not saying," Bok said. "There is something you are keeping to yourself."

"Yeah, I suppose so," I said. "It's a matter of your pride."

Bok frowned until he brightened. "I understand. You do not want to flip me, as you feel I will then have to kill you in order to restore my honor."

Bok surprised me with his insight. "That's it exactly," I said. "I don't want you to stab me later."

Bok stared at me, and now his lips thinned. "You think I'm stupid."

"What?"

"You don't think I can kill you, do you?"

"Sure, you can kill me."

"You mean to say, 'Yes, you can kill me but only while I am asleep.'"

"That isn't what I'm saying," I said. "You're the nephew of the Chieftain. You have to retain your dignity. I do not yet belong to the tribe. Thus—"

"Say no more," Bok said, raising a hand. He had huge hands, twice the size of mine. He would have made a great big-time wrestler on TV back on Earth. No one would have bothered about his grotesque Neanderthal features either.

He turned away, gazing at the mountains. Soon, he faced Yakov and me. "You will teach me everything. You will throw me as you have the Feral. You," he said, staring at Yakov. "I will kill you if you ever speak about this to anyone. But if you are loyal to me, I will reward you greatly."

Interesting. Bok had the makings of a leader—not just the stick, but the carrot too.

Yakov nodded sharply. He had a fat lip and his right eye had puffed shut from our practice bouts. I hadn't been easy on him, as I'd tried to show Bok exactly what to do.

Now began a hard time of teaching Bok a few basic throws. First, I tried to teach him about the correct stance, and maintaining good balance. He quickly grew impatient with that.

"Fine," I said, deciding he needed a lesson. "Come at me again."

He charged. I flipped him higher and faster than I'd done earlier. He slammed onto his back on the ground, bouncing off before landing again.

He rose slower this time.

"While you were down, I could have grabbed a rock and bashed it against your face," I said.

He stared at me, and I noticed that his eyes had become bloodshot.

"Look, Bok," I said. "This isn't working. You're getting mad. We can't do this if you get mad at me."

"Show me again," he said in a hoarse voice.

I knew he was going to try something tricky. I'd wounded his pride. He was huge. He was the tough guy, and me—the hairless freak from Dirt—had shown him up as a fool—at least in his eyes. These Neanderthals were fighting specimens, but they couldn't control their tempers very well. Might that have

140

been how Cro-Magnons had defeated them during the Ice Age on Earth, goading them into reckless or stupid actions? Wouldn't that have been something if Neanderthal bad temper had done them in?

Bok charged me, but slower than he had in the past. As I reached for him, he tried a rabbit punch in the side. I might have let him hit me in order for him to keep his dignity, but I wasn't sure I could take such a shot, or that he'd stop there. Thus, I chopped-blocked his wrist, both to cause him pain and to block the rabbit punch.

He tried kicking me in the shin next. I skipped back and used my foot to lift his kicking foot higher, causing him to fall onto his back.

He climbed slowly to his feet, glaring at me, his bloodshot eyes shining with suppressed rage.

Yakov took that moment to snicker.

Bok whirled toward him. "You laugh at me?"

Yakov instantly wiped away his grin, shaking his head.

"Don't take it out on him," I said. "It's your fault you fell."

Bok whirled back to face me. "That is a death insult."

"No, it's not," I said. "You're pissed off because you can't beat me hand to hand. You can't because you won't learn the things I need to teach you. And that's one of the reasons the Ophidians hunt you instead of you hunting them."

"Why?" he snarled.

"Because they're smarter than you are," I blurted.

Bok blushed crimson. He turned, raced to his spear and picked it up.

I closed my eyes for only a moment. Why couldn't I keep my big mouth shut sometimes? I'd needlessly alienated an ally.

"Now, we'll see!" Bok roared, shaking his spear. "Now, I'll gut you and rip out your heart, leaving it for the animals to eat."

I raised both hands. "Bok, I'm sorry. I shouldn't have said that."

"It's too late," he roared. "I'll water the ground with your blood. You are inferior. I thought you might know things. But you're afraid to teach us anything."

141

"Hey, dumb shit!" I shouted. "I've been trying. You're so touchy, though, you can't learn. If you could get something through your thick skull, you could run your tribe and clean Saddoth of the Ophidians. But no—"

He bellowed at the top of his lungs, racing at me madly. His spear was leveled at my chest to run me through.

When I'd first started yelling at him, I'd lost control of the situation. I realized I had to do something risky to regain it. Thus, I'd goaded him beyond endurance, deciding I'd try the Cro-Magnon trick.

Bok raced at me, stumbled over a stone—I grinned. But in a flash, I realized this Neanderthal brute had tricked me, as that had been a fake stumble. He thrust his spear where he figured I would shift because of the stumble. I would have, too, if I hadn't understood what he was up to. Instead, I dropped and tensed my muscles as I felt him kick me in the side.

It was not intentional on his part. He tripped against me, and he went flying over my prone body.

I scrambled up, my side throbbing from his kick.

Bok slid across the ground, his spear snapping in half. He must have hit his head as well, as he seemed dazed.

Yakov jumped up, grabbed his spear and charged Bok. His eyes blazed with rage. "Nephew of the Chieftain, you have met your match."

"Feral!" I bellowed.

Yakov glanced at me.

I scooped up a rock. I'd been the best pitcher on our high school baseball team in Turlock. The rock felt good in my hand, and I heaved it like the time I'd pitched a no hitter against Downy High.

The rock sped true and hit Yakov in the face. It would have dropped a normal person, probably knocked him unconscious. This guy—he screamed as blood dripped from his swollen eye. He changed direction, coming for me instead of Bok.

I scooped up another rock as I saw death sprinting for me. Yakov had his dander up—I hurled. He closed his eyes. The rock did not hit him in the face, as I hadn't been aiming there. I'd had this guy from Beyer High charge me on the mound three different times. The last time he'd charged, I'd done as I

142

was doing to Yakov. My rock hit the Feral in the groin where I'd aimed.

He went down screaming, releasing his spear and clutching his bruised balls.

I wasn't sure what to do next.

Bok was. He rose, wobbled to Yakov and went down onto one knee, stabbing the man in the back of the neck, pinning him to the stony ground. Then, he pulled out his flint knife and finished the Feral.

I still stood there. All this killing, this running around, this freakish planet with hot-tempered Neanderthals and sly Ophidians—

"Jake Bayard," Bok said.

I regarded the Chieftain's nephew. Bok held his half-spear and the Feral's spear as he stood before me.

"You saved my life just now," Bok said.

I nodded.

"I would repay you," he said.

"Okay," I said. "I know a way. Have you ever heard of blood brothers?"

He shook his head.

I explained the concept, and he understood just fine. Then, under the shade trees up in the mountains, Bok and I mingled blood and swore an oath of brotherhood that I made up on the spot.

"Blood brothers must always defend the other," I said.

"This is of Dirt…of Earth?" he asked.

"Yes," I said.

His flattish nostrils flared. "You are my blood brother. Now, will you teach me how to fight as you do?"

"I need to rest first," I said. "After that, yes."

"Good," he said. "Because now that I have lost two fighting slaves, my uncle will be furious with me. Unless I defeat him, we will both die roasted over the fire as the others watch."

I swallowed, understanding the gravity of the situation, realizing the stakes had risen once again.

-27-

It was interesting how much better I felt wearing a simple loincloth. I'd taken Yakov's. I would have preferred a shirt, pants and boots as well, but the loincloth meant I wasn't running around naked anymore, with my stuff hanging out for the world to see.

I carried the Feral's spear as well, and used the strips of leather for crude sandals. I did not sunburn as badly as I thought I might. Perhaps the thicker atmosphere saved me.

It took us four days trek to reach the higher mountainous terrain. There were narrow valleys with trees, deer, rabbits and lynxes, definitely peculiar-eared lynxes with their customary large paws. It showed that either Earth creatures had come here at some time in the past, or creatures had come to Earth and here from a similar place.

I hadn't seen an air-car for two days now, and I asked Bok about that.

"The..." He frowned with concentration. "How do you say...?"

"Ophidians," I said. "What do your people call them?"

"Masters. But I hate that word."

"Ophidian is better," I agreed.

"The Ophidians seldom come this high."

"Do you know why?"

Bok shook his head.

144

We practiced his combat hand-to-hand technique, and he'd gotten better, although not terribly so. I let him flip me a few times, showing him how to land so it wouldn't hurt as much.

As we journeyed, I learned that his tribe did not live in tents or huts, but slept in the open. The women carried the tribe's belongings in leather sacks. The men carried spears and water-skins. They ate seeds and fruit, and deer, rabbits, gophers, mice and birds when they could catch them.

Occasionally, Ophidian hunting parties scoured the mountains for Neanderthals. Sometimes, they used specially bred trackers and brought along fighting slaves to aid in the hunt.

Bok considered the meat cattle or meat Neanderthals as a different species. They were bigger, but slow-brained, only able to speak a few words. The fighting slaves and trackers were much smarter than the meat cattle.

I quizzed Bok about the Ophidians: how they lived and what they ate.

"Ophidians eat meat cattle," Bok said. "During some mountain hunts, they feast on Original People."

"Where do they live?"

"In the valleys, in…structures."

"How many are there?" I asked.

Bok spread his arms as far as they would go. "They fill the planet."

I had a feeling the Ophidians numbered in the hundreds of millions, or billions, while the Original People were probably scattered throughout Saddoth in the tens of thousands at most. That was only a rough guess to be sure, but it seemed reasonable from the little I'd seen.

With that being the case, I didn't see how the Original People or Neanderthals could throw off the yoke of meat-slavery. If I showed Bok's tribe a better way to fight, would I be consigning them to an Ophidian eradication campaign? I mean, if Neanderthals learned to steal guns, or what passed for guns around here, and steal air-cars and raid the cities, wouldn't the Ophidians simply gather an army and burn the Original People out for good?

I mused upon that as we traveled. Could Bok be right about the Original People, or had his tribe originated from Ferals? I suspected that was how the free tribes continued to survive, fed by Ferals, who escaped captivity because of the innate human drive for freedom.

If that was the case, a kernel of Original-People information had survived the eons, passed from one free Neanderthal to another, the children of each escaped Feral group believing they'd actually come from the Original People. And if that was the case, the free tribes might be ubiquitous for as long as the Ophidians kept meat slaves. The only way the Ophidians could eradicate the free Neanderthals was to abolish the vast herds of cattle Neanderthals.

I thought about that and saw a ray of hope. Maybe introducing a better way of fighting would trickle down through the ages, kept alive in the same manner as the Original People knowledge. I wouldn't be able to grant true freedom to the "free tribes" today, but I might start the process that would over the decades and centuries help the free Neanderthals kill more Ophidians.

It would be like the Spanish conquistadors bringing horses to the New World, some escaping here and there, and eventually the Plains Indians of the Old West becoming a horse-riding nomad people. The Comanches had been fantastic light-horse warriors, among the best that had ever lived. The industrialization and numbers from European civilization had finally crushed even the Comanches. But if Americans had kept vast herds of tame Indians around—

I shook my head, believing that my analogy had finally broken down.

The point, I suppose, was that I was going to aid the Neanderthals. Maybe I'd never leave Saddoth. In that case, I wanted to harry the foul Ophidians for the rest of my life. If I could leave—I wanted to give the Neanderthals a method to carry on the war against the serpent men that would work better for them.

I found the situation here disgusting, to say the least. In truth, I found it morally repugnant or evil. Was I judging Ophidian culture? You bet I was. I did not adhere to the idea

146

that everything was relative: that you have your truth, and I have mine, and they were inherently equal. I rejected such thinking as foolish and obviously false, at least regarding the most fundamental issues.

Let me explain it this way. Were the Soviet Communists wrong in murdering millions of Orthodox Christians in the gulags?

I give that a resounding yes! And if someone couldn't say that was evil, I knew he or she was morally bankrupt and did not understand truth, beauty and the good versus the lie, ugliness and the bad.

I suppose my point was that I had no qualms about upsetting the Ophidian applecart by helping my Neanderthal cousins here on Saddoth.

That didn't make me an altruist or crusader, but it did mean I would help the free tribes with my whole heart.

I smiled. I suppose I was becoming Spartacus, or thinking about it anyway.

Spartacus had been one of my heroes ever since watching the old movie about it as a kid. I'd later read Plutarch's history on the man. Spartacus had been a Thracian and a gladiator in Italy. Seventy or so of them had escaped the training camp and gathered hordes of escaped slaves around them, teaching them how to fight. They'd smashed several Roman legions that had come to finish them. That in itself was amazing, unheard-of— to beat the hardened professionals of Rome. But they were fighting for their freedom. That made them formidable.

Finally, though, Crassus and others had thoroughly routed the freed-slave armies, crucifying thousands of them along the Appian Way.

I didn't want to see the Ophidians crucify the free-tribe Neanderthals, but I did want to give them the knowhow to fight back better than they'd been doing. Maybe that would result in their eventual destruction—but anything was better than being made cattle. So, I'd teach them how to fight a superior enemy—and win.

First, though, Bok and I would have to survive his uncle the Chieftain.

-28-

We reached the tribe the afternoon of the fifth day.

Bok and I trekked through a forest of birch-like trees, squirrels watching us pass. Suddenly, Bok stopped and raised a hand.

I halted.

He faced me. "The tribe is near."

I noted his troubled look. He had a healthy fear of his uncle.

"Stick to what I taught you," I said. "When your uncle lands on his back the third or fourth time, and he looks dazed, that's when you pick up a rock, bash his head in and become the new Chieftain."

Bok nodded, but I wasn't sure he really heard me.

I clapped him on a thickly muscled shoulder. He flinched. I frowned. Maybe he was too frightened to do this.

"Do you want me to fight your uncle for you?" I asked.

"You?" he asked.

"Yeah, me. Do I become the Chieftain if I defeat your uncle in battle?"

Bok kept staring at me, clearly dumbfounded by the idea.

"Let's go," I said. I could see that he was working himself up into a blue funk. Either he could grab his balls when the time came or he was going to fold. Then, I'd have to talk my way into a challenge fight.

We continued, and two hundred feet later, I heard a sharp whistle.

Bok groaned with dread.

"Come on," I said, leading the way. "You can do this."

Suddenly, five brutish Neanderthals appeared before us from the surrounding brush. Each held a spear. Others came up from behind to surround us.

"It's Bok," one said.

Bok looked around, and he seemed to regain his courage. He pointed at me. "This is Jake Bayard. He walked down from the Ziggurat of Ubo Tan."

"The hairless one did this?" a Neanderthal asked.

"Bayard comes from Earth," Bok said, "from a different world than Saddoth."

The warriors glanced at each other and murmured among themselves.

"I must take Jake Bayard of Earth to the Chieftain," Bok said.

"Yes," the second-biggest Neanderthal said. "Follow us."

The others circled us, although none of them attempted to take my spear from me.

We soon entered a clearing, and I spied females and children huddled in groups, the women scraping hides with bone tools or crushing something in crude stone bowls with round rocks.

There was a different, singular group with an older, bent Neanderthal wearing a feather headdress similar to those some Plains Indians had worn back in the day. Beside him was an even older, white-furred Neanderthal with many knotted strings dangling from his belt.

In the center of all this was a massive Neanderthal, a veritable giant. He sat in some kind of leather chair, the only chair here. Around him huddled other bull Neanderthals, each of them holding a spear.

The giant raised a vast hand, one missing half of its middle finger.

Everyone ceased speaking and working.

"Bok," the Chieftain said, in a deep bass voice that sent chills down my spine. He was a monster of a Neanderthal. No wonder Bok was so scared. He had a huge gut as well, which meant he was well fed. But this boy was plain frightening.

149

"Uncle," Bok said with a quaver in his voice, raising his half spear.

The Chieftain eyed me and made of show of looking around. "Where are Qal and the Feral?"

Bok swallowed as if he'd been dreading the question, which he undoubtedly had. He licked his lips, stammering, "T-They died."

"Died how?"

Bok swallowed again. "Qal—Qal challenged Jake Bayard of Earth."

The Chieftain's eyes narrowed, and he pointed at me. "That white-skinned, hairless slug slew Qal?"

"B-Bayard defeated Qal in battle," Bok said, temporizing.

"What happened to the Feral?"

"The Feral treacherously attacked me when my back was turned."

"And?" the Chieftain asked. "Finish the tale."

Bok glanced at me. "Jake Bayard stopped the Feral."

"You mean the hairless one killed the Feral?"

"No. I killed the Feral for his treachery. Bayard of Earth protected me when my back was turned."

There were glances and murmurs from the assembled warriors.

The huge monster of a Chieftain bent his head in obvious thought. Finally, he looked up. "Historian, come here."

The old white-haired Neanderthal with knotted strings dangling from his belt rose painfully from his circle of attendants and hobbled to the Chieftain.

"I would know the status of the hairless one," the Chieftain said. "What do the histories say about such a one?"

The old bent Neanderthal peered at me. One of his eyes was milk-white and blind. "You...you walked down from the Ziggurat of Ubo Tan?"

"Yes," I said.

The old one fingered his strings, pulling one up and feeling the various knots. His sloping brow furrowed, and he began to mutter to himself. He let go of the string and felt another, mumbling more as he fingered other knots. Finally, his hoary

150

head bobbed up and down and he looked at me with his good eye.

"Are you a Traveler?"

That he named me one put goosebumps on my arms. How could his knotted strings have retained any ancient histories? Or did the strings and knots act as mnemonic devices for his memory?

"I am a Traveler," I said.

He nodded. "You arrived on Saddoth inside the Ziggurat of Ubo Tan?"

"I did."

The Historian shuffled around to face the Chieftain. "The Traveler is a great one, a man of mighty deeds. The thunder and lightning we saw and heard several days ago foretold his coming."

"Why has he come to Saddoth?" the Chieftain asked.

The Historian shook his head. "I do not know."

"I know why," Bok said.

The Chieftain stared at his nephew. "You court death by speaking out of turn."

Bok trembled, looking down, but he did not make an excuse.

"You lost two fighters," the Chieftain added. "You were in charge of the scouting expedition. You should not have let them perish so easily. Good fighters with heart are hard to find."

The Historian made a motion.

"What?" the Chieftain said.

The Historian winced at the harshly asked question, but the old one held his ground. "If it pleases the Chieftain, I would like to ask Bok a question."

The Chieftain's eyes narrowed once again, as suspicion swam in them. In the end, though, he nodded.

"Why did the Traveler come to Saddoth?" the Historian asked Bok.

"To teach us things."

The Historian's interest sharpened further. "Like what things?"

151

"He has told me the name of the so-called Masters," Bok said, looking around. "They are really called...Ophidians."

The Historian tried the word soundlessly until he turned to the Chieftain.

"Well?" the Chieftain demanded.

"I don't know what Ophidian means," the Historian said.

"Like a snake," I said. "Ophidian means like a snake. The best thing to do with snakes is stomp them to death."

Once more, the warriors seated on the ground glanced at each other and murmured among themselves.

"He is bold, this hairless one," the Chieftain said, as he eyed me.

"He is a cunning fighter," Bok said.

The Chieftain raised his eyebrows as if he doubted his nephew. "Is he strong?"

"Strong enough," I said.

The murmuring this time was more than before.

The Chieftain noticed, and he pushed himself off the leather chair to tower among us. He had to be at least seven feet tall and was immensely wide. It looked as if he could take three warriors at a time and toss them around at his leisure. No wonder Bok feared him.

Maybe it would have been best to let the Chieftain have his say first. But I decided to exploit my novelty to the hilt and lay my claim while I could.

"I have also come to show you *how* to kill Ophidians," I said loudly. "They eat you, and that is evil."

"Evil?" the Chieftain asked.

"It is wrong," I said. "The Ophidians should not eat you. They should not keep Neanderthals as cattle."

"We know how to kill...Ophidians," the Chieftain said. "We drive a spear through their bodies."

"How often have you done that?" I asked.

His brow thundered. "You dare to question *me?*"

"No, Chieftain," I said. "I highly respect you as the ruler of your tribe."

He grunted, giving me a slight nod.

"I mean among your people. How often do your people slay an Ophidian?"

The Chieftain stared at me, and I could see that his eyes were becoming bloodshot. He liked the respect, but clearly hated these questions. Even so, I decided to make one more stab for rank among them.

"I can show you how to kill *many* Ophidians," I said loudly.

The Chieftain grunted, and he pursed his lips. "If we kill many of them, they will come to the mountains in hordes to hunt us."

I nodded. The Chieftain was more than just a giant Neanderthal; he also had brains.

"We could do this in secret," I said. "We could do this so the Ophidians would not know the killers came from the mountains. In time, you could send others to different tribes, gathering more warriors until you had...hundreds." I would have said thousands, but I wasn't sure he could envision that. "If you do this in secret, building up strength, training others in the new ways of battle, you could surprise the Ophidians in their structures and slaughter all of them at once."

"You speak of *magic,*" the Chieftain said. "We are warriors, not shamans."

Many of the warriors grunted as they nodded in agreement.

"I do not speak about magic," I said. "I speak about warrior skill and cunning and new strength."

"New strength?" he asked.

"I can explain the method to your Historian so the tribe will never forget," I said. "Then, if you wish, I will lead some of your warriors to the low country and kill Ophidians in secret, bringing their weapons back to you to teach you their skills."

The Chieftain cocked his head. I could see the wheels turning in his crafty mind. "Is this why you came to Saddoth: to teach the Original People how to conquer the Ophidians?"

"It is," I said, wondering if I was damning myself for lying. No. I would *make* it true, and thus it *would* be true.

"What do you say, Historian?" the Chieftain asked. "Do you think he speaks the truth?"

"He is a Traveler," the Historian answered. "Our histories say that Travelers often help those in need. I think..." The Historian threw his ancient hands into the air. "The Traveler has given us their secret name. Ophidian is like a snake and they *are* like snakes, even having fanged maws. By naming them, the Traveler has given us authority over our terrible and relentless enemies. Yes, I believe him, because we saw the portents in the skies foretelling his arrival."

The Chieftain's flattish nostrils flared as he turned back to me. I saw distrust in his black eyes, but maybe hope there as well.

"You will sit among us, Jake Bayard the Traveler, and tell us these tales. Afterward, after we have feasted, you will take Bok and others and hunt Ophidians in the low country, in the Slave Lands. And then we shall see if you can do as well as you boast."

I doubted I would get better terms than that. The Chieftain hadn't acted as Bok suggested he would, killing us for losing the two Ferals. This was a good start...except...I would remain on my guard, ready for anything, just in case the Chieftain decided to try to kill me in secret.

-29-

My fears concerning the Chieftain were unwarranted, as the next day, three other warriors joined Bok and me as we headed back toward the Slave Lands, as they called them.

I wore my own loincloth now and better supple leather wraps around my feet. The fact was the Historian had given me the seal of historical approval by naming me the Traveler. It meant we might try my tactics, and it meant our troop didn't mock me about wearing these pseudo-sandals.

I'd debated constructing bows and arrows or even slings. Instead, I had a premonition about that after watching the Neanderthals throw rocks yesterday. They had all proved indifferent pitchers, which was hard to watch. Pitching was why I'd gone to college for a year. I loved baseball, and I'd always berated myself for not trying out for the Big Leagues.

We'd tossed spears after that, and I noticed that I threw far better than any of them did, and this was new for me in a sense. All my pitching came in handy with spears. Short casts, I noticed, they could do. Longer javelin-like throws...not so much.

I wondered again about Neanderthal-Cro-Magnon wars in the last Ice Age. The Neanderthals had struck me as more emotionally primitive, less able to control their tempers. Now, I wondered if they had also been lousy archers and slingers. Perhaps their hand-eye coordination with distance weapons lacked the finesse that Cro-Magnons had possessed or even as we modern *Homo sapiens* had.

If that were so, would the Neanderthals prove indifferent pistol shooters? That might degrade my grand idea of teaching them how to use the Ophidian dart guns, air-cars and balloon-wheeled vehicles with rocket-assisted cannons.

Perhaps that was why the Neanderthals each had such awesome physical courage. They needed it for hunting. I could envision these boys surrounding a cave bear, lunging in like snapping dogs and stabbing with their spears. Cro-Magnons had likely stayed out of range of the terrible claws, hurling spears or shooting arrows into the beast.

Well, maybe my ideas were off about that because these Neanderthals had never had the opportunity to cast long-range javelins or fashion bows and arrows. If I was staying around, I would teach them.

We trekked single-file through the birch-tree forest, a lone band of humans setting out to change the balance of power on Saddoth. It was a heady feeling, even if it was ridiculous. I—

"Wait," Bok said, as he held up his left hand. He carried the spear in his right.

I'd noticed that most of the Neanderthals were right-handed, which was interesting if you thought about it.

I was behind Bok and heard him clearly. Some of the others must not have. I turned and held up a hand. "Stop," I stage whispered.

The other hunters stopped.

I faced forward again. Bok was cocking his ugly head one way and then another.

"Is something wrong?" I whispered.

"Down," Bok hissed.

The others threw themselves flat. I hesitated, and I heard a whine ahead of us.

Instead of falling right there, I jumped to the left and went down among foliage.

Seconds later, a band of Ophidians in camouflage gear and holding long-barreled guns came down the game trail.

I saw them, and my gut went cold. This could not be good for us.

Bok scrambled upright, screaming.

The Ophidians stopped and then drew back.

I jumped up and hurled my spear at them. It must have been beginner's luck. The spear arched perfectly and took an Ophidian soldier in the back. He hissed, flopping into heavier brush.

"Charge them," I bellowed, yanking out a flint dagger. "Kill them before they gain their balance and slaughter us."

Bok glanced at me. Then, he gripped his spear with both hands and shouted, charging. One other Neanderthal followed us. The last two took off running, screaming in fear.

I strained to reach the Ophidians in time. The one still thrashed on the ground. The others blinked and seemed to be recovering from their shock.

Bayard, stop it, a voice said in my mind. *You can't win this fight.*

It took a second for me to realize that Psi-master Spencer was telepathically speaking to me in my head. Was he part of the Ophidian band then? I didn't see him among them.

This is your last chance, Bayard, Spencer said in my mind. *You'll never get home unless you surrender.*

Instead of heeding him, I ran even harder at the Ophidians, and I almost made it, too. I'd already killed the one. If I could—

Ophidians leveled their long-barreled guns at us. They fired as darts hissed from the rifles. Three took Bok in the chest, which he ignored as he kept coming.

Two of the darts struck me. I could hardly feel them, and I laughed internally, as these were piss-poor weapons. Then a horrible sense of disorientation struck. I stumbled and my eyesight blurred.

You're not going to die, Bayard. They're tranks. They shot you with tranks.

"What?" I slurred, as I struck a tree and bounced off it, falling onto the ground.

I couldn't afford to have them kill you, now could I?

"Why are you doing this?" I said.

You didn't really think you escaped from us, did you? You fool. I've been tracking you via telepathy the whole time.

"No," I said, managing to turn over and start crawling.

157

I didn't get far before hideous Ophidian feet swam into my vision. I tried to strain upward to see them. This couldn't be happening. I was going to save the planet for the Neanderthals. I was going to free millions of meat slaves. I was going to take down the Ophidians, even if over the course of many centuries of warfare. At least I would get the revolution started.

Instead, as reptilian three-clawed hands gripped me, as Ophidians lifted me, I lost consciousness, wondering if I was going to wake up as the main course for a party of serpent-men hunters.

-30-

I awoke with an awful headache. I sat in the back seat of a grounded air-car, my hands handcuffed behind me. I wore a shirt, pants and boots again, and my skin felt scrubbed and clean.

I was witness to a wretched sight, one I believe I'll never forget, as much as I wish I could. A cavalcade of big balloon-wheeled vehicles was parked in an open area outside a birch-tree forest. From out of the forest stumbled lines of neck-chained Neanderthals. Beside them were Ophidians in leather gear, many of them with the double-pronged shock rods and power backs. Whenever one of the big brutish creatures took too long moving forward, an Ophidian applied the shock rod. The Neanderthal would cry out in agony, unable to retaliate because his or her hands were wired behind their hairy backs.

The slave drivers brought the Neanderthals to the trucks, driving them into the open back areas. There, other Neanderthals wearing shock collars chained the formerly free tribe-members onto benches. Perhaps the worst sight was seeing Bok and his uncle, the Chieftain, driven onto one of the slave wagons.

The Chieftain caught sight of me in the air-car. He straightened his gigantic frame and bellowed, "You traitorous scum! You were never a Traveler, but a fiend in human guise. You came to trick and enslave us!"

The massive Chieftain might have said more, but several Ophidians lashed him with the double-pronged rods, shocking him until he roared with anguish and stumbled up a ramp into a slave wagon.

I hung my head in shame. I'd failed horribly. If my memory about what Spencer had said was correct, I'd helped lead the Ophidians here through the psi-master's vile telepathy.

For the next thirty or forty minutes, I witnessed the dismal scene. I'd had such big plans, such hopes to be a Spartacus-like champion for these primitives. I should have known better. I should have realized—

I shook my head as my stubbornness reasserted itself. I would not allow myself to wallow in self-pity. I would—

"What will you do?" I whispered to myself.

What do you want *to do, Bayard?* Spencer asked in my mind.

I looked up, seeing if I could find Spencer. I didn't spot him anywhere.

Do you want to leave Saddoth?

"Yes," I said, feeling bitter about that. Bok, the Chieftain, the Historian—the Neanderthals would remain meat slaves to the Ophidians. That struck me as so terribly wrong. Did that mean I wanted to share their fate, though?

I exhaled. Maybe I deserved that, as I'd failed these people so awfully.

"Hey," I said to myself. "Get a grip, Bayard. What could you have ever done? Nothing. The Neanderthals were doomed anyway."

Ah, Spencer said gloatingly in my mind. *That's what I love about people. Do you know what our one great gift is?*

"No," I said.

Rationalization—it is mankind's only true genius.

"That's seems awfully cynical," I said.

Wouldn't you expect a born telepath to be a cynic? I can read people's thoughts. I know what they're really like.

"Are all psi-masters cynics?"

I suspect they are all realists. Come now, Bayard. The Neanderthals here on Saddoth are the sub-species. The Ophidians, as you've named them, are the dominant race. That was never going to change, never will change in the entire history of the planet.

160

I didn't want to believe that. But maybe Spencer had a point.

This is one world out of many, Bayard. I think Saddoth once belonged to the Harmony. Here, however, events took a terrible turn for humans, for the Neanderthal branch, anyway. If you play your cards right, though, you'll leave this hell world.

"And take you with me?" I said bitterly.

I accept the invitation, provided you help both of us to leave.

I looked away from the final stages of the Neanderthal boarding. I had to do something to help these poor souls. I couldn't just run away and leave them to their sorry fate. Is that what a Traveler did: run if a planet became too hot to handle?

I frowned, thinking about what Spencer had said. "What about Charmalos? Does he want to leave here too?"

We won't worry about him, eh.

My frown deepened. "You're cutting and running out from your ally?"

I'm not an idealist like you, Bayard. Survival comes first. Surely, you finally realize that.

"Why did you send me back here the second time, Spencer? What's your game?"

Tut, tut, I can't tell you all my secrets. Did you speak the wretched language of these creatures?

"That should be obvious," I said.

Oh, you did. How marvelous. Charmalos was—Spencer's thought quit on the instant.

I closed my eyes and hunched my head. Spencer was playing me. There was more going on here than I understood. If he told me truths, they must be half-truths. What had happened to Charmalos? The idea he might be an Ophidian—I shook my head. That had been a ploy on their part. Spencer wanted to confuse me…for some reason.

"Hello, Bayard," Spencer said.

I jerked up. The doctor wore green garments and a hat, and he wore sunglasses. He smiled, but I could tell that it was strained.

161

An Ophidian guarded him, one taller than the rest. This one had glowing red eyes indeed. For a moment, there seemed to be something familiar about him.

I snorted. That was a ridiculous idea.

The Ophidian hissed and indicated the air-car.

"Are you ready to leave, Bayard?" Spencer asked me.

"Do you understand the guard's hissing speech?" I asked.

"To a degree," Spencer said.

"Did you really use telepathy to keep track of me?"

Spencer's smile grew, but seemed even more strained than before. What was going on? What was Spencer really doing out here?

A group of Ophidians clumped near with a red-robed bastard leading the way. That one regarded Spencer's keeper, and he hissed imperiously at him.

The guard looked down.

Spencer stepped up, hissing, as he seemed to concentrate.

The red-robed Ophidian looked from the guard to Spencer. Finally, he regarded the doctor, and they had a quick and heated talk, or so it seemed to me.

In the end, the red-robed Ophidian turned to his party, raised his skinny arms and hissed for a time. Several asked what seemed like hissing questions. The red-robed Ophidian seemed to grow impatient, gesturing more urgently. At last, the others relented, and they all turned away.

I noticed that Spencer had a sweaty brow, and he seemed decidedly winded.

"You feeling okay, Doc?"

"Shut up, Bayard," he whispered. "We're far from out of this yet. If you make a scene…I may not be able to save you."

"Why didn't you just tell me that through telepathy?" I asked.

Spencer shot me an ugly glance.

I was sure then that he was mentally exhausted from speaking with the Ophidians and couldn't use telepathy for the moment. Hmm. What had happened to Charmalos? I would have dearly liked to know.

Spencer turned to the tall Ophidian guard, nodding sharply. Both the guard and the doctor entered the air-car, with Spencer in the driver's seat. Something seemed very wrong about that.

The balloon-wheeled vehicles started up. And the slave-hunting cavalcade started back for the low country with their prisoners.

We joined several other air-cars, leaving the slower, grounded vehicles behind.

Spencer gripped the controls with a white-fingered hold, showing that he was under extreme tension. The Ophidian guard also sweated, which seemed odd. Impossible, even...

"Where are we going?" I asked from the back seat.

"That will depend," Spencer whispered.

"Depend on what?" I asked.

"Why don't you shut up, Bayard? This is tricky enough as it is."

"I—"

The Ophidian guard whirled around, aiming a taser at me.

I stared at the taser, him, and for an instant, it seemed as if the guard's facial scales shifted and blurred. My mouth opened in surprise as understanding struck me—

A purple bolt zagged into me from the taser, sending me into unconscious oblivion.

I eventually woke up, and as had happened before, I felt groggy and disoriented from the tasing. I was still in the back seat of the air-car, my wrists cuffed behind me. My right shoulder hurt because of the way I'd slept. I felt the passage of wind on my face and realized the air-car flew over uneven ground.

The jostling of the air-car must have been what had woken me up.

"Bayard?" Spencer said from the front passenger-side seat.

I said nothing, deciding I'd pretend to still be sleeping.

"Jake Bayard," Spencer said.

I remained still and silent.

"If I must," Spencer said, "I'll inject you with a painful substance that will force you awake for days. I don't think you'll enjoy the suffering, which will continue for a week or more."

"Uh…" I said, pretending to come awake, opening my eyes and raising my head.

Spencer had twisted back and now grinned down at me. "That did it, eh?"

"What's going on?" I said, ignoring the question.

"Sit up," he suggested. "Take a look around."

I sat up and saw that we'd left the mountainous terrain far behind. We flew alone across green rolling hills, covering much more territory than Bok and I had while traveling back to

Original People. I also noted that the tall Ophidian drove the air-car—if he really was an Ophidian.

Spencer must have noticed my glance. "You have questions, I imagine."

I closed my eyes and sat against a corner. The enormity of what I'd caused to Bok's tribe hit me all over again. They had all become slaves, likely fodder for the arenas, for gladiatorial games. I imagine the Ophidian masses would love seeing the Chieftain fight. Would they feast on him when he eventually lost, selling choice pieces from the famous gladiator?

"It's hard on the psyche traveling to a strange world," Spencer said. "Their norms can be quite different from our own. You must possess a supple outlook to endure such journeys. I'm not sure you have such plasticity of thought."

"Uh-huh," I said. "You don't mind that the Ophidians eat people?"

"I suppose they do have some serpent qualities, which makes the name fitting after a fashion."

"They're hideous," I said. "The Ophidians feast on another intelligent species."

"Yes. I suppose they do at that."

"Don't you care?"

Spencer shrugged. "You forgot. Before all this, I was a professor at MIT. As it turns out, I had two doctorates. One of them, fortunately for me, was in philosophy. I say fortunate because it has taught me plasticity of thought. Modern humanity would shudder in horror at Ancient man's beliefs. I put it that way because women were considered inferior in olden times. So, you should realize that a different world with a different species would have decidedly different mores than ours."

"Spencer, the serpent men *eat, devour, feast upon* people."

Spencer shrugged. "Earth has produced more than one cannibal culture."

"Sick cultures," I spat.

"Come now, Bayard. You don't hold yourself as superior to cannibals, do you?"

"Yes!"

"Ah, I see. Well, I suppose you wish to destroy Ophidian culture then?"

"No," I said.

"No?"

"I wish to destroy the Ophidians."

Spencer laughed with delight. "You have no idea how provincial you sound."

"I couldn't care less. I know right from wrong."

"That proves you're a rube. Right and wrong are relative. And it's clear that you plan to remain a rube and will wallow in it to your heart's delight for all your days."

"Have you eaten Neanderthal steaks then?"

"No," Spencer said. "I'm too fastidious for that. And I'll be honest, I find the practice repulsive. That doesn't mean I set myself up as morally superior to the Ophidians. This is their world after all. It runs how it runs. I wish to leave, and that is where you come in."

"We tried that before," I said. "Remember what happened? Charmalos took his magic toy and bailed on us. Have you found Charmalos?"

Spencer laughed once more, a superior and annoying laugh. "Bayard, Bayard, Bayard, you really are a funny fellow. I know you know what happened to Charmalos."

I squinted at Spencer.

"I didn't read it in your thoughts," he said. "I can't unless you verbalize—"

The driver glanced sharply at Spencer, and the good doctor ceased talking.

I pretended not to notice that, but I did all right. Had Spencer just admitted that he couldn't read my innermost thoughts? Or had the two of them set that up to get me to believe Spencer couldn't read my thoughts unless I...spoke aloud, I guess. I decided on a test.

I'm going to rip out your throat, Spencer! I thought with great vehemence.

The doctor didn't twitch a muscle. Hmm. I didn't think him physically brave enough to have maintained a placid pose with such a sudden and violent threat, not with me right beside him. Thus, I didn't think he'd read that in my mind.

166

"Spencer," I mouthed, so low that there was no chance he could have heard me.

"What?" Spencer said.

"What happened to Charmalos?" I said, more loudly.

"As I said, you already know what happened to him."

I jutted my chin at the driver. "Are you telling me *he's* Charmalos?"

"I don't have to tell you that," Spencer said. "You already know."

"Charmalos!" I shouted at the driver.

He twitched. Then he glanced back at me, his red eyes aglow.

"Is it just happenstance that both Charmalos and Ophidians have red eyes?" I asked.

"Indeed so," Spencer said.

"Enough," the driver said in Charmalos' voice. "Don't give him any more data than he needs."

I stared at the Ophidian, and I believe I finally understood the situation. A Krekelen was a shape-shifter. When my hands were free, I'd feel the being's skin. If it were hot, I'd know without a doubt that it was Charmalos.

Was it impossible to hide the red-glowing eyes, though? It must be. On Earth, Charmalos and the others had gotten away with it because they'd worn heavy shades. On Saddoth, it didn't matter, because the Ophidians also had red eyes. Theirs didn't glow to such an extent, however. But that seemed not to matter.

"Are we headed for the obelisk?" I asked.

"Would you prefer to stay on Saddoth and fight for your Neanderthal friends?" Spencer asked.

"What else could we do?"

"Why not go home to Earth," Spencer suggested.

"Don't you remember?" I said. "Charmalos told us years have passed, at least twenty-six years so far. If we go to Earth, it will be…fifty-two years since we left."

"Don't you want to see what's happened on Earth since then?" Spencer asked with a lilt to his voice.

I turned away, staring into the distance. I might have stared for some time, but Spencer's chuckles began to get on my nerves.

"What now?" I asked. "Was Charmalos lying about the time dilation effect?"

"Yes," Spencer said amid his laughter.

"What?" I said. "You're kidding?"

"But I'm not," Spencer said. "Charmalos said that…" The doctor glanced at the driver. "He said it for his own reasons. If he wants to tell you what they were, he can."

"I already know why," I said.

"Oh?" Spencer said.

"Charmalos is the worst bastard I know," I said. "Krekelens by nature are deceivers and liars. Think about it: they're shape-shifters."

"That doesn't necessarily mean they're liars and—"

"Silence!" the driver hissed at Spencer.

The doctor shrank back from the Ophidian, laughing nervously a few seconds later.

I watched the interplay, and I began to ponder all that had happened to me since Charmalos and his buddies had picked me up at the U.S. Embassy in Santiago, Chile. As I did, I realized that not many days had passed since then, assuming the time dilation idea was a lie. In fact, I was still officially a U.S. Marine. But the real point was this: years hadn't passed since we left, after all. I could go home again. I might even get a belated date with Juanita Bolivar.

I frowned. I no longer deserved that date after what had happened to Bok and his uncle. There had to be something I could do for Bok. I was his blood brother. That meant something. It hadn't been a one-way trick on my part.

"Can we attempt it?" Spencer asked Charmalos.

The shape-shifter glanced at a device he kept beside his door. "It's possible we may have a small window of opportunity. We're…fifteen kilometers from the obelisk. If we hurry—"

"Go!" Spencer said.

Charmalos as an Ophidian turned the air-car sharply, and he increased speed.

168

"What's going on?" I said.

Spencer gave me an ugly smile as he drew and aimed a taser at me.

I closed my eyes and held my breath. After a few seconds, I opened my eyes. I expected Spencer to blast me then.

"Listen closely," Spencer said. "Are you listening?"

I nodded.

"Then wriggle your handcuffed hands under your butt and let me unlock them. You're going to need both hands to do this."

I frowned.

"It's going to hurt," he said. "But after all that has happened, it's the only way."

-32-

The air-car raced across waving fields of grass. Neanderthal cattle looked up in places, contentedly munching on seeds. There were meandering streams, stands of trees and groves of intensely bright red and orange flowers. Far in the distance I could see a highway, and upon it were balloon-wheeled vehicles. Farther beyond that, I saw city spires, an Ophidian metropolis, I suppose.

Spencer had unlocked the cuffs, and I rubbed my sore wrists.

He now aimed the taser at me as he brought up a smaller device. "I'm going to insert a locator in you," he said.

"What are you talking about?" I said. "You're not putting anything into me."

Spencer raised an eyebrow. "I can tase you and then put the locator in you. You have no say in this."

His threat was all too real. I nodded, saying, "Just tell me what the locator really does."

Spencer gave me a toothy grin. "Are you ready for the injection?"

"What does it do?" I said more loudly.

"What do you think it does?"

I wanted to keep calm, but was having a hard time and blurted a threat: "Spencer, you can tase me, but I can still probably grab you and toss you out of the air-car before I'm unconscious."

"I'm wearing a seatbelt, you idiot. So, you can't do that."

"Okay," I said, getting more anxious by the second. I didn't want any detector bug in me. "I can still jump out myself and break my neck."

Spencer's smile vanished. "Bayard...do you really want to die?"

"I want to know what's actually going on," I said. "What is a Traveler? I know I am, but what does that *mean?"*

Spencer glanced at Charmalos.

The shape-shifter shook his Ophidian head.

"Sorry," Spencer said. "I'm going to put the locator in you. You have to hang onto the injector for twenty seconds so this works. It will be painful, although not for long. It's much harder to do if you're unconscious, and tasing you again could slow our departure time. Why else do you think I've un-cuffed you if not to speed up the process so we can *all* get away?"

"All right," I said, slumping back, in desperation mode now. "You win. I want to get home, and I don't want to ever be tased again."

Spencer nodded curtly and moved the injector toward my chest. I swear I could see a tiny tentacle in the aperture. Was he putting a biological locator into me?

"Remember," he said, "you have to hold the injector in place for about twenty seconds."

"I know," I said, maybe with too much vehemence.

At the last second, Spencer tried to pull back, as I think he understood what I planned to do. I grabbed the injector—it was hot—ripped it out of his skinny hand and hurled it from the air-car.

"No!" Charmalos shouted, immediately braking, slowing down.

Spencer almost tased me in retaliation as he shifted back so he leaned against the front dash—his seatbelt pulled far up—the taser aimed at my chest.

"You tase me," I said, "and I can't go through the obelisk until I'm awake again."

"Do we have time to search for the injector?" Spencer asked Charmalos.

For an answer, the air-car picked up speed again.

"That was stupid," Spencer told me a second later.

"Yup, I can see that," I said, grinning anyway.

"We'll have to break his arms," Charmalos said. "Tase him first."

"No," Spencer said fast, possibly to forestall any violent actions on my part. "You said the obelisk is presently open. We may not get another chance while we have him. The venerable one is going to want to interrogate him, remember?"

"Who's that?" I said.

"The red-robed serpent man outside the forest," Spencer said.

"Bayard is unstable," Charmalos said. "We cannot afford any mix-up back at Prime."

"Prime," I said. "Where's Prime? Is that Earth?"

"You should shut up for once," Spencer told me. "You're making Charmalos nervous, and that's a bad idea."

"Is Charmalos really from long ago?" I asked. "Were he and his kind in stasis chambers in subterranean Antarctica? Or was all that smoke you've been blowing in my face?"

Neither of them said anything.

"Are we even using the obelisks the right way?" I asked. "I don't believe in Mu and Antarctica colonists from that mythical land. This is something else, isn't it?"

"I really worked at MIT," Spencer said. "I didn't know about any of this until seven, maybe eight months ago. My mother really did have relations with a psi-master in 1968. There really was a place called Mu."

"A different planet called Mu or a sunken continent in the Pacific Ocean?" I asked.

Spencer stared at me for a pregnant moment. "You're not as stupid as you look, are you?"

"Shut up," Charmalos told Spencer. "You are far too garrulous with data. Remember, you are not essential to The Plan."

"So, who built subterranean Antarctica?" I asked, trying to mask my interest in that last little tidbit.

"I don't know as much as you think." Spencer glanced at Charmalos and then back to me. "A team belonging to DARPA—"

Charmalos gave him a quick warning glance.

172

Spencer nodded. "Look, Bayard, you're going home. That's the essential thing. You get to leave this place. Forget about the Neanderthals. Forget about the U.S. Marines and any nobility you think you possess about being able to stop this. If you do this our way, you'll get to live in luxury for years. If you screw up and try to thwart us—"

"Us?" I said with a laugh. "You mean Charmalos. He's in charge. You're his boy. That's all."

"I'm a psi-master," Spencer said proudly. "You have no idea what I've been doing—"

"That's it," Charmalos said. "I will now—"

I bellowed as I launched myself at the shape-shifter. I'd finally noticed that he wasn't wearing a seatbelt like Spencer. Would Spencer tase me later at the Krekelen's orders? Would they break my arms before I went through the obelisk? If that was so, *this* was wiser than doing it their way.

The Ophidian was hot-skinned like the Charmalos of old, confirming everything. He still had muscles like steel, and in those seconds of grappling, I realized he was stronger than I was. Still, I had the element of surprise. I wrenched his neck, wrenched it again and managed to shove him half out of the air-car. Then, using my legs, I shoved both of us out of the car.

We fell a short distance, and then the two of us were tumbling over grassy ground. I didn't bother trying to hang on to him, but concentrated on rolling so I didn't get hurt. Finally, I stopped and lay gasping on hard dirt.

Knowing I had to move while I had the advantage, I sat up, groaning. It didn't appear I'd any broken bones, but I hurt all over.

The air-car plowed into dirt a short way away to the left. It didn't explode. It didn't do anything but sit there. I couldn't see Spencer.

I did not see Charmalos anywhere either. Maybe he was injured, hopefully badly.

I climbed to my feet, a mass of throbbing bruises. In the far distance…that seemed like the right direction for the obelisk. I couldn't see it yet, but I could start moving. So, I did, shuffling with a limp. In a few moments, I forced myself to run-stagger, covering ground fast.

I heard a gunshot behind me.

I glanced back and saw an Ophidian in a shooter's stance, using two hands to fire another round from a Glock. Incredibly, I heard a bullet hiss past me.

Charmalos was a pistol marksman, it seemed.

I broke into a sprint to put more distance between us. They'd made a tactical mistake in taking off my handcuffs, even if they'd needed my help holding the injector against me. Had that been sheer arrogance on their part? I shrugged as another round hissed past.

As Winston Churchill had once said, "Nothing in life is so exhilarating as to be shot at without result." I laughed with glee, finding that to be exactly the case. In fact, I gave Charmalos the finger. Then I concentrated on running, on reaching the obelisk before anyone could stop me.

-33-

I staggered onward, panting as I moved through tall grass. In the near distance, I saw the same vine-covered obelisk as before. I'd been running for quite some time, with a horrible stitch in my side and sweat pouring from me. So far, I did not see a following air-car. I—

I yelped. I saw the air-car. It was far out there, but it was flying fast. I had no doubt that Charmalos and Spencer were in it. If they could, they would tase me and break my arms and maybe my legs now, too.

I put my head down and forced myself to continue running. I would find a way to warn those on Earth. Then, I would tell someone in authority and he would figure out a way to help the Neanderthals on Saddoth. Surely, we would want allies in this fight. Surely, we could bury the ancient hatchet and help these poor suckers.

I had to hope that even our wretched politicians would side with people over Ophidians.

That would all be moot if I couldn't reach the obelisk in time. Why did I think it would send me to Earth, though? Last time, it had sent me right back to the Ziggurat of Ubo Tan.

I grinned horribly. I figured I could get to Earth because I should be able to talk to the obelisk or the intelligence behind it this time. I would use the Neanderthal tongue, and hope the crystal capstone would know what the words meant.

That was the thing. Who'd made the planet-hopping monuments? If Ophidians had made them, wouldn't they know how to use them? Why had the Neanderthal Historian known the name of the step-pyramid?

My questions were guesses as I tried to put pieces of the puzzle together.

I flung sweat out of my eyes and continued running. Glancing back—my eyes narrowed. The air-car was gaining fast. They might shoot me before I reached the obelisk.

Come on, Jake, I told myself. *It's time to run like you've never run before.*

I don't know where I called up the stamina, but I actually increased speed. I seemed to fly through the tall grass. I became one with running, no longer feeling the stitch in my side, the ache due to the lack of air—

Bayard, can you hear me? Spencer said in my mind. *You have to listen to me.*

I had no intention of listening to him, or letting him know I heard him. Instead, I concentrated on sprinting; telling myself that humanity back on Earth and the Neanderthals on Saddoth all depended on me reaching what Charmalos had called Prime.

Bayard, this is a mistake, Spencer told me. *Even if you get back to Earth, you'll likely be in subterranean Antarctica.*

"Likely? You mean you don't know for sure?" I gasped.

Bayard, listen to me. Charmalos is willing to make a deal. You have no idea how rare that is. A deal, man, you can have a deal with the greatest species in existence.

"A deal with a liar and a cheat," I gasped.

No, no, you don't know him. You've just seen his dark side. He's willing to overlook your murdering of the others—

"Spencer."

Yes? he said hopefully.

"Charmalos wasn't in stasis in Antarctica, was he?"

He was; he really was.

I sensed a lie in that, but also the truth.

I didn't have the energy to figure out what Spencer meant. Once more, I flung sweat out of my eyes and I staggered because of a hidden divot in the ground. That exploded the stitch in my side. I was near the end of my endurance, having used most of it up in this last mad dash.

Bayard, if you don't stop, Charmalos is going to do more than break some bones. He's ready to give you—

Despite my exhaustion—or maybe because of it—I discovered an ability I hadn't known I possessed. It was like a switch in my mind, a power that I'd always had but hadn't known how to access. I blocked Spencer's telepathy, shearing it cold from my mind. I actually felt his presence depart.

Perhaps there was more to being a Traveler than I realized. My dad had done things I still didn't understand. I sucked down air, feeling a great weariness descend upon me, and my clarity of purpose waver. To counteract this, I brought up the mental image of a pack of Ophidians electrocuting the Chieftain, making him bellow as they drove him to the slave wagon.

Purpose reinvaded me, filling my mind. My mind attempted to shackle my body to its high and noble resolution. I would reach the obelisk and access it before the air-car arrived, before Charmalos was near enough for a pistol-marksman shot.

I knew this would cause intense fatigue later. Perhaps it was something akin to the *berserkergang* of old. That had been a Teutonic thing from the olden times, when Germanic or Viking warriors had called upon Odin and gone into a frenzy of battle madness. The ancient Celts had done likewise—one of the reasons the Romans had developed an early dread of them.

I heard the thud of my feet on the ground. I felt air burning in my overtaxed lungs. I sensed a higher elation as I knew I would beat the Krekelen and his pet psi-master to the obelisk.

Would I reach Earth in subterranean Antarctica? Would I appear inside the Giza Pyramid in Egypt or would I walk off one of the ancient Mayan ziggurats in the jungles of Central America?

The next phase of this felt surreal possibly due to my heightened senses. I reached out with my mind to the obelisk. It wasn't a psi-master skill, but something Travelers could do. How I knew this, I do not know, but it was a positive sensation.

"This is Jake Bayard of Earth," I said in the Neanderthal tongue of Saddoth.

A beam of red light reached out from the top of the obelisk. It stabbed true, striking against my forehead.

I understand, I heard in my mind.

"Can you send me to Earth?" I said aloud.

There was the sense of relays clicking and calculators tumbling. Power surged within the obelisk.

"It is the third planet from the star Sol," I said.

Your references are odd. Ah. This might be it.

I was not an advanced Traveler. I was Jake Bayard, a novice in this. There were precautions I could have taken, but I was out of time.

"Send me," I said.

The Obelisk of Ubo Tan beamed a stronger red ray at me. And as I ran toward it, as the air-car strained to reach me, I felt myself begin to waver and turn into traveling energy.

I left the ground of Saddoth, reached the glowing red pyramidion of the obelisk and shot outward to Earth, or so I believed. I saw in that moment how I left a trail for others to follow. I'd opened a way…

I strained to know more, but I lost consciousness as I sped outward into deep space.

-34-

I awoke with a start surrounded by red energy. I floated upon it, realizing that the energy was being reconstituted into my body.

Where had I arrived? Was I back on Saddoth in the Ziggurat of Ubo Tan? Had I journeyed back to the Planet of the Dead that orbited Epsilon Eridani? Or had I reached home, Earth—

I thudded the few inches upon a dais, and in that moment, darkness became complete as the last particle of red mist entered the funnels above me. Fortunately, the greater octagonal chamber was much like the others. I recalled the shape and stumbled in the darkness until I found a latch. Turning it, I heard the grinding of sliding stone as the latch pulled out of my grasp.

I felt ahead, going through a short corridor, and then into emptiness.

I stopped, as I'd always landed upon the top of a high step-pyramid. It wouldn't do to fall down steep stairs, injuring myself, or tumbling over the edge and killing myself far below.

Surely, Charmalos and Spencer would be following me soon.

I nodded in the darkness, realizing it would be a good idea to get off the step-pyramid before lightning and thunder demolished me.

Knowing that time could be critical, I went down onto my belly and slithered for a distance.

179

"Oof," I grunted, yanking my hand back. I'd felt over an edge into nothing. Slowly sliding forward, I felt downward for a step, but didn't find one.

Moving along the edge, I continued searching, about ten minutes later finding steps leading down. I was sweating even though I'd regained all my lost energy and strength. The process of traveling had once again invigorated me.

I swiveled around and crawled backward down the steep steps. I felt like a child again, when I used to maneuver like this up and down stairs in our old two-story home. I wanted to be cautious, and I wanted to get off the step-pyramid as fast as I could.

I ended up being more worried than cautious, for I pushed too fast and began to roll and tumble down the last fifty or so steps. I lay gasping at the bottom, bruised but otherwise unhurt.

That had been stupid...well, maybe not. I climbed to my feet and strained to see anything. I could not. It was pitch black.

"Hello," I said.

I listened to the sound of my echo. I was definitely in an enclosed space. The lack of stars might have proven that, unless heavy cloud cover blocked them from sight. I thought about my situation, and it came to me that it was warm in here.

Did that mean I was far under the Earth? Was this even Antarctica?

Okay. I didn't have any answers right now. Shuffling slowly, hoping I did not stand upon a greater terrace, I moved in one direction. I did this—

I cried out, stumbling over an object in the darkness. I crashed suddenly upon my hands and knees, striking stone. I was lucky that I hadn't twisted or broken a wrist.

I turned and felt...the thing I'd tripped over was metal, twice the length of a body and maybe four times as wide. It...I closed my eyes, concentrating. I definitely felt the slightest vibration from it, which indicated...

I shook my head in the darkness. I did not know. Making a fist, I rapped my knuckles against it, listening. The tubular object was hollow and made of metal—no, part was glass, sounded like glass.

What I wouldn't have given for a flashlight or even a torch. Heck, a match would have been a godsend.

I imagine you can tell what I was thinking. Had I stumbled upon a stasis unit? It seemed like the right size for one. But why would a stasis unit be here in the subterranean chamber with a step-pyramid?

A dreadful sensation surged through my body. It was— lightning roared into existence, and titanic thunder boomed through my body, shaking my bones and rattling my teeth in my jaw. The intense light was too much for my eyes. I cried out, squeezing my eyelids shut and clapping my hands over my ears. The process continued with savage intensity.

As the last thunder reverberated, I peeked through my slit fingers. I had a momentary image of the place, a vast chamber with a gigantic ziggurat before me. On the floor before the steep steps were fifty or more brass-colored cylinders. They were littered as if they'd tumbled down the steps in a mass.

Then, swirling glowing red particles up there gave off greater light. I stood, looking more closely at the brass cylinders, stepping near one. Through a glass window, I spied a still, large-headed woman. Could she be a psi-mistress as Spencer's father had been a psi-master?

The swirling particles sped faster, but the light from them lessened. I divined the reason, as the particles began to ooze into the block temple on top of the step-pyramid.

I twisted around, searching for an exit. There, several hundred yards away, was a high arch leading somewhere.

I broke into a sprint, hurtling over cylinders, wanting to use the light while it lasted. I noted prehistoric scenes painted on the nearest wall showing mammoth riders with lances facing others on T-Rexes.

How I hoped I'd reached Earth. That I was deep underground gave me hope.

I glanced back. The last of the red particles were flowing into the block temple on top. I faced ahead, and made it through the high arch, entering a tunnel, I suppose. I wasn't sure because everything turned pitch black again as I slowed to a walk, feeling my way, knowing I needed a weapon. If

Spencer and Charmalos freed those in the cylinders...I and maybe the entire Earth were doomed.

I stumbled through darkness for hours, finally sitting and gasping against a granite tunnel-wall, with my forehead pressed against my up-thrust knees.

It had gotten cooler, although it hadn't bothered me yet. Perhaps moving around as I had kept me warm. Sitting, I began to shiver, and realized if I trekked any higher, I'd need a jacket or parka if I hoped to survive. That led me to believe I reached subterranean Antarctica, but I hadn't fully confirmed it yet.

It would seem there was a fantastic maze of tunnels in this subterranean world. Once again, I wondered who had built it and when. The mammoth and T-Rex riders would seem to indicate a time before normal human history had begun.

I raised my head, blinking. Wait a minute. Didn't accepted natural history tell us that dinosaurs had lived millions of years in the past? But if mammoth riders had battled T-Rex riders, then obviously dinosaurs had been around much more recently. That didn't fit with the science I'd learned in school, though.

Of course, was it science strictly speaking? Science meant the scientific method: an exact process that said if you conducted a certain experiment many times over, it would always come out with the same results.

For instance, if you released a stone it would fall to the ground. That proved the law of gravity. You could try the experiment a thousand times, and it would come out the same each time.

What experiment had the scientific community practiced that showed us dinosaurs had gone extinct millions of years in the past? Instead, people with theories and expectations said this geological strata—the one the dinosaur bones had been in—proved the bones were millions of years old. The testers did no tests, but followed their assumptions, and others in authority agreed with them, dismissing anything that said otherwise.

What did that have to do with anything? I don't know. I'd seen the prehistoric pictures on the wall. That's all. It shook my understanding of early life on Planet Earth. I'd trusted my schoolteachers to know what in the world they taught was really true. I bet most just trusted those who had told them, "This is the way it is. And if you don't believe that, you're a moron." From the teachers I'd had, that would have been more than enough to cow the vast majority of them.

I shook my head.

The ancient Greeks had taught that the bottom of the sea was smooth and that there were four basic elements: earth, air, fire and water. And if you didn't believe that, you were a barbarian moron who probably believed the gods hatched from eggs, or something equally bizarre.

I climbed to my feet.

It didn't matter what I believed about Earth prehistory. I was down here. The cave paintings showed dinosaur riders and I'd been to two other planets using an obelisk launcher and a ziggurat lander. Ancient monuments had filled one dead world. The second world had had a one-sided race war with Ophidians dominating poor Neanderthals.

I just wanted to surf in Kauai and live the life of a knight-errant, maybe becoming a private detective in time. I didn't want to have to kill anyone anymore, and I didn't want to climb a corporate ladder with a bunch of woke bastards and Karens making my life miserable. They'd already done a number on the Marines.

I started walking again, feeling along the wall and—

Bayard, can you hear me?

That was Doctor Spencer's voice inside my head. I thought I'd turned that off back on Saddoth. Maybe arriving here had reset my mind back to normal.

I feel as if you can hear me, Spencer said in my mind. *We must work together. There is still time to patch this up. Charmalos has a proposal for you.*

I thought about that as I moved through the stygian tunnel. What I wanted was to kill Charmalos and interrogate Spencer for several weeks.

Yeah, I know. I'd said a few moments ago that I no longer wanted to kill anyone. I guess I meant no more killing of regular Joes on Earth. No more wars over mindless stuff...when there was a galactic battle secretly taking place under our noses. Ophidians were eating Neanderthals twenty-six light-years away on Saddoth. *That* was worth fighting about. Stopping the shape-shifting Krekelens from maneuvering covertly on Earth—

I stopped suddenly. Had that been taking place?

I scowled. I had no idea. Still, there was a possibility that Krekelens with psi-master puppets had started to move among us. That might explain some of the craziness of the past few years.

I thought about the brass cylinders lying askew at the bottom of the step-pyramid. If I had to guess...what would I think that represented? Hmm. If I had to guess...I would say those in the stasis tubes had made a journey between planets. Those in the tubes hadn't been Travelers, but ordinary guys in the traveling sense. The process worked differently if a Traveler didn't make the jump or blaze the trail for others to follow...if they did so soon enough after the Traveler jumped or jaunted.

I snorted. This was more guessing on my part, but it had a feel of rightness to it. Perhaps the Krekelens had found a way back onto Earth. Maybe there had been a galactic war back in the day, or between those of the Harmony. Maybe Earth was one of the few planets that had really advanced since the bad old days.

Okay, okay, I told myself, while shaking my head. It was time to stick to facts. I had to do something about Spencer and Charmalos. If Spencer had used telepathy—

I activated the cut-off switch in my head—that's how I thought about it, though it was obviously not mechanical—to foil Spencer from using his psi-master power on me. If he'd been talking to me, he was close. If he was close…maybe he'd been using his telepathy to track me.

I held myself perfectly still, and I listened with everything in me. I strained—

There! I heard a shoe scape against stone. Spencer and his hot-skinned shape-shifter overlord were following me.

My breath came raggedly.

Let the games begin, I thought to myself. There were two of them and one of me. I lacked any weapons except for myself. They had at least one taser and a Glock. I was a United States Marine, a lethal mass of bone and muscle. I wanted to crack my knuckles in anticipation about what was to come. Instead, with my cut-off telepathy switch in place, I turned back to deal with these two villains.

-36-

I turned back, but I must have taken a different corridor somewhere. I'd tried to be thorough and rational about this, but in darkness so utterly devoid of any semblance of light, there came to be a feeling of material blackness. I bumped into this darkness, stopping, and then reconsidered and felt with my hands...nothing in front of me.

Perhaps the darkness disoriented me. I was getting hungry and thirsty, and shivering more often. Finally, in desperation, I reconnected the telepathy part of my mind and went so far as to say, "Spencer? Can you hear me?"

I didn't receive a reply. I didn't feel any connection with the psi-master.

"Don't panic, Jake," I told myself. "You can do this."

I felt before me and yearned for freedom. I wanted to get out of here so badly—I froze. Before me, I heard the grinding of stone on stone, a distinctive sound.

I swallowed hard.

Had a stone door opened before me? I would guess so. Who had opened it? Or what had opened it? I could only believe that it had something to do with my Traveler genes.

With fatalistic resolve, I stumbled through the opening, and I felt the faintest stir of air against my face.

Behind me, the grinding sound resumed. The door or path must have closed again. I turned back, feeling—yes, the way I'd just used was blocked.

I faced forward—the stir of air being the marker—and began to trek earnestly. I soon became aware that I trudged upward at a slight angle. Hope filled my breast and fear as well. I had little doubt now that I'd reached subterranean Antarctica. That being the case, how would I survive the hideous cold?

"One thing at a time, Bayard," I said.

I continued the stygian journey, shivering and rubbing my shoulders, my teeth chattering eventually. Yet, doggedly, I continued onward. I had no food or water. This was the time to finish the trek. If I slept, I might recoup some energy, but lose that much more sustenance as my body lost liquids and devoured my fats.

I stopped as I realized—

"Light," I said, sounding like a madman with the glimpse of sanity in his grasp. There was the faintest illumination before me.

I held my hands before my face, and detected their outline.

I'd been shuffling for a time. Now, I resumed with a steady gait, no longer using my hands, but using my eyesight to guide me.

The illumination grew by the slowest of degrees. Finally, I could see myself, and I'd become cold, quite cold. I couldn't stop my teeth from chattering.

I debated breaking into a sprint, but held myself back. I would trudge with resolution until I dropped. I'd heard stories about Old West gunfighters ambushed by so-called friends who had crawled fifty miles through the desert all so they could gain their revenge. I had a greater goal. My blood-brother Bok was in an Ophidian gladiatorial camp.

I was still a Marine. We did not willingly leave our own behind. I had visions of myself leading a platoon of Marines, mowing down the Ophidian guards as we rescued our Neanderthal brothers from captivity.

Perhaps that doesn't sound like me, the surfer-to-be living the knightly life. Well, I was a born warrior. The captain had said so in Bhutan. I'd fought hard there, had made something of a reputation among the others. If the war had actually been worth fighting—

Yada, yada, yada, I was talking big. Let me leave it at this, I trekked. I walked, stumbled, staggered and continued to rub my shoulders. Man, it was cold down here. I could see my breath, white mist. I could—

I stopped.

Three people in parkas down the tunnel—up the tunnel—shined flashlights at me. I couldn't see their faces because each of them wore scarves. They stared blankly, though.

Had I reached Spencer's psi-master zombies that we'd met the first time I came to Antarctica?

One of them waved, and shouted, "Over here. You must be freezing. Who are you?"

I broke into a run then, staggering and shouting, weeping a little, I'm afraid. He'd spoken English like an American. I was back on Earth. I had to be. They didn't strike me as zombie soldiers, but regular guys exploring in subterranean Antarctica.

Soon, I stumbled into the arms of a bushy-bearded man. My knees gave way, but he held me up.

The other two were women. One looked to be in her forties and watched me closely. The other had a gun in her right hand, the only hand among them that didn't wear a glove. She might have been in her mid-thirties.

"Who are you?" the man said.

"Sergeant Jake Bayard, U.S. Marine Corps," I said.

The man glanced at the woman with the gun. She in turn glanced at the other.

"Just a minute," that one said. She pulled out a computer slate, checking—her head whipped up. "What name did you say?"

"Sergeant Jake Bayard," I said.

"Where are you stationed?" she asked.

"The U.S. Embassy in Santiago, Chile," I said.

"That's right," she said. "That's one of the names."

"You're really Jake Bayard?" the man asked.

"I am. Is there a problem?"

"Why aren't you wearing a parka?"

"I lost it. Please," I said. "Do you have an extra one? I'm freezing."

The three of them traded glances.

189

I groaned, with my knees unhinging again as I slumped to the tunnel floor.

The man shed his parka. He had more layers on underneath. He knelt and wrapped the parka around me. "Put this on," he said.

I struggled up, put on the parka and began to laugh hysterically.

"No, no," he said. "You're okay. Are you hungry?"

"Yes," I whispered.

"Left pocket," he said.

I tried it, found a Snickers bar and ripped off the wrapper, devouring it in seconds.

The woman put her gun away and her mitten back on.

"We need to get him back to the base camp," the man said.

"Just a minute," the armed woman said. "Is there anyone else down here with you?"

"Two others," I said.

"Do you know them?"

"The one," I said, retaining enough wariness to know I could easily say too much. "His name is Doctor Spencer."

The other woman checked her slate. "Yes," she said. "He's on the list, too."

"You don't know the second one's name?" the gun-woman asked me.

I shook my head.

"Let's get him to the base camp," the man said.

"Yes," the armed woman said. "And I suggest we hurry. There's something strange—" I didn't catch what else she said, as she lowered her voice.

They led me into ice-hewn tunnels, and eventually we reached a cage. A crane drew us up, and I became convinced that this was the same cage I'd used coming down.

It was daylight, thank goodness, when we reached the surface. And it was so cold, the bite hurt my face. I had no idea how the man was standing it without a parka, but he didn't complain.

There were U.S. soldiers everywhere in parkas. Soon enough, my Good Samaritan shrugged on an extra parka a soldier gave him. We passed the area of white humps in the snow and ice. I saw no indication of the gunfight a week and a half ago. There were several large cargo planes on an icy tarmac. One of them was the C-130 I remembered. There were two Chinooks as well.

As we headed for the trenches that held the buildings, I did see one area with splotches of frozen red. Had someone spilled blood there when the Chinooks had landed? Had there been a bloody battle? There was no evidence of that now.

They helped me down a ladder, and I stumbled into a barracks. I rushed immediately to a heater, absorbing the lovely warmth. The bearded man led me to a table, and I wolfed down food and drink. Afterward, extreme exhaustion claimed me. I yawned so much that the man showed me where I could sleep.

Then, I fell into a cot, pulling the blanket over me before unconsciousness claimed me.

***

I think I dreamed, and I don't think I liked my dreams. I woke up with a start, frightened and sweaty, looking around.

The door to the bedroom opened, and I saw three MPs with helmets, batons and sidearms. Had I known they were coming? The timing was odd to say the least.

"Sergeant Jake Bayard," the toughest-looking said, a man with thick neck, a flat-top cut and a tattoo on his left wrist.

"Yes?"

"You're to come with us."

"Uh…I just woke up."

"Now," the MP said.

"How about you let me take a piss first?"

He studied me. "You're a funny boy, are you? Fine. I'll join you."

"You have to drain the lizard too?" I asked.

He didn't crack a smile. He did follow me into the john and stood watching as I whizzed into the toilet.

"Is there a reason for this?" I asked. "I'm unarmed, there are three of you, and no way out of this head…I mean, latrine," giving him the Army word for a restroom with a slight sneer. I really wasn't in the mood for their crap right now.

He said nothing.

"What if I take your gun and baton and just leave the base camp?" I asked.

He quit leaning against the sink, his right hand falling onto the butt of his holstered sidearm.

"Just kidding." I stepped beside him, washing my hands in the sink. Instead of using a towel, I wiped my hands against his shirt.

He tried to shove me, the obvious move. I shifted out of the way so he stumbled. As he did, I took his baton. He righted himself and whirled around. I handed him back his baton.

"We can handcuff you," he said, as he put the baton away.

"Sure," I said, moving past him, forgoing giving him a hip check. I'd just wanted him to know I could crack his skull any time I wanted.

192

In the main room, I donned winter gear and so did they. We climbed the ladder, walked along the top of the trench and soon reached the parked planes. They led me to an LC-130H, the main difference being that this one had skids instead of wheels and the interior was much, much different from the first 130. There were all kinds of machines in operation in here and a staff of at least six. The MPs took me down a tight passageway.

Tough Guy knocked on a door.

A second later, it opened. The gun-toting woman from the tunnels stood there.

"Jake Bayard, Colonel," Tough Guy told her.

So, she was a colonel.

"Thank you," she said.

"He, ah—" Tough Guy quit speaking when the colonel turned back and stared at him.

"You can wait in the heat shack," she said. "I'll be fine."

Tough Guy nodded briskly. It seemed he didn't want to contradict the colonel.

"Come in," she told me.

I squeezed past Tough Guy and closed the door behind me. It was close in here. She had a desk and it was loaded with gizmos and computers, with a single open lane between the chair before the desk and the one behind it. She sat in the one behind.

I took the one in front.

She was tall for a woman and quite lean. In her early to middle thirties, I'd guess, a bit young to be a colonel. She had brunette hair to her shoulders and clear skin without any hint of wrinkles, and dark brown eyes. She seemed deadly serious with thin lips and a thin nose.

I looked her in the eyes to see if I could detect contact lenses. I wondered now why Krekelens wouldn't wear contacts instead of dark sunglasses.

"Is there a problem?" she asked.

"None," I said.

"Why are you studying me so closely. You think I might be an enemy agent?"

"Bingo, Colonel. I hope you're not." I slumped back in the chair and looked around her office with its various computers and other equipment.

"My name's McPherson," she said after a moment.

"Jake Bayard," I said, inclining my head politely, as if to an equal and giving her my attention. "But you already know that." I felt better for having slept, but was hungry now. I wouldn't have minded some coffee either.

McPherson stared silently at me, obviously sizing me up.

I stared back, waiting for it.

"You've been down in the tunnels for eleven days, Sergeant. How have you survived all this time?"

"Before we get into all that," I said, "do you mind if I ask you a few questions?"

She said nothing to that. So, I figured it was okay.

"Are you Army?" I asked. "Because you're sure no Marine." The female Marines I knew were all whipcord-lean and tough. They had to be to put up with the males…and the Navy had no colonels. The Air Force did, but somehow she didn't strike me as blue.

She folded her hands on the desk. "I'm with DARPA."

"Oh?" Still didn't answer my question. Civilian agencies didn't have colonels either, except as the services assigned them to work there.

"You know about DARPA?"

I nodded.

"Do you care to answer my question now?"

"But you didn't answer mine."

She grimaced. "All right. Technically, I carry an Army commission. Now, how did you survive down there for eleven days?"

"Did you work with Doctor Spencer?" I asked, ignoring her question.

McPherson leaned back, fingering her chin. "I did not. Why do you ask?"

"Uh-huh. So you *know* about Doctor Spencer?"

"In what manner?" She seemed guarded, so it was quite possible she did know. Or maybe she was just being cagey, learning more from my questions than I was.

194

"Spencer had his men take me from the American embassy in Santiago."

"Yes, I know about that."

"Did Doctor Spencer have authorization to do that?"

McPherson sat forward as her thin nostrils drew inward. She'd come to some kind of decision about me. "How much do you know about Doctor Spencer?"

"More than you, I bet."

"Hmm. We should stop being coy. You tell me the truth and I'll tell—"

"Colonel," I said, interrupting, "there's no way I'm going to tell you anything unless I think you might believe me."

"Oh. Why's that?"

"Because when I tell you...anyone would think I'm a lunatic. Unless they already know some...fantastic things."

For the first time, McPherson's features softened just a bit, and I knocked a few more years from her age. She hunched even more forward, staring intently. "I have a TS/SCI clearance, with more codewords and compartments than you probably ever guessed existed. Yet you're acting as if you know even more secrets.

"I don't have that kind of clearance, but I do know...things you'd probably call classified secrets."

"I see." She seemed nonplussed for a moment, then took a breath, let it out. "Does the year 1968 mean anything to you?"

"Don't you mean 1967, when the survey team first found the stasis unit?"

She jerked as if I'd punched her in the gut. The little color she had in her face drained away. She slumped back in her chair, and her eyes seemed glassy for a moment.

She recovered quickly, though. "How did you learn about that?"

"Spencer told me," I said.

"You're lying."

"Colonel, let me give you a compound word. If you know what I mean by it, I might be able to tell you a few things."

"What word?"

"Psi-master."

195

Her eyes narrowed into a gunfighter's squint. Soon, she nodded, and she began to relax, as if this were now a conversation instead of a struggle of interrogations.

"Doctor Spencer told me he was a product of the union between the man in the stasis unit found in 1967 and his mother, a linguist," I said.

"Yes," McPherson said.

"From the stories Spencer told me, I figured DARPA scientists would have kept him under lock and key for the rest of his life instead of letting him run around."

"We tried to intern him. He used his…psionics to escape." McPherson watched me closely as she said that.

"His psionic powers are quite real," I said. "He must have used them—"

"I know all about that," she said, interrupting.

"Really. All about it?"

"More than you, I bet. Frankly, I'd rather that you tell me about *your* father."

The statement took me by surprise, and I must have shown it.

McPherson gave me a wolfish smile. She had very white teeth. "When I learned about you, Sergeant, I requested a deep search into your past, which included your unusual father. Do you know that the FBI and CIA were unable to find any evidence of his birthplace?"

"How about that," I said. "Hey, it was pre-internet, almost pre-computers. No big surprise."

"Where was your father born?"

"I don't know."

"Don't know or won't say?"

"Don't know. He never told me."

McPherson nodded slowly. "I would prefer to have you hooked up to a lie detector as we proceed. However, for now, I'm going to trust my instincts about you and your answers."

"All right," I said. "Let's cut to the chase. How much have you seen down there?"

"A complex of unexplainable tunnels," she said.

"Have you come upon any drawings or wall pictures?"

"No. Have you?"

"Yes."

"Where are they, and what did they show?"

"What do you know about Mu?"

She gave me a funny stare. "Are you talking about the mythical Pacific Ocean continent?"

"Up until a day ago, I would have said yes. Now, I think Mu is the name for another planet."

"What?"

"Colonel, what if I told you I've spent the last eleven days on two different planets? Would you believe me?"

"Of course not. Why ask me something so foolish?"

I felt unaccountably saddened by her answer. I suppose I wanted someone to believe me, to know what I'd been through. But I couldn't afford to have her think I was crazy. That would have been a mistake—maybe I'd already said too much.

I thus shook my head. "I asked because I'm trying to determine how gullible you are."

"No, I don't believe that." She drummed her fingers on a small open area on her side of the desk. "Do you really believe you were on different planets?"

"Of course not," I said, mimicking her. "Why ask me something so foolish?"

She stared at me, and began to nod slowly. She opened her mouth—

A klaxon began to blare from within the plane. Then, others sounded from outside.

McPherson jackknifed to a switch on her desk. Pressing it, she asked, "What's the situation?"

"We appear to be under attack, Colonel."

"An air assault?" she asked.

"No. I just got word that aggressors have boiled up from the main excavation point. I suggest you escape the base camp immediately."

"Alert the team," she said.

"I have. I think we're outnumbered. I suggest you leave while you can. We'll hold them as long as we can."

McPherson looked up at me. "What do you think we should do, Sergeant?"

"Kill them all," I said, thinking about the brass cylinders in the main ziggurat chamber. "They're aliens in human guise, some of them anyway—and not the friendly kind. If they leave Antarctica, the world is going to be in a desperate mess—a worse desperate mess."

She stared at me.

"Colonel," said the man on the other end.

McPherson spoke into the intercom: "Defend the base camp. Fall back if it becomes imperative. See if you can capture one of the aggressors for interrogation."

"Yes, ma'am," he said. "I still think you should lift-off. Remember—"

"That will be all," she said, cutting him off and staring at me.

"He was going to say remember the others," I said, antsy to help defend the base. "He must meant those who acted like zombies eleven days ago—or however many days ago you took over here."

Colonel McPherson drummed her fingers on the desk, thinking deeply, it seemed like. "Kill them all?" she asked.

"That's my recommendation," I said, squirming, ready to bolt out of here and find a gun to help fight.

"It would seem you have definite opinions about all this. Why is that?"

"The base is under attack," I said. "Shouldn't we be go our way? Or maybe you should go out there and supervise, if nothing else?"

She watched me, her eyes darting back and forth.

"Oh," I said, getting it then. Colonel McPherson was a cagey and clever woman. "The base isn't really under attack, is it? That was to test my reaction, see what I'd tell you." I thought about the implications of all the klaxons blaring at her command. "Does DARPA control the base camp?"

McPherson shook her head, still observing me.

"Fine," I said. "You tested me, heard my recommendation and heard me say some crazy crap. Now, what happens?"

"I want you to tell me what really happened to you these eleven days."

"I wandered down there, lost."

198

"I don't believe you."

"You also didn't believe me when I tried to tell you the truth." I looked up at the ceiling. I was hungry and thirsty, and this woman had just tricked me. I no longer trusted her. She was more than cagey; she was dangerous.

"Colonel, before we continue, how about I get some chow? I can't think on an empty stomach."

"Yes," she said, "as that will give me time to hook up a lie detector for further questioning."

"Whatever," I said, standing.

"The MPs will keep you company while you eat."

"Sure," I said, reaching for the door handle.

-38-

After exiting the 130 and walking across the snow for the housing trench, I noticed two other big Air Force planes coming in for a landing. A C-17 and a C-5, I think. We were having a regular convention. Had my arrival begun a process? Hmm. I wonder if earlier there had been the cosmic lightning outside, or had that only occurred down in the ziggurat chamber? Something like that might bring more top brass out here.

I shrugged, hurrying across the ice for some chow, the three MPs keeping me company. I figured I'd find out soon enough what was happening. Right now, I needed food.

Maybe twenty minutes later, I was scarfing down bacon, eggs and toast, and drinking strong hot coffee. It was utterly refreshing and comforting to eat normal food with a plate, knife and fork. The company could have been better, but as I started on my second cup, I decided to use the MPs to my advantage.

We were in a base cafeteria, with another group at a farther table. The MPs sat at my table, being stiff as they tried not to just stare at me. It was odd, too, as no one wore a surname tag on his uniform.

"How long have you guys been here?" I asked.

Tough Guy scowled. "You trying to pump us for information?"

I put a hand on my chest. "I'm Jake Bayard. Sergeant Jake Bayard. Who are you guys?"

Tough Guy shook his head.

"Come on, Campbell," one of the others said. "What can it hurt to talk to him?"

"Campbell, huh?" I said. "Glad to make your acquaintance."

"Look," Campbell said. "You ought to know this is a strange assignment. The colonel is a Defense Department hotshot and you're a weirdo lost down in the tunnels for eleven days. Before we arrived..." Campbell scowled at his two friends.

One of them shrugged.

Campbell was obviously a weightlifter, with big arms given his size. He was considerably shorter than I was and maybe I intimidated him. I would bet he knew several martial arts and practiced pistol marksmanship a lot. He would be the kind of civilian cop that would swagger when coming up to a driver to give him a traffic ticket, and he would likely enjoy staring down at people while he wore his mirrored sunglasses.

"What happened when you first arrived here?" Campbell said. "What were the base personnel like then?"

"You trying to pump for information?" I asked, mimicking him from earlier.

"Hey, tough guy," he said. "I was trying to make conversation. Isn't that what you want?"

I took a sip from my second cup of coffee. "Okay. I'll play. You could have called them zombies. They weren't the living dead. They were still alive. I only mean, none of them talked or acted normal. What happened to them?"

"They're all dead," said the one that had shrugged. He had a red mustache, so in my mind I called him Red.

"Dead?" I asked.

"Delta guys came in to regain control of the base," Red said. "They ended up killing most of them, they say. I heard strange things about the prisoners."

So, they hadn't *all* died. "Strange things like what?" I asked.

"Like that's all we're going say about it," Campbell said in a rush, glaring at Red.

201

I looked over at the entrance as it opened. Two men walked in, their parkas already unzipped and the hoods thrown back. Most people did that *after* coming inside. One of them had gray hair at the temples. He was a square-jawed man in his fifties with—ah, he was a general, according to his uniform.

The man beside him was lean, with a hand resting on his holstered sidearm.

"Jake Bayard," the general said in a crisp voice as he scanned our two groups.

"That's me, sir," I said, raising an arm.

"You're coming with me, son," the general said.

Campbell jumped to his feet. "Begging your pardon, sir, but he's in my custody. I'm under specific orders to keep him in sight at all times."

"I'm giving you new orders," the general said.

Campbell hesitated. "Sir, I'll have to call Colonel McPherson for instructions. Or get those orders in writing."

I raised an eyebrow. Old Campbell here had more balls than I'd originally given him credit for. Standing up to a general was not an easy thing to do.

The lean man with the general stepped forward as if to press the matter.

"No," the general told him, using an arm to hold the lean man back. "The man's just doing his duty. Sure, you three MPs come along. I'm going to see Colonel McPherson anyway. I may need you to place her under arrest. Any more questions?"

Campbell glanced at the other two. They lacked his grit, and did and said nothing. "No, sir," Campbell said.

***

Outside, I saw that the two big planes had landed, with armed soldiers in parkas and setting up heavy weapons. Did I say that I didn't like the feel of this new development? Well, I didn't like it one bit.

After the six of us crossed the ice, nearing the planes, several hard-eyed soldiers intercepted the MPs. Campbell complained to the general. Two soldiers grabbed his arms, marching him away. Red and the other MP followed the rest of the soldiers. Once away from us, I noticed the soldiers disarming the MPs.

"This way," the general told me, snapping his fingers for my attention.

I looked at him and nodded, following the general and his bodyguard. We soon climbed an airstair into the larger of the two planes. I had a bad feeling that I'd never see Campbell and the other two again.

The general and bodyguard escorted me into a large room with a conference table. Two soldiers eyed us as we entered. They looked tough and professional, with MP-5s held at the ready. To my surprise, Colonel McPherson already sat at the table. She looked unhappy, staring at one of the porthole windows.

"Sit," the general told me, indicating that I take a chair beside McPherson.

I did so, all too aware of the two soldiers standing at attention behind us.

The general shed his parka as if he found it uncomfortable, tossing it onto a small sofa to the side. The bodyguard did likewise before taking up station at the door to the conference chamber.

The general sat across from McPherson and me, his hands near a closed folio. "Sergeant Bayard, Colonel McPherson, I'm General Stanton. He smiled coldly. "I am under direct authority from the Joint Chiefs of Staff with the authorization to look into any unusual activity. Colonel, I must say, you have acted hastily and brazenly here."

Her head snapped up. "I'm on a top secret mission, General, with direct—"

"Colonel," he said coldly, interrupting her. "You will contain yourself. I'm not interested in your emotional outbursts. You will answer questions, but until then, you will remain silent. Is that clear?"

She nodded stiffly.

He eyed her, glanced at me and opened the folio, extracting a paper. He laid this on the table. "According to this report, your people murdered American soldiers on January two, this month, eleven days ago to be precise. The survivors of your assault are under severe mental stress."

I glanced at McPherson. She stared woodenly at the table. What the general had just said didn't jibe with what Campbell had told me about Delta Force members assaulting the base. Old weightlifting Campbell could spin a tale on the spot. I was impressed. There was something else, though, that I needed to check.

"Could I see the report, sir?" I asked as meekly as I could.

The general glanced at me. "I don't see why."

"Please, sir, it's germane to the situation."

General Stanton raised an eyebrow.

I couldn't be sure, but he might have been wearing contact lenses.

"Aren't you trying to get down to the mystery, sir?" I asked. "I believe I can help you."

"A cheeky fellow, are you? Fine." Stanton picked up the paper, passing it to me.

I leaned across the table and grabbed his hand, half crumbling the report in the process. "Oh, sorry," I said, taking the paper from him.

Stanton snatched his hand back, scowling at me.

McPherson glanced at me.

With my heart pounding, I put the paper on the table and smoothed it out. "Ah," I said, as I bent over the report, reading it. "Yes. It does talk about a firefight."

I looked up to find Stanton staring at me. I could feel others and glanced behind me. The bodyguard was directly at my back, with a pistol aimed at my neck.

"Is something wrong, sir?" I asked the general.

Stanton opened his mouth, perhaps reconsidered what he was going to say and closed his mouth. He gave the barest of headshakes.

The bodyguard stepped away from me, holstering his pistol.

"Your man is rather edgy," McPherson said.

"Hmm," Stanton said.

I went back to smoothing out the paper. I'd felt General Stanton's hand. It had been hot like a Krekelen's would be. He didn't need his parka to stay warm. The general was obviously an alien shape-shifter wearing contact lenses to hide his red glowing eyes.

The bodyguard was likely a Krekelen too. I wasn't sure about the two soldiers. I doubted it, and I doubted the entire complement of soldiers were frauds, but the real deal directly from the U.S. of A. I would even bet General Stanton worked for the Joint Chiefs.

I had to do something. Otherwise, I was sure Stanton was going to take over and find a way into the subterranean maze in order to retrieve all those stasis units, and recover Charmalos and Spencer to boot.

-39-

I thought of myself as a badass Marine. Still, I wasn't sure how to overpower a hair-trigger Krekelen bodyguard and two elite armed soldiers. The general probably had his own sidearm, too. All I had was McPherson, and she might not understand in time that aliens had hijacked the base camp. The only weapons I possessed were my trusty hands, and feet, when it came right down to it.

"Colonel," Stanton was saying. "I'm afraid I have to relieve you of command. You will immediately take your people and fly directly to Panama, to Fort Enrique, and surrender to the MPs there. From there, you and your staff will be transferred to Camp Bravo in Alabama."

"What?" she said, while sitting straighter. "That's highly unusual. I thought you wanted to hear my testimony."

"I'm afraid we're under an accelerated time schedule," Stanton said.

McPherson glanced at me, the paper and then at the general's hand, the one I'd grabbed.

Stanton observed her doing so. "You don't understand the true situation, Colonel. For you own good—and that of your people—you should depart immediately...while you're able to."

She put both her hands on the table. "General, sir, I would like you to bear in mind that I—"

"Stop," Stanton said. "I don't want to hear any more."

I kept smoothing the paper and pretending to scan it. The tension in my gut had coiled into something monstrous. Two vile Krekelens were in the room with me. I wanted to destroy them with extreme prejudice. These two would open a floodgate so more of their kind could insert themselves into our government and military. What would that mean for the future of Earth? The problem was, I didn't have a good plan to stop these two.

"It was a mistake bringing you here, Colonel," Stanton said. "Captain LeMay, escort her off the plane and prepare for her departure."

"Just a minute," McPherson said.

The bodyguard—Captain LeMay, obviously—had stepped up behind McPherson's chair.

"I've given you an order," Stanton told her.

"First, I would like to know what happened a moment ago," McPherson said.

"Really, Colonel," I said. "Don't be an idiot." I put the paper in front of her face. "Look at what you did: killing innocent Americans. Don't you have any shame?"

She pushed my hand and the paper out of her face.

"Stop," Stanton said. "This isn't working. LeMay, kill her."

Did the order surprise the two soldiers standing guard? It might have. It didn't surprise me, as I was wound as tightly as I could be, ready to explode into action. The second the general gave the kill order, I moved out of my chair, grabbed the back of it and swung it around as hard as I could. It crashed against Captain LeMay as he drew his pistol, hurling him to the side so he tripped and fell.

I jumped after him and kneed him in the throat as he sprawled on the carpet. Reaching across his body, I grabbed the fallen automatic. LeMay spasmed against me with the steely strength of a Krekelen, launching me higher than anyone had a right to think someone his size could.

That might have stunned the two soldiers. I noticed one of them with his mouth agape as I sailed past him.

LeMay jumped up, gurgling in pain from the hard knee against his throat, one of his eyes glowing red like some demon from hell. I suppose I'd jostled loose a contact lens.

207

Landing on my back, skidding across the carpet, I brought up the automatic. I assumed LeMay had already chambered a round.

McPherson did not scream at our interplay, but jumped up and launched herself across the table at the general.

I barely saw that out of the corner of my eye. She grappled with General Stanton, who had drawn a heavy pistol.

I aimed and pulled the trigger three times with three loud retorts as LeMay charged me. Each bullet tore chunks of alien flesh from the Krekelen's chest.

One of the soldiers finally gained enough presence of mind to fire his submachine gun at me. LeMay got in the way, his back riddled as he collapsed upon me.

Stanton was roaring orders and firing his gun. I don't know what McPherson was doing.

I hurled the smoking Krekelen from me, and saw the bulging-eyed soldiers aiming their submachine guns at me.

"Stop, stop," I shouted, letting the automatic fall to the floor. "I surrender."

The two had enough presence of mind to keep from shooting me.

Stanton was shouting orders for the soldiers to pull the wildcat off him.

I remained on the floor, my hands up, as I heard McPherson scream and Stanton shout hoarsely in agony.

The two soldiers glanced over there, and they wilted at whatever they saw.

Then, I saw McPherson stumble backward off the table with bloody hands. She panted, her features drawn into a stark mask.

General Stanton's body thumped upon the conference table. Was he dead?

One soldier began spewing a string of profanities. The other turned ghost-white, blinking his eyes and shaking his head in disbelief.

"Listen!" McPherson shouted at them. "Are you two listening to me?"

The wildly cursing soldier shut up. The other stared at her.

"Look at him," McPherson said. "He isn't human. He's something else, something that used you, used your officers." She pointed emphatically at the dead LeMay Krekelen on the floor.

He was gray-skinned and lumpy, changing in the last few seconds, maybe mutating back to his normal form because he'd died. His mouth was wider than seemed possible. The firing soldier must have shot him in the back of the head, which was fortunate. That must have destroyed enough of the brain to kill the Krekelen permanently, as the braincase was a wreck.

"Stanton isn't human either," McPherson said, now pointing at the krekelen lying on the table. "Do you two understand that? Your chief officers were aliens pretending to be humans. They were aliens using the U.S. military for some nefarious purpose."

The man who'd been cursing used a sleeve to wipe sweat from his brow. He looked badly shaken and out of breath. "Okay, an alien. I can see that. I can hardly believe it. It's crazy, but—" He looked at me, and his eyes narrowed. He aimed his submachine gun at me. "What about him? Is he an alien too? Should I shoot him? I think I should shoot him."

"No!" McPherson said. "He's human. His actions just saved our lives. Put down your weapon. Let him up. All three of us owe him our lives."

The soldier stared at me, but he didn't seem convinced as he continued to aim at me.

I smiled as best I could under the circumstances. "How 'bout them Yankees?"

"Listen to me," McPherson said. "You two are now under my command. I need your help so we can get to the bottom of this alien conspiracy as quickly as we can. Do you both understand that?"

The sweaty soldier glanced at McPherson and then his fellow soldier, who just stared at the dead Stanton-alien on the conference table.

McPherson stepped up to them, and with her bloody hands, she grabbed hold of their weapons. The sweaty soldier resisted a moment but then relented as she took the submachine guns.

I climbed to my feet, trembling due to the adrenaline rush, wondering what we were going to do next. That was when I saw the knife sticking out of the gray alien's forehead, the alien wearing a bloody general's uniform and who lay permanently dead upon the conference table.

-40-

I told McPherson about the hot flesh, had her touch each of the dead Krekelens to verify the truth.

The two soldiers knelt and touched the one I'd killed. He was still hot, much hotter than a human would be.

"That was why you grabbed his hand," McPherson said.

I nodded. "There could be more of them in the general's unit. It's possible he also has a psi-master along."

"Like Spencer?" she asked sharply.

I nodded again.

McPherson rubbed her jaw. "What do you suggest we do?"

"Are you two convinced?" I asked the soldiers.

"Yes," the sweatier of the two said, Thompson. "They're aliens. There's nothing else they could be. What did you call them again?"

"Shape-shifters," I said.

Thompson nodded, asking, "Like a werewolf?"

"Yeah, like a werewolf," I said. Did those legends hold more than a grain of truth? How long had Krekelens been on Earth, anyway? Legend held you had to use silver to kill a werewolf. Was that because some people had noticed Krckelens surviving otherwise killing wounds?

"Stanton's unit," McPherson, while shaking her head. "We must retake control of the base camp. Stanton must have come to help Spencer and the other one."

"Good point," I said. "We also have to stop the ones I saw in stasis units from reviving."

211

"I'm open to suggestions," McPherson said.

I plopped into a chair, amazed she'd had the presence of mind to bring a knife aboard and then use it on the general. This was one tough cookie. Yeah. Punching a knife through forehead-skull into the braincase took some serious strength. It was lucky she'd done that, been able to do it.

"Sergeant Thompson," McPherson said, "who's in charge after Stanton?"

"That would be Colonel Van Kiep," he said.

McPherson looked at me, as the wheels seem to turn in her mind.

***

McPherson worked fast. I could see why those in the Defense Department had chosen her for the assignment.

She cleaned up at a sink and had Thompson go search for the three MPs. When they arrived—rearmed and ready—McPherson had them look at the dead aliens.

Soon after that, the three MPs and two soldiers brought Colonel Van Kiep into the plane.

Thompson nodded significantly to McPherson. He'd made sure to jostle the colonel in order to make sure he had regular temperature skin.

McPherson showed Van Kiep the two dead aliens. After he overcame his shock, she asked if he recognized the uniforms.

Van Kiep had to sit down and drink two glasses of water before he could speak again. Finally, though, he realized—deduced, really—the aliens were General Stanton and Captain LeMay.

McPherson left me out of it, but she explained that these two had been acting against the interests of the United States military and against humanity in general.

"What should we do?" Van Kiep asked.

"You should leave and take your soldiers with you," McPherson said.

"To where?" he asked.

212

"Fort Benning," she said, writing on a piece of paper. "Give this to the general in charge of Benning."

Van Kiep read the scrap of paper, looking up afterward. "Shouldn't we stay and help you here? This is some weird stuff."

"That's true," McPherson said. "But I have enough soldiers to take care of this because I've vetted all of them. Your men—" She indicated the dead aliens. "They might have others embedded among your men. And this isn't the time or place to do the vetting."

"I understand," Van Kiep said. "You're right, of course. We'll leave as fast as possible—within the hour."

"Yes," McPherson said. "That's for the best."

The colonel moved fast. She had a few of her soldiers come in and examine the two aliens. She explained about their shape-shifting power and the heat of their skin. She said the aliens must have had something to do with the zombie-like mentality of those who had held the base camp eleven days ago.

Less than an hour later, the two big planes taxied down the runway, taking their people with them, including Thompson and the two dead Krekelens. The alien corpses were going to be a big surprise to those in Fort Benning and later to others in the military. This would have *huge* ramifications.

After the planes had dwindled to small specks in the sky, McPherson turned to me. "I need to talk to you, alone, in my office."

"Yes, sir," I said.

"Then let's go."

* * *

"That was good work, Bayard," McPherson said in her office aboard the C-130H.

During the walk to the plane, I'd been thinking about how calmly she'd accepted the presence of gray-skinned, shape-shifting aliens suddenly taking the place of U.S. officers, how calmly her people had accepted the Krekelen corpses. There was something weird going on here I didn't understand. The aliens should have freaked everyone out as they'd done to Thompson and Colonel Van Kiep. McPherson's reaction had been unusual, very unusual. Yes, McPherson knew about psi-masters and psionics, about the complex of tunnels here in Antarctica. But did she know about aliens, about Krekelens? If she hadn't known beforehand…how could she accept this latest revelation so calmly?

I didn't ask her about that, but said, "When did you learn to use a knife like you did?"

McPherson shook her head as if that was unimportant.

"I know Krekelens are overpowering strong," I said. "I've fought their kind before. I'm stunned you could defeat him the way you did."

"That's what he was called, a Krekelen?"

"According to Doctor Spencer," I said.

"Well—"

"Colonel," I said interrupting. "You don't seem surprised shape-shifting aliens controlled an elite group of U.S. soldiers. You don't seem surprised these aliens tried to foil you or that aliens secretly move among us."

McPherson stared at me.

"You've faced Krekelens before, haven't you?" I asked. "You already knew about them."

She still said nothing.

"Uh-huh," I said. "Do you suppose it's a coincidence that some people talk about disguised reptilian types being among us?"

"You're referring to crazy conspiracy nuts?"

"How can it be crazy when you just killed an alien shape-shifter?"

"Look, Bayard—"

"The Krekelen was strong, maybe stronger than me, and yet you defeated him hand to hand, shoving a knife through his skull, which was exactly the correct move to make, by the way."

"That's the second time you've mentioned their unusual strength in relation to me. What are you suggesting? That I'm an alien too?"

"The thought has crossed my mind."

214

McPherson reached over the desk. "Feel my skin. It's normal."

I reached out and felt her hand. It was normal.

"Thanks for the vote of confidence," she said.

"You still haven't explained why finding aliens impersonating U.S. officers didn't freak you out."

"I'm here to question you. You're not here to question me."

"Don't give me that," I said. "You went after the general, drawing a hidden knife and stabbing him in the chest and then through the forehead. You must have known that's the only way to kill a Krekelen permanently, that you have to destroy the brain. How were you able to out-muscle a Krekelen? There has to be an explanation. Otherwise, I'm thinking you're a new type of alien I've never met before."

McPherson looked at me, sighed, and began to unbutton the cuff of her long left sleeve. She rolled it back, showing a complex webbing of mesh around her wrist and forearm.

"What's that?" I asked.

"A type of exoskeleton armor," she said. "It gave me the strength I needed."

"Uh...like when did the U.S. Army start manufacturing that?"

She shook her head.

"It's experimental?"

McPherson looked away, sighed, and regarded me. "Bayard, you're right about a few things. I was hoping you wouldn't notice, but you did. I'm not quite who I appear to be."

"Oh boy," I said. "I knew it."

"No, it isn't what you think. I do belong to the Defense Department, but I don't belong to DARPA. I'm part of the most hush-hush organization there is. We know a little about...extraterrestrials, the Krekelens in particular. This mesh on my arm is actually quite ancient. Our scientists believe it predates Ur of Sumer or Jericho. Do you have any idea what that means?"

"Isn't Jericho supposed to be the oldest city on Earth?"

"Supposed to be, yes," McPherson said. "Oldest one actually discovered, anyway, and not just written of in legends."

"Wait a minute. Are you saying that mesh is from Mu?"

"I'm not saying it's *from* the time of Mu, as we're still not sure the place ever existed. But there was something going on before regular human history began."

That shouldn't have been a kick in the gut, but it was. In a way, I didn't feel quite so alone anymore. Others of my kind knew about this crazy stuff.

"So, umm," I said, "do you know about the step-pyramid deep in the subterranean maze?"

McPherson leaned forward with interest. "I do not. You've seen this step-pyramid?"

"Not only have I seen it, but about fifty brass cylinders with various bigheaded people in them are near the steps."

"You think those are stasis units?" she asked.

"That's my theory so far."

"Who else is down there?"

"Charmalos the Krekelen and Doctor Spencer. At least I think they both are."

"And you still say you've been to other planets?" she asked.

"Would you believe me if I said I had?"

"If I saw this ziggurat, I might."

"How long have you been in this secret organization?" I asked.

"Two years, three months and five days," she said without hesitation.

"How long has it been around?"

"Since 1968."

I nodded. Since they'd found the original psi-master.

"Are you ready to help us?" she asked.

"If you're ready to help me."

"I think our goals are aligned."

I stared into her eyes a moment, trying to be sure of her. She didn't flinch. "All right."

"Then let's get started."

216

-41-

McPherson decided to keep the commando group small, too small, in my opinion. I wondered what the real reason was for only a handful of us going down.

The rest of the base would be on high alert.

I equipped myself with body armor, an M27 with many extra magazines and several fragmentation grenades. Then I put on a thick parka and mittens.

We went down by crane in the cage: McPherson, the bearded man by the name of Suvorov, the woman with the computer slate called Qiang, and me.

We wore helmets with lamps and had spare flashlights. Everyone had weapons, Suvorov what looked like an old-time elephant gun.

"You planning to hunt dinosaurs with that thing?" I asked.

"You see any down here?" he asked.

"Colonel," I said. "Are you sure there are enough of us? What if Spencer and Charmalos have opened the stasis units, revived and armed the occupants? That's at least fifty people to our four."

Bearded Suvorov's head snapped around. "What did he say? He saw stasis units?"

I felt a prickle against my back and looked behind me.

Qiang had a strange gun aimed at me. It didn't have an orifice but a glass rod with diodes around it.

"Hey," I said, facing her. "What is that thing? Who are you people?"

"What do you mean?" McPherson asked me.

"Yeah, right," I said. "You have fancy mesh armor that made you strong enough to beat a Krekelen. Suvorov here has a freaking elephant gun, if that's what it is. What, is it really some kind of laser weapon?"

Suvorov's eyes widened.

"And Qiang has some Buck Rogers kind of raygun," I finished. "Are you guys even human."

"Quite human," McPherson said. "I thought I'd already passed that test with you."

"Are you going to tell me that you're all Americans?" I said.

"Naturalized," McPherson said.

"What?"

"We weren't born Americans," Suvorov said. I finally noticed his slight hint of a Russian accent. "But we're Americans now. We were naturalized and took an oath to uphold the U.S. Constitution."

"You were all born on Earth, though?" I asked.

Suvorov laughed. "What kind of question is that?"

I jutted my chin at Qiang's gizmo. "The raygun and exoskeleton mesh-armor make me wonder."

"What do we do now?" Qiang asked McPherson.

I glanced from Qiang to McPherson and then to Suvorov. "All right," I said. "Maybe you three are good guys, maybe you're not. But you're not part of any top secret Defense Department team."

"But we are," McPherson said.

I stared at her. "Yeah, I get it. The top-secret team is your cover. You've conned someone high up, and you run it on the straight and narrow, I'm guessing. But in reality…you three are from somewhere else, somewhere not from Earth. Or you get your orders from off-world, anyway, right?"

"Colonel," Qiang said sharply.

McPherson studied me.

"Are you Travelers?" I said.

"What did you say?" Qiang asked, sounding shocked.

"Who is he?" Suvorov asked McPherson.

218

"From what I can gather," McPherson said, "his father was a Traveler."

"Oh," Suvorov said. *"That* explains a lot. This Charmalos must have known about that."

"I'm beginning to think so," McPherson said. "Yes, it wasn't a bad plan on their part either."

"Where's Prime?" I asked.

The three traded glances.

"What's really going on?" I asked. "What are you three trying to do?"

McPherson eyed me, glanced at the other two. "I'm going to tell him. It's on my authority."

"It isn't a good idea," Qiang said.

"I disagree," McPherson said. "When has our group ever spoken to a Traveler?"

"We don't know he really is one," Qiang said. "Just that he brags he is."

"He told me he's been to two other planets in the last eleven days," McPherson said.

Qiang regarded me anew. "What planets?" she asked.

"One orbits Epsilon Eridani," I said. "I called it the Planet of the Dead because it was filled with ancient monuments: pyramids, ziggurats, obelisks, terraces, plinths, monoliths, you name it. And there were no people around except for me, Spencer and three Krekelens."

Qiang stared at Suvorov.

"Go on," Suvorov said quietly.

"The other planet was Saddoth," I said. "It's twenty-six light-years from Earth. Ophidians or serpent people have vast herds of Neanderthals there that they keep as cattle for food."

"What?" Suvorov said, aghast.

I nodded. "The Ophidians feast on the Neanderthals. It was horrible. I have a blood brother there by the name of Bok. I'm hoping to go back with several battalions of Marines so we can clean up the planet and free the herd Neanderthals."

"This is incredible," Suvorov told McPherson. "He's actually a Traveler."

"That's what I'm saying," McPherson said.

"With a Traveler—" Suvorov said.

"You trust him?" Qiang spat, interrupting. "I don't. Look at him. He's a moron, a big dumb Marine. You two are telling me he had enough presence of mind to defeat three Krekelens and a psi-master each time?"

"We checked his father's records, remember?" McPherson said. "It was the kind of bio a stranded Traveler would have. This is the kind of break our group has been waiting for."

"Hey," I said. "Let's cut the crap. Just tell me who you guys really are. Because the way you're saying it, I know it's not a top-secret Defense Department organization."

"See," McPherson told Qiang. "Despite his size and appearance, he's pretty smart."

Qiang eyed me again, shaking her head, although she holstered her raygun, if that was what it was.

"If it means anything," Suvorov told McPherson, "I agree with you. Use your authority to tell him what you think is wise."

McPherson faced me. "Our group is older than the U.S., and it has always been small. In the grim past, people called us witch hunters, but we didn't hunt for the poor souls medieval peasants burned at the stake. We hunted for those creatures who people might have named vampires or werewolves. They weren't supernatural creatures, however, but Krekelens and psi-masters."

"Uh…that's crazy," I said.

McPherson nodded. "We didn't know how the Krekelens landed on Earth until 1967. The survey team that found the stasis unit gave us the great clue. We've pieced together some of the data about obelisk launchers and ziggurat landers. The ones on Earth, those visible above ground, never had that purpose. There was a Mu, but not how it was portrayed in the legends. Some of our most antiquated and useful tools come from that era."

"The mesh armor like you said?" I asked.

McPherson nodded. "We're all Earthlings. All our ancestors, as far as we know, were Earthlings. You're the only one among us who has alien ancestry."

"My father was human," I said.

"Alien in this instance simply means from a different planet," McPherson said.

"Okay," I said. "My dad fits that description. Go on."

"Doctor Spencer is like you in that way," McPherson said. "We didn't know about his mother until six months ago. He escaped DARPA captivity before one of us could get to him. We've been trailing him ever since. How Charmalos found him…" McPherson shook her head.

"What's the Harmony?" I asked.

McPherson shook her head. "I don't know. We don't know, as we've never heard of it before this. We've been operating in the dark for centuries, for millennia. Now, though, with you, we might broaden our horizons."

"What are you thinking?" Qiang asked her sharply.

"Isn't it obvious?" McPherson said. "We have a Traveler. We've already learned some amazing facts. After we stop Charmalos and Doctor Spencer—and capture the stasis units—we can send Bayard back out there."

"What?" I said.

"To learn more," McPherson said. "To build up our data so we can become part of the greater human race again."

"You think there's a greater organization out there," I asked, "a group of good guys?"

"I don't know," McPherson said. "Certainly, that's one of the things we need to learn, to discover."

I inhaled deeply, unsure if I wanted to do that, but knowing I would in the end, if for no other reason than to help my blood brother Bok on Saddoth.

"Hey," Qiang said. "I'm picking up something." She had her slate out.

"Right," McPherson said. "Let's get going. We've dawdled here long enough."

-42-

Bearded Suvorov took the lead with his elephant gun, with Qiang behind him giving directions. I followed her and McPherson brought up the rear.

In the wash of our helmet lamps, I tried to exam the elephant gun. It had a few gewgaws attached, cylindrical objects to the sides where you might shove shells into a shotgun. Wires went from the cylinders to the gun.

"What's it fire?" I asked.

"What?" Qiang asked over her shoulder.

"What does the elephant gun fire?" I asked.

"Never you mind," Qiang said testily.

"It doesn't fire bullets," McPherson said behind me.

"I didn't think so." After several steps, I added, "It seems kind of risky to bring it out in the open like this."

"One of the reasons I didn't bring any more soldiers down with us," McPherson said.

After that, I mulled over what they'd been telling me. The big question was this: did I believe them? The story sounded farfetched. But then again, so did mine. There were elements I could buy, as it held together after a fashion. People always said there were secret organizations with hidden motives. And I did recall a philosophy class I'd taken once where they'd talked about Hegel and his idea of thesis, antithesis and synthesis. A person propounded an idea, the thesis. Someone else over time disagreed vehemently with the thesis, the antithesis, and out of that over time developed the synthesis between the two.

In this case, the Krekelens were the thesis. They'd introduced themselves into the mix of humanity on Earth. The little group that Colonel McPherson presently led was the antithesis to them. What the possible synthesis of that could be, I did not know.

But it made sense that someone on Earth had risen to resist the Krekelens and their psi-master puppets. And it also made sense that at least one arm of that group had found me.

In fact, it was more than a little thrilling to be part of this. I knew things no one else on Earth did.

I'd done things I doubted anyone else on Earth had done, well, not since the time of the... I was going to say Mu people. Perhaps the better way to say it was since the time whoever had built the tunnel complex in subterranean Antarctica. Maybe using the term Mu could be shorthand for those people.

I mean, who had ridden mammoths and T-Rexes, fighting each other with lances? Who had ridden giant pterodactyls? Someone had painted those cave walls. Someone had painted the dome of the obelisk chamber.

Suvorov stopped suddenly, turning around and aiming his huge rifle at me.

"What's wrong?" McPherson asked.

"How do we know he isn't playing us?" Suvorov said. "Maybe this was all staged to get us down here. If the Krekelens could capture and question us..."

"He's real," McPherson said. "It still could be staged, but Bayard isn't part of it. Do you think we should get more soldiers?"

"I do," Suvorov said.

McPherson nodded noncommittally.

"How about pointing that thing somewhere else," I said.

"I'm...I'm still not convinced you're really with us," Suvorov said.

I looked into his eyes. His seemed—the answer struck me. I turned to McPherson. "Could you ask him to point the gun elsewhere?"

"Suvorov," McPherson said. "Lower the gun."

"I…can't," Suvorov said. "I…I want to shoot him. I'm fighting the compulsion, but I don't know how long I can resist the pressure."

I heard a buzz of noise. Something flashed. I hit the deck as fast as I could. I needn't have bothered. Suvorov collapsed onto the icy floor of the tunnel.

Qiang lowered her raygun.

From the icy floor, I said, "That was Doctor Spencer's doing. Do you have any way of combating telepathic commands?"

"Qiang," McPherson said, "is your inhibitor on?"

"Yes, Colonel," she said.

"So is mine," McPherson said. "Could you check Suvorov's?"

Qiang knelt beside Suvorov and unzipped his parka, checking something inside it. "The battery must have died. It's on red." She stood, contemplated a second, and drew the raygun again, pointing it at me. "How can we be sure the psi-master won't control him?"

"I can block his telepathy," I said.

Qiang looked to McPherson.

"It makes sense," McPherson said.

"Do we want to trust our lives to that, though?" Qiang asked.

"Put a new battery in Suvorov's inhibitor," McPherson said. "I'll think about the situation as you do it."

Qiang went to work.

McPherson regarded me.

I raised my palms upward. "I can block Spencer. I learned to do it after he tracked me to the Original People's camp."

"Who?" asked McPherson.

"Never mind. I can block him. If you doubt me, send me back up."

"Then why would we be down here?" Qiang said. "I thought the whole point was to ambush these suckers. Now, it's clear the psi-master knows about us."

"Look," I said. "Spencer is close. He has to be in order to influence someone. Now's the time to attack: to find and defeat them."

"What about Suvorov?" McPherson asked.

"We leave him for the moment," I said.

"I vote against that," Qiang said.

"Then, stay here with him, and I'll go kill these two," I said. "I'm itching for some revenge about now."

"Qiang," McPherson said. "Wake Suvorov and then stay here with him. We'll be back soon."

"Splitting up is always stupid," Qiang said.

McPherson studied her, nodded, and said, "We're going to do it anyway. The payoff—this is what we've dreamed of finding. We roll the dice and hope this lug of a Marine knows what he's doing. Do you, Bayard?"

"You can count on it," I said.

Qiang gulped, nodding, saying, "Stay safe, Colonel."

"You too," McPherson said. "We'll see you soon."

Then, the two of us continued deeper into the icy tunnel.

-43-

McPherson and I reached the granite tunnels. It was so much different with a helmet lamp switched on. In a way, it was worse, but I couldn't explain why.

"This is risky," she said.

I put an index finger in front of my lips. I'd just sensed something. Quietly, I removed my mittens with my teeth, putting them in my pockets. Then, I gripped the assault rifle. After several seconds, I went down onto my stomach.

From the sounds behind me, McPherson did likewise.

I began to crawl with my elbows and knees, doing it as quietly as possible. I stared intently ahead into the tunnel. Inspiration struck the next moment.

I turned back and whispered, "Colonel?"

She crawled up beside me.

"I'm shutting off my lamp," I said. "I want you to do likewise."

"How do I follow you then?"

"Sound," I said. "The darkness will heighten your hearing."

For the first time since I'd known her, a modicum of fear entered McPherson's eyes. "I hate the dark," she whispered.

"The light is giving us away."

"You think Charmalos and Spencer are near?"

I nodded.

She swallowed and then nodded, clicking off her helmet lamp.

I turned mine off next, and we were cast into pitch-blackness.

A second later, McPherson grabbed my left boot. "Bayard," she whispered.

"I'm right here."

"This…this…you're sure you know what you're doing?"

"Stick with me, Colonel. This is what I do best."

She didn't respond, but she kept a gloved hand on my left boot.

We now began to slither down the long tunnel. We moved by slow degrees. I paused every so often, listening and using other senses to try to detect our foes.

I'd switched my mind back to receiving any telepathic thoughts from Spencer. I don't know if he'd try but—

Bayard, I can feel you out there, Spencer said in my mind.

"How about that," I said so quietly that I doubt McPherson heard.

Ah, so it is you, Bayard. You came back down into the tunnels. You're even stupider than I thought.

"Quit lying, Doc. You tried to get Mr. Elephant Gun to take a potshot at me. It failed, though. You're pissing yourself in fear at the idea I might be tracking you."

Tut, tut, you really are a moron, thinking far too highly of yourself. Perhaps a Traveler must possess arrogance to try what he does. But you're a fool if you think the adventurers can save you from Charmalos. They're part of the losing side. Come join the winners, Bayard.

"Your dad is dead."

So is yours.

"What are you saying: that Charmalos had a hand in my dad's death?"

Your father was on the losing side. I don't know the exact reason for his demise. But a Krekelen certainly had a hand in it.

"Hey, I have an idea. Why don't you join humanity in fighting the aliens? Or does psi-master mean traitor?"

You aren't clever, Bayard. The Krekelens and their allies won the war a long time ago. These are merely mopping up operations.

"Uh-huh," I said, "like I believe that."

Don't believe me. Believe your blood bother.

"Bok?"

If that is the name of the Neanderthal you befriended.

"What about Bok?"

The Neanderthals have lost the war on Saddoth. Homo sapiens *have lost the war on Earth to the same extent. They just don't know it yet.*

"Spencer, why don't you use your head for once? Your father was a traitor, and he failed. You have half Earthling blood. Stick with that part instead of being a slave-race traitor to your breeding masters. Quit licking Charmalos' hand. Bite it for once and help us. Use your gift of psionics for your own people."

"What did you say?" McPherson asked from behind.

"Shhh," I said. She must have finally overheard me.

Ah. One of the adventurers is with you, Spencer said in my mind. *I do believe you think you're tracking me. Don't you know that in reality—?*

I ceased crawling, and I concentrated until I flipped the switch in my mind, shutting Spencer out.

"He's near," I whispered.

"Have you been talking to him?" McPherson asked.

"I have. But I'm not anymore."

"Have you betrayed me?" she asked.

"Lady, that's the last thing I'm ever going to do. Now, are you in or out?"

"Don't leave me in the dark," McPherson said fast, pleading.

"I'm not. But we're going to have to crawl fast. Are you ready?"

"I don't think so," she said. "But let's do it anyway."

I grinned. I was starting to like McPherson. She had *moxie.* Then, I put that from me as I concentrated, straining for a scrape, a sigh, anything to give me Spencer's location.

I slithered, listening, wanting to find the traitorous—the grinding of stone on stone sounded from ahead. It had to be a door opening.

"Did you do that, Spencer?" Charmalos asked from ahead.

"No," Spencer said.

I aimed at the sound of their voices and depressed the trigger. Flashes of light flamed from the barrel of my M27, showing the horrified faces of men and women crouched in a stone corridor. I thought I recognized the bigheaded woman I'd seen in a stasis unit.

I kept firing, knocking down what I believed to be psi-masters and Krekelens until my rifle emptied. I slung it as I scrambled to my knees, pulled the pin on the first grenade and hurled it. I added two more before I roared at McPherson, "Back up."

I slithered back and covered my head with my arms.

Grenades exploded. There were more screams and cries of agony. I was butchering them in the close quarters. The flashes, the explosions—

I yanked out the empty magazine and shoved another into the M27. As the explosions died away, I rose to my knees and fired again, using the flames of my shots to see what I aimed at. It wasn't pretty. It wasn't nice. It was war underground, one of the worst and nastiest ways to do battle. When the weapon was empty again, I speed-yanked the mag and slammed in a third, continuing to fire into the mass of alien and traitorous psi-master bodies.

This was like Bhutan all over again. The ambushes, the close quarter fighting—the gore rose in my throat. I refused to acknowledge that as I tore out the third magazine and inserted my fourth. The M27 was hot, and it was going to get hotter still.

I stood, and I waited, seeing faint light appear up ahead: maybe something was burning, or someone's machines were glowing. The light allowed me to see others rise in the tunnel, likely to race away.

I emptied this magazine, too, catching a few of them in the back as they ran. I needed to make headshots, though. The Krekelens and their slaves did not like this type of face-to-face combat. I didn't like it either, but it was getting the job done.

Finally, I backed away, clutching in the dark and dragging McPherson with me.

"What's happening?" she shouted.

229

We were deafened from all the blasts in confined spaces. I clicked on my helmet lamp just in time to see the door slide closed, the one that had opened in the dark to reveal them. When it shut, it looked exactly like the wall in the corridor.

"Did you cause that?" McPherson shouted into my ear.

"Yes."

"How?"

"By wanting it," I said.

"What?"

"Keeping going," I said. "We have to regroup. We have to get our bearings."

She nodded, and together, we scrambled back to a new position to figure out our next move.

I checked the number of magazines I had left: three. I had one grenade left as well.

"You're a natural killer," McPherson said.

I rested against a tunnel wall, the back of my head against the wall as well. I opened my eyes and looked at her.

She stood in the middle of the tunnel, staring at me.

"I'm a Marine," I said.

"No. You're a natural killer. A Marine is a professional, a man or woman trained to do a job. What you did back there—" She shook her head.

"It's no different from what you did with General Stanton."

McPherson laughed mirthlessly. "I fought for my life, terrified every second of it. You—you were in your element back there."

"Balls."

"I'm serious, Bayard. You're a natural killer."

"All right, lay off already."

"A killer good at what he does," she added.

"Hey, Colonel, I'm defending my planet from invaders."

She nodded emphatically. "I agree to that. I'm glad you're on our side. I can see now how you survived the other planets. Maybe successful Travelers have to be born killers. How else can you hop from one planet to another and live to tell about it?"

"That's not the issue," I said, tired of the talk. "We have to finish them while we can. I'm afraid some of the Krekelens I shot are going to survive. I needed to shoot each of them in the head to make sure they stayed dead."

McPherson laughed in a half-strangled manner. "That's exactly what a killer would say. Aren't you satiated just a bit?"

"Look, I don't eat them. I'm defending the rest of humanity from infiltrators, from mind-masters and shape-shifters who for all I know take over different countries. Knowing what I do now, I wouldn't be surprised to learn that Hitler and Stalin were Krekelens, busy murdering as many humans as they could and starting wars to get the rest to kill each other, to weaken the human race. I bet the bastards who started World War One were Krekelens as well."

McPherson wiped her nose and then plopped down beside me. A few seconds later, she put a hand on my right knee. "I'm sorry I said all that. You did the right thing. It's just...I've never seen anything like that, and I never want to see anything like that again."

I nodded.

"How did you know they were there? How did you find them?"

"I didn't," I said. "I've discovered that there's an intelligence behind the subterranean complex. There's an intelligence in the obelisk. Maybe some kind of AI or machine. It's talked to me each time I traveled."

McPherson moaned in dread.

"Hey," I said. "It isn't that bad. The intelligence, or whatever it is, is on our side. That's a plus, not a minus."

McPherson nodded fast. "Do you think we should get out of here, go back?"

I gave her a look of surprise.

"I guess not," she said. "You want to finish this, huh?"

"We've gained the initiative. That means we have to keep attacking while they're unbalanced."

"How do we attack? They're behind the walls. No wonder we never found the obelisk and ziggurat. We'd have to blast our way through. But I'm not sure I could find the spot again, are you?"

"Maybe I can."

McPherson blinked several times, nodding, rubbing her runny nose.

"We should get to it," I said. "We should hit them again before the Krekelens heal from their wounds."

"I'd like to leave you to it, but I feel morally bound to tag along. You've probably killed more Krekelens in the past few minutes than our group has in the last five centuries. This is more than a win. This is a strategic victory with possible new directions. We can start taking the offensive—or you can, traveling to other worlds and discovering what you can."

"Sounds grand," I said, getting up. "Is your inhibitor at full strength?"

McPherson opened her parka and checked, looking up at me and nodding.

"Okay. Here's the plan," I said, outlining our next move.

***

An hour later, far deeper in the tunnels, with both our parkas unzipped, I suggested we start crawling again.

"Wait a minute," McPherson said. "I'm bushed. I need to eat, drink and rest a few minutes."

"We can't wait too long."

She stared at me, shaking her head. Then she sat cross-legged, devoured a ration pack and guzzled water before hunching forward with her eyes closed.

I ate a ration pack too, sipped some water and closed my eyes. I let myself go blank and try to feel Spencer or another of the psi-masters. I didn't feel a thing.

I knew what was wrong. I needed to need it desperately.

McPherson opened her eyes. "I can keep going."

"Listen, we're going to have to go dark again."

"Turn off our helmet lamps?" she asked.

"Yup," I said.

A look like pure terror entered her eyes, but she agreed. "Tell me when."

"Let's get into position first." I stretched out on the floor, with the M27 in my hands.

McPherson lay behind me, a hand on my left boot. "Okay," she said in a tremulous voice.

I clicked off my helmet lamp. She did likewise with hers. It threw us into pitch-blackness.

"It's worse this time," she whispered.

"That's in your mind. You're fine."

"Not if you get killed."

I would have said, "Not going to happen." But as a Marine, I didn't want to jinx myself. Thus, I said nothing as I began to slither through the tunnel.

I strained to sense Spencer as I opened the link in my mind. "Hey," I called, so softly that McPherson wouldn't hear.

There was no response, no feel, no nothing but the loneliness of the deep. I inhaled and continued to crawl, wondering how long we would have to do this.

What if they escaped from the tunnels?

I shook my head. They were down here somewhere. It was my job to find where and eliminate them for good.

-45-

We took a break a little later, shedding our parkas and tying them around our waists. Instead of crawling again, we held hands and shuffled in the dark, feeling ahead of us.

"Were you this far down before?" McPherson whispered.

"I'm not sure."

"I wonder why the original builders made these tunnels down here in Antarctica. What was going on above ground that they had to hide all this?"

I stopped and turned my head in McPherson's direction.

"What's wrong?" she asked.

"That's a good question. I'd really like to know the answer."

After a second, we continued walking.

McPherson squeezed my hands. "I just had another idea."

"Yeah?"

"You spoke about an intelligence before."

"That's right."

"Maybe you can talk to it from here."

I raised my eyebrows. "Sure. I'll try." And I did, mentally calling out, telling it I was grateful for the trips to other plancts. I received exactly squat in return.

After a long time, McPherson stopped. "I'm bushed, and I'm sick of moving in the dark like this. I-I don't think I can keep going. And I don't want you to say that you're going to leave me here and trek ahead. I'll start screaming and I don't think I could stop."

"What are you suggesting?"

"That we go back to the surface."

I considered the idea. I could use more ammo and grenades. But marching up and then down again…I'd need to rest, and that might give them too much time to regroup, and it would give the wounded Krekelens time to fully heal. Surely, Charmalos had his computer slate. I'd bet they had flashlights. What else was stashed down here they could use?

"Bayard, I'm serious. Let's turn around."

"I'm going to turn on my helmet lamp instead."

"What difference does that make?"

"I want to take a look around."

After a second, McPherson sighed. "Sure. Fine. Turn on your lamp if you want."

I did, and I winced at the sudden brightness of it. As my eyes adjusted, McPherson made an exclamation, what sounded like wonder.

I rubbed my eyes to hurry the process, studying the cave painting she saw. It showed mammoth riders, with pterodactyl riders whirling above. They moved among pyramids and plinths.

"This is incredible," she whispered, glancing at me and moving further down. "Look!" she cried, pointing. "Spaceships, these must be spaceships."

In the painting, flying saucers shot beams at exploding pyramids.

McPherson turned to me. "What does it mean?"

I shrugged. "Other than people fighting, I haven't a clue."

"Bayard, look, is that a crossway?"

I saw where she was pointing. Fifty feet down the tunnel was a three-way junction. "Do you still think we should go back up?"

"Suvorov and Qiang must have been waiting for hours," McPherson said. "They might think we're dead."

"That doesn't answer the question."

She peered into my face and then studied the three possible paths. "This changes things, doesn't it?"

"It makes it more likely the others could find a way out without any tunnel-wall doors having to open for them."

"Do you really believe that?"

"I wouldn't have said it otherwise."

McPherson took a deep breath and expelled it with force. "If we can keep our lamps on, yes, I'm for continuing the search."

"Then let's go," I said.

She stopped me as I started forward "We can keep our lamps on, though, right?"

"Yes. Let's just hope we don't walk into an ambush."

***

We took the left passage. It led us to an underground lake of warm water. I didn't see any paths around the lake, so…

Backtracking to the three-way junction, we took the right passage next. This one continued in a mazy path, giving us more murals. I kept thinking about McPherson's question. Why had whoever gone to such trouble to build these tunnels, and why in Antarctica? It would have taken intense labor. Could Antarctica have been ice-free back then? When had there been such a time?

I found myself thinking about my father. Why hadn't he come to Antarctica? How had he reached Earth if not through the ziggurat lander down here? Did that mean there were more ways to travel? The paintings of spaceships would seem to say so. The stasis unit with Spencer's father, in the snow above ground, would also suggest that.

"My feet are killing me," McPherson said later. "I haven't walked this far in ages."

I was tired, too. This was much longer than I'd expected to take.

We continued anyway, and twenty minutes later —garbled speech rebounded up the corridor toward us.

I whirled around to McPherson, my face feeling tight. Her eyes went round. I clicked off my helmet lamp. She kept hers on. I reached up and shut her lamp off as well. In an instant, she clutched me, breathing in my face. I was tempted to kiss her, even though this was a lousy moment to do it. Just body stress, looking for relief.

"Keep calm," I said instead.

"I can't."

I could feel her trembling. "Okay," I said, stroking her head. "Listen to me. I need to keep both hands free."

"I'm not letting go of you."

"You won't have to. But I'm going to turn around and face the others."

"Are we going to lie on the floor again?"

"No," I said. "We're going to stay right here, as I think they're heading toward us."

"If that's true, we should go prone."

I nodded. "You're right. We'll go prone. You hold onto my boot again, okay?"

"Okay..."

"How many weapons do you have?"

"A handgun and a knife," she said.

"Give me the knife."

"Why, what are you thinking?"

"Let's lie down. After that, give me the knife."

"Why?"

"Because once I'm out of ammo, I want more than just my hands and feet. I also have to smash the blade into Krekelen foreheads to make sure they're dead."

"You'd actually charge the enemy?" she said in a small voice.

I was thinking about Bok, about the Ophidians shock-rodding the Chieftain into a slave wagon. I was thinking about how helpless I'd felt then and how this was my time for revenge on someone.

"I'm getting onto my stomach," I said.

McPherson followed me onto the ground, passing me her knife and then holding onto my left boot. After that, we waited.

-46-

What do you want to hear, every gruesome detail? I hope not, as that might make you too much like me.

We waited, and we heard them shuffling along before we saw flickering light. One of them wore a helmet with a lamp. That lamp was dim. It showed…thirty of them, I'd guess. Some limped. Some needed others to help them.

By the looks of it, two-thirds of them were Krekelens, gray, lumpy-skinned aliens with wide mouths. They were ugly. Had that been their evolutionary need to become shape-shifters, to hide their hideous aspect from others? Where did they ever pick up such an ability? Maybe they were vat-created creatures, made centuries or millennia ago in a laboratory.

I guess here in the dark, the Krekelens had no need to be others but showed their true selves.

The rest were bigheaded humans, psi-masters, I'm guessing. Only one of them looked familiar: good old Doctor Spencer. He didn't limp, have a wound, cut or even bruise. Had he gotten lucky, or was he a good at staying in the back when bullets flew?

"Bayard," McPherson whispered in the softest voice I'd ever heard.

I grunted in response.

"Here you go," she whispered.

I heard her slide her automatic to me.

"What's that for?" I asked.

239

"If you charge them with the knife," she said, "maybe it will help you to have a pistol, and you can use it for head shots."

"What about you?"

"I'll shine my lamp on them if you want."

I thought about what she was suggesting. It was actually a good plan, but it would put her in jeopardy.

"When that happens," I said, "I want you to hold the lamp to the side—in case they take potshots at you."

"I'm not usually like this," she whispered. "It's the deep tunnels that unnerve and frighten me."

"You're doing great," I said.

After that, we waited longer, as the alien-psi-master company approached.

I couldn't tell if Charmalos lived. No. I take that back. I saw one of the gray-skinned Krekelens holding a computer tablet. Capturing that seemed important.

I held the M27, judging the right moment to cut loose. They were walking straight into an ambush. I considered setting the selector switch to single fire, but voted against it. When the moment came, I was cutting loose on rock and roll.

Shock and awe, baby, that was the plan.

They jabbered among themselves. They limped. The psi-masters cowered whenever a Krekelen noticed them. The helmet lamp—

McPherson hissed as the lamp washed down the corridor toward us. Did it shine upon something reflective we held?

The group stopped.

I depressed the trigger, the M27 sending bullets smack-dab into their center mass. I didn't keep the trigger down for a quick spray of all my bullets. I used machine-gun-fire marksmanship, firing three-round bursts.

Krekelens and psi-masters tumbled, torn by the brutal bullets. Every time anyone aimed a weapon in our direction, I cut them down. I was even more brutal than earlier. I could see them. That made this so much easier.

I was hardly aware of swapping out the empty magazine for a fresh one. I continued the three-round bursts until all of them switched off their helmet lamps.

I tore out the pin and hurled my lone grenade.

"Move with me," I told McPherson.

I rolled left. She rolled left with me.

The enemy got off several shots. Then the grenade exploded among them.

I stood up and fired into them, switching to the last magazine.

"Wait here," I told McPherson.

I headed toward the mass of screaming wounded.

The colonel was surprisingly brave. Her helmet lamp clicked on, shining into the mass. I spied several Krekelens and Spencer trying to sprint away.

I used the last magazine to blow them apart. After that, I tossed the M27 aside and walked purposefully toward them, the automatic in my right hand and the knife in my left.

This became gruesome, and I don't care to report in minute detail how I punched the knife into Krekelen foreheads. I wanted to save the automatic's ammo for emergencies.

I'd hit, hurt and killed far more of them than I'd realized. I think a few of them must have shot each other too. Maybe they'd become thoroughly demoralized in the dark after all this time. I don't know much about Krekelen psychology. But this became like shooting fish in the barrel.

It was so easy, this last part, that McPherson picked up her helmet and ran up behind me, shining it on the writhing mass.

I finally turned and gave her the pistol. "You're on overwatch. If you see any of them raise a weapon, shoot them."

I walked among them like the proverbial Angel of Death. I used the knife, a very sharp tool, and it was a mess, a bloody mess.

I thought about the Neanderthals as I did this. I thought about how Charmalos and Spencer had helped the serpent men against humans. Did I feel pity for these aliens and their puppets?

Yeah, I actually did. But I suppressed the emotion and did what needing doing.

Finally—

BOOM! BOOM!

I flinched from the shots, turned to see McPherson holding the smoking pistol, and turned again to see a man slump to the tunnel floor.

I hurried to him, finding Spencer coughing up blood. He had a gun beside him. I suspect he'd been aiming it at me.

Spencer opened his eyes. I know he saw me, because he said, "Bayard."

I knelt beside Spencer and grabbed an arm.

"What are you?" he whispered. "It wasn't supposed to go like this."

I didn't know what to say.

He arched upward, opened his mouth and vomited a glob of blood. After that, he died.

It left me deflated instead of elated. "Doctor Spencer," I said, "rest in peace." In truth, I was glad McPherson had shot him instead of me.

I got up and found Charmalos' computer slate. It was smashed and useless.

A little after that, the Krekelens began to dissolve as if their bodies were made of acid. Some of them must have been like the walking dead. The same thing had happened, by the way, to General Stanton and Captain LeMay. We'd learned that by radio from the two planes.

Yeah. I suppose the dissolving was a key reason humanity as a whole hadn't learned about the alien shape-shifters. One could never show people a dead specimen after more than an hour.

McPherson came into my arms and began to weep. I patted her back, wondering if we'd gotten all of them.

-47-

We backtracked for a long time, did not find Suvorov or Qiang waiting for us in the tunnels and had to radio down the cage.

It turned out that Suvorov and Qiang had gone up hours ago. They'd searched for us, eventually giving up and heading up for reinforcements. They were overjoyed finding us alive. We discovered that in our absence the President of the United States had ordered the expedition home.

That seemed more than a little strange.

"A Krekelen in high places must have gotten to the President," McPherson told me. "It happens more than I'd like to admit."

"Why hasn't your unit been disbanded then?" I asked.

"It almost was—by General Stanton. The longer answer is that the Krekelens like to remain behind the scenes. This move shows their hand, and in time, I might be able to discover who convinced the President to give the order for us to leave."

Stanton's two planes didn't have dead aliens to back up our story. That might have had something to do with the Presidential order.

"Is there going to be an inquiry into Stanton's killing?" I asked McPherson.

We were in her office aboard the 130H. We were already in the air, as Suvorov and Qiang had been loading everyone up when we returned. No one had remained behind. The base camp was presently off-limits to all U.S. military personnel.

"We might have to disappear for a time," McPherson said.

"Who's we?"

"Suvorov, Qiang and me," she said.

"What about me?"

McPherson shook her head. "There was no mention of you in the order. Frankly, you can do what you want."

"How can I travel to other planets if I can't get to the obelisk in Antarctica?"

"You can't get to the obelisk today. Who knows what's going to happen tomorrow, though."

"Okay… So, do I join your group?"

"Unfortunately," she said, "that isn't my call."

"Whose is it?"

McPherson shook her head. "I can't tell you."

"That's it then? We just part ways?"

"I'm sorry, Jake. That's how it has to be for now."

"All this work and then, bam—nothing?"

"It isn't nothing," McPherson said. "We stopped them. That was huge, as the fifty stasis units would have given them a great influx of personnel."

"Okay," I said. "So, we stopped them for now. But some Krekelens might have survived down there. You know that, right?"

"It's possible, but believe me when I say this is the biggest blow we've ever given the Krekelens. And it was all because of you."

I thought about that, but didn't find it satisfying enough. "What about the talk of me traveling to other planets? This isn't helping Bok and the Neanderthals on Saddoth."

McPherson looked troubled.

"What should I do now?" I asked. "After this, I'm not sure what to do next."

"Do you want to remain in the Marines?"

I looked away, thinking about that, and finally shook my head. The Marines was no longer an option. I'd made that decision quite some time ago.

"What then?" she asked.

I stared off into the distance as conflicting ideas raged in me. "I have to think about this. Maybe I'll surf for a while in order to clear my mind."

"Then we should probably drop you off in Santiago."

"Back in Chile?" I asked, incredulous.

"So you can pack for the States and get your honorable discharge. Believe me, you'll want that. You don't want to be labeled a deserter. Once the paperwork's done, you're free."

"And nobody here will mention what I did in the South Pole?"

McPherson shook her head gravely. "It will be better for all involved if we keep you out of the official story."

"Fine," I said, feeling let down but figuring she was probably right. Talk about an anticlimactic ending.

"Jake—" she said.

"Naw," I said, standing, interrupting her. "I have to think about all this."

She stared at her desk, looking up as I opened the door. "I understand. This isn't the end of it, though. I promise."

"Sure," I said, walking out, feeling…I don't know. Feeling like it had all been a great big waste of time.

They dropped me off in Santiago, Chile at the Comodoro Arturo Merion Benitez International Airport. It seemed like a lifetime ago since I'd left with Doctor Spencer.

I took a taxi back to the embassy, let them know I was alive, spoke a few minutes to Master Guns Hendricks and soon found that I was packing to go back to the States.

I thought about calling Juanita Bolivar, but never did. I'd blown my chance with her and it was time to leave the Southern Hemisphere. What would I say to her other than, "Hi, I'm leaving? It's been real. Bye."

The plane ride to the States proved seriously uneventful and boringly long.

I suppose I expected a Krekelen or two to waylay and try to interrogate me under threat of death, or maybe drag me to a secret place and hook me to a lie detector and generator to give me electro-shock incentives.

No one gave me any dirty looks, other than the old lady I sat next to on the plane ride home.

Later, I got my honorable discharge. And yeah, I bought a ticket to Kauai, leaving rainy Central California at the end of January. It was raining in Kauai too, when I got there, but it was warm rain.

I decided to spend a couple of weeks at the Sheraton on the ocean. The main lobby was a hoot, as it lacked any doors to close. Even when it was raining outside, it was comfortable in the lobby.

I swam, surfed and used snorkel, fins and mask to chase small fish along the beach. I bought a kayak and went miles out to sea, paddling once among a pod of killer whales. One old fella gave me the eyeball but otherwise left me alone.

I was free. *Yeah, right,* said a weak voice in my head.

After all the things I'd been through—

I shook my head as I pulled my kayak up the beach, realizing I was bored with this existence. I mean, the relaxation was fine. Eating and sleeping all I wanted—I liked that. I lifted weights, swam, surfed, kayaked and did more snorkeling. I was a Gawain, doing exactly whatever I wanted to do—and I knew I needed something more.

I went to a church service and listened to the preacher expound on the word of God. Singing with them was the most fun, as I felt like I was a part of the group.

But I really wasn't. I was an outsider now. I didn't even have the Corps anymore.

At times, I thought about my old man, how he'd died in the middle of Nevada in a desert, killed by electricity where there had not been any storm.

I thought about heading to Nevada, but decided I'd do it in the springtime when it was warmer.

Two weeks later, I realized I'd spent the last four days in a library, reading everything I could find on Mu and Antarctica. I didn't want to get a library card, didn't want to leave any traces or records, so I did my reading in the library.

I read up on reptilian imposters among us, how President George Bush—the last one, the one with the drawl—had supposedly been a reptilian creep in disguise. I did not find the conspiracy theory argumentation convincing. If anyone was a Krekelen, it was someone near him, someone whispering in his ear—the Vice President or the Secretary of Defense, maybe. I read up on vampires and werewolves. That was more interesting. Vampires and werewolves were hard to kill, as they could take incredible punishment and keep on living.

Witch hunters, huh, I'd been hooked up with old-fashioned witch hunters. Only, they hadn't hunted little old grannies with warts on their noses, but nasty aliens with hot skin, great strength and the ability to take on any shape they wished—well, I guess within reason.

Did I get soft during my stay at the Sheraton in Kauai? I didn't have a gun, although I kept a flick-knife on me, one on the larger size.

I'd tested it several times, so I knew the blade wouldn't fold back on my fingers if I were trying to stab a Krekelen in the forehead.

Three and a half weeks into my stay in Kauai, I was eating lunch at a burger joint. I made the order and sat outside at a table waiting. I watched women pass by, checking them out, not trying to be too obvious about it. A few smiled at me. I smiled back and even waved at one, a true hottie. She was roller-blading and thus didn't stick around.

The waitress brought out my burger and fries. I devoured them, used the john afterward to wash my hands, and then strolled away along the sidewalk.

I walked a long time, eventually finding myself near the ocean along the side of the road. There were no buildings anywhere, although cars passed from time to time.

It was the off-season for tourists.

I had my hands in my pockets and don't remember what I was thinking about. I heard a tire squeal, turned to my right and saw a white van slowing beside me. I hadn't seen the driver—

The side-door, a big slider, opened fast. My reflexes must have been off. Three big guys jumped out, true Hawaiians, I'm guessing. They were heavy-set guys, youngish as in their twenties and not yet turning to fat.

The biggest lunged at me.

I twisted aside, and he went stumbling by. I yanked my hands out, and caught the wrist of the next guy swinging a sap. He was strong, but I was stronger and twisted his wrist. He bellowed, dropping the sap—the third guy slammed against me and all three of us went down. We rolled over grass. One tried to grapple with me. He got an elbow in the face for his effort. I pulled back and gave him a second elbow so he grunted in pain.

I twisted up—the other guy who had first missed me slammed me from behind, and we both rolled.

248

I was breathing hard, disoriented and thinking—*Krekelens, these are Krekelens trying to kidnap me.*

My knife came out. I used my thumb to flick it open and slashed the latest attacker. He screamed and scrambled away from me.

It gave me time to get up.

The driver had stopped the van. He opened the door, stepped out and drew a snub-nosed .38. He was the same size and shape as the others.

I didn't wait, but started sprinting like crazy away from him. Pistols are notoriously hard to aim well, and the more distance, the worse they became.

Pop, pop, pop, pop, pop, pop, went his Smith & Wesson.

None of the slugs hit me. I thought about turning back and teaching him a lesson, but maybe they had more guns. Thus, I ran into some bushes and started putting more distance between them and me.

Soon, I panted, waiting, but when I looked for them, the van was gone.

So, what had that been about: just local Hawaiians angry with the big white guy tramping around their territory? Krekelens hiring the local talent?

Or a test by McPherson's group?

I was the living the dream, the chivalric lifestyle. It had its pluses, but it had its minuses.

As I headed back to the Sheraton, I decided it was time to move on to different pastures.

-49-

Three weeks later, I piloted an old rowboat, moving offshore along tropical Guadalcanal. If the name sounds familiar, it was the famous island of WWII where the U.S. Marines first faced the Imperial Japanese Army.

I did not use an outboard, but rowed. I had a good tan going and felt very fit. I'd been traveling by rowboat about these South Sea Islands, with my worldly goods stashed in my trusty vessel in two duffel bags by my feet.

This time, my goods included firearms: an ancient single-shot shotgun and a snub-nosed .38 with a shoulder rig. I'd bought both cheaply, and had a limited supply of shells and bullets.

I'd been thinking hard these past few weeks. I was sure now that I was going back to Antarctica. I wouldn't do it right away, as I had yet to figure out how to reach near the South Pole. I planned to try again for the obelisk.

It was going to need a ton of preparation first.

I didn't care for the idea of my world under alien invasion. I didn't like waiting for Krekelens to hire local muscle to try to kidnap me. I was a Traveler by heritage. If nothing else, I would like to find out where my dad had been born. Maybe his people could teach me about Traveling, about how to do it right.

I also wanted to know a few things. Had Mu existed? How did the obelisk do what it did? How—

250

I heard the buzzing of a helicopter and looked around. Ah. This one flew low, from the direction of Guadalcanal. It was a small chopper with a bubble canopy, a single rotor thing. There was one person inside, a woman by the look of it. The chopper had pontoons for skids.

As the chopper veered and headed for me, I happened to turn and see a yacht, a biggish yellow one. Its bow churned the placid water and aimed in my direction as well.

I studied the yacht after rummaging in my belongings and picking up a pair of binoculars. I trained it on—snipers climbed onto the front, lying down as spotters watched me.

I picked up the oars and began rowing hard for shore. I didn't know about the chopper, if the woman was on my side or not, but those boys looked as if they wanted to splash me.

It became a race.

I looked up as the chopper eased down toward me. The machine dipped forward and I saw...McPherson waved to me—if it was McPherson and not some Krekelen in disguise.

At that moment, it dawned on me the fearful advantage the aliens had over us.

McPherson or her lookalike brought the chopper down beside me.

I looked back, and saw small splashes from the sniper fire. There were still too far out to reach me.

McPherson hunched her head as she climbed out of the pilot's seat, probably because of the wash of the still-spinning blades. As she stood on a pontoon, she tossed me a line.

I took it, and I hand-over-hand hauled the rowboat to the pontoon.

"Hurry up," she shouted, with her hands cupped around her mouth. "Get in while you can."

I grabbed my two duffel bags, tossing them one at a time to her. She pitched them into the bubble canopy. Finally, I accepted a hand onto the pontoon. Her flesh was warm, but not too warm.

"It's really you!" I shouted.

"Yes. Now, get in. Hurry."

I obeyed, clicking on a seat belt as I sat down.

Soon, McPherson applied power and the helicopter rose into the air.

I put on a pair of headphones and adjusted a microphone. "Can you hear me?" I said.

"Just a minute," she said through my headphones.

I craned over, pulled up my binoculars and saw that someone on the yacht had a handheld SAM—surface-to-air missile.

McPherson took us skimming low, racing for the treetops on Guadalcanal.

The SAM launched with a puff of smoke, and the missile sped for us.

McPherson pressed a switch, and I suspect flares and chaff—metallic strips designed to confuse radar—billowed behind us.

The missile did not take us out. We dropped below the treetops, using them to hide from the yacht and more SAM launches.

McPherson turned to me. "That was too close."

"Krekelens?" I asked.

"More likely their hired guns."

I nodded. "So, you've cleared me with your secret team leader?"

McPherson's features fell. "I'm afraid not. We all voted, and it was close, but they voted you're too risky. Qiang never really trusted you."

"You're kidding."

"We're actually a very conservative organization," she said.

"What's does that mean? You're here."

"Suvorov and I feel differently about you."

I think I understood. "It's just the three of us then?"

"Until we can prove how valuable you are to us and Earth," McPherson said.

"How do we do that?"

She nodded and smiled. "I think you know how."

"By my successful traveling to another planet and back," I said.

"Yes."

"That means I have to go back to Antarctica."

"When the time is right," McPherson said.

"And when is that?"

"Yes," she said. "That is the question. We have to make plans. We must assess what you learned at the Planet of the Dead and on Saddoth. We've got to keep you alive. I think the Krekelens finally understand how dangerous you are to them."

"What about your organization? Won't they try to kill me once they know what you're doing?"

"I hope not."

"That's not a cheery answer," I said.

"Do you want out?"

I considered that, and I already knew the answer. I was going to find a way to help my blood brother Bok and the Neanderthals on Saddoth. I was a Traveler. I also had to help Earth against the Krekelens. I needed to discover…well, we had to figure out what I needed to find. I had a team, McPherson and Suvorov. That was better than going it alone. And if I could learn something really cool, I might swing the rest of the secret organization onto my side.

I would still be a knight-errant, a Lancelot or a Gawain, but one with a great purpose. Finally, I'd found my calling in life. It felt good, really good.

"Thanks for coming back for me," I said. "Thanks for believing in me."

McPherson nodded. "I have ever since the tunnels. This is the chance we need. And I know you want to help Bok and will thus give it your all."

I grinned. McPherson was right about that. And there was something else. Colonel McPherson, she was good people.

"So how are we going to do this?" I said.

We began to plan as she flew, knowing there would be Krekelen traps along the way. The last thing they wanted was for us humans to know more. But that was *exactly* what we were going to do.

THE END

SF Books by Vaughn Heppner

LOST STARSHIP SERIES:
The Lost Starship
The Lost Command
The Lost Destroyer
The Lost Colony
The Lost Patrol
The Lost Planet
The Lost Earth
The Lost Artifactt
The Lost Star Gate
The Lost Supernova
The Lost Swarm
The Lost Intelligence
The Lost Tech
The Lost Secret
The Lost Barrier

THE SOLDIER SERIES:
The X-Ship
Escape Velocity
Final Odyssey

Visit VaughnHeppner.com for more information